ALSO BY MARK SLOUKA

Lost Lake

GOD'S FOOL

GOD'S FOOL

MARK SLOUKA

Alfred A. Knopf
New York
2002

This Is a Borzoi Book Published by Alfred A. Knopf

Library of Congress Cataloging-in-Publication Data
Slouka, Mark.
God's fool / Mark Slouka. — 1st ed.
p.   cm.
ISBN 0-375-40216-0
1. Bunker, Chang, 1811–1874—Fiction.   2. Bunker, Eng, 1811–1874—Fiction.   3. North Carolina—
History—Civil War, 1861–1865—Fiction.   4. Rural families—Fiction.   5. Married people—
Fiction.   6. Siamese twins—Fiction.   7. Freak shows—Fiction.   8. Farm life—Fiction.
9. Brothers—Fiction.   I. Title.

PS3569.L697 G63 2002
813'.54—dc21   2001053975

Manufactured in the United States of America
First Edition

For my wife, Leslie, and our children, Zack and Maya,
who make this world all a man could want,

my parents, Olga and Zdenek,
who know about the ties that bind,

and for Sacvan Bercovitch,
who introduced me to America.

Into the air, as breath into
the wind. Would they had stay'd.
—William Shakespeare

Acknowledgments

My sincere thanks—yet again—to Sloan Harris, Jordan Pavlin, and Colin Harrison, exhorter extraordinaire, my students and colleagues at the Columbia University Writing Division, for providing encouragement or commiseration as needed, and the National Endowment for the Arts, for shrinking the bills.

I am indebted, however, not only to friends and governmental agencies, but to certain books as well, particularly Lawrence Weschler's *Dr. Wilson's Cabinet of Wonders,* which sharpened my sense of the nineteenth century's appetite for "curiosities," and Henry Mayhew's magisterial *London Labour and the London Poor,* which made the costermongers' stalls along Petticoat-lane as vivid and familiar to me as anything on Broadway.

PART ONE

I.

In a vertical world, a world of men like pines, or posts, more separate than they know, we were born with a bridge. A small, fleshy bridge, a handspan long and half as thick (thick enough for a boy to march his soldiers across if he watched their steps and they kept in file), forever connecting our two principalities like an act of God, the will of the citizens to hate one another be damned. If a life were measured by the number of metaphors it gives occasion to, the opportunities it presents to journalistic hacks and carnival barkers, ours has been rich indeed; in the field of grammar alone we have been wealthy beyond measure, a veritable primer made flesh. We were the hyphenated twins, as that nice young man writing for *La Quotidienne* once put it. We were a living conjunction, an *if* or an *and* or a *but* where a full stop would have been both correct and kind. We were separate sentences spliced with a comma, an error come alive. I could go on.

The day we were born, the midwives ran from our monstrous birth, leaving our mother to cut her own cord, untwist and bathe us. Twenty years later, the citizens of two continents came running to stare. I despised them about equally. I never changed. I see this now as my essential trait: Pushed to the wall by man or God, I pushed back. If the world showed its teeth, I rubbed it against the fur. I was born that way, and if I were to live to be as old as Methuselah, I'd be that way still.

Little Charlie Stratton, who could stand in a teacup, once preached me a sermon on Christian acceptance. "We must accept our fate with humility and gratitude," he hectored me in that mad-duck voice of his, and I remember being tempted to add, "and milk it like an udder until it runs dry," but didn't, distracted, I suppose, by the furious little digit he poked at my stomach with each stressed syllable (ac-*cept* our *fate* with hu-*mi*-lity and *gra*-titude), like a schoolteacher trapped in a child's dream. Oh, but how he made us cringe, Barnum's "little brick," posing and primping for councillors and queens: now Romulus bravely attacking a vase, now Cain with a club the size of a quill, now Crusoe in furs like a shipwrecked squirrel. But we were separate cases, Charlie and I. Humility is prudent when you're the size of a hat.

Acceptance was not in my nature. Even as a young man it seemed to me that everywhere the world conspired against the heart, and though I knew the heart would lose, I couldn't bear to call it right. It seemed unjust to me that those we had come to know should have to leave us, that the mowers resting in the shade had to rise, that perfection passed. Gideon liked to claim that my melancholy grew the more I watered it, but it wasn't the wine that made the passing of things so hard for me, just as it isn't the port by my side that makes me miss him now. No, like God, I had a jealous nature. I would have kept him here, you see. Drawn a circle around him, as I would around all the ones I've known and loved. And some besides. And in that circle, their heads thrown back through a warm ray of sun (the mark of my benediction), the mowers could laugh forever, one leg up and one leg out as the handles of their tools slowly moldered to dust and the blades of their scythes sank down in the grass. But the circle didn't hold. I couldn't hold it. Except once, maybe.

Before the attack on Cemetery Ridge, they say, Pickett's men waited in the woods by the edge of the open fields, watching the milkweed drifting in the air like a lost squall. They knew. Every man and boy among them. Some scribbled quick notes against the stocks of their rifles or their brothers' backs or the stones of the old mossed walls that ran through those woods like a stitch through a quilt, marking borders long forgotten—"To Miss Masie," "To My Father," "In Case of My Death"—then pinned them to their shirts. Most just sat with their backs against the trees, their caps hung lightly on their bayonets, waiting.

No one spoke. A bee buzzed on a turtlehead blooming in the damp, climbed up the tongue. A hot blade of sun lit the moss on a boulder, cut the toes off a boot. Here and there men lay sprawled on the previous season's leaves, staring up through the layered branches as if into the milky eye of heaven itself. Further off, where an old road cut light through the roof of leaves, a photographer in a black vest and a wide-brimmed hat went about his business, hurrying back and forth from a small, square wagon.

Suddenly a canteen went over with a clank; a cut leaf twirled slowly to the ground. Like sleepers waking, they raised their heads. A private's hat flew from a branch. They leaped to their feet. The floor of the forest, an overgrown orchard, was stippled with apples, small and hard as hickory nuts. Within seconds the shade was alive with joyful, savage shouting. Men sprinted for the breastworks of pasture walls and broken trees, one hand holding their caps to their heads, the other cradling their bulging shirts, lumpy with ammunition. Some said afterward that a strange sort of dream seemed to come over that glade. For a short space of time, they one and all seemed to forget where they were. The wavering heat, the ridge, the order—soon to come—to advance across the open fields (an order Longstreet himself would have to give with a nod, unable to bring himself to speak): All these faded away like distance on a summer afternoon, and they played. As children will play. As though death were a story to scare them to bed, and scarce worth believing.

And I ask you: What manner of God would stop them? Would bring down his foot? Would turn them, laughing, to blood and bone?

I see Christopher there, my little boy grown tall and lean, his wrists protruding a full three inches from the sleeves. I can feel his thrill at a solid hit, the sting of a little green ball in his side. I've imagined myself there so often now that my imagining has taken on the color of memory. You say this is wrong? Who was it, I want to know, who first divided history from dream, who ran his finger down the ranges of the past and decreed a frontier where none had been? When was the treaty that gave us this damnable map, and who gave it authority? No, I'll say it once and be done with it: There is no frontier, in this world or any other, that love or desire or pain can't cross.

II.

He's asleep, the old fool, his face pressed into the crimson pillow, his hands hanging between his knees. How he grumbled and spit when I woke him, sitting on the edge of the bed like a big gray child, fumbling with his buttons, grousing at the cold. The fire started quickly. We have a good store of applewood left from the fall. He asked if it was the pain again. I lied. I'll not go traipsing about the country of a night like this. The sound of the ice comes in from the dark; the dogs' bones have welded themselves to the dirt. As though the Yankees, having imposed their will on us, now felt free to impose their weather as well.

Gideon could tell me what it is that clenches my heart like a tomato in a vise. With Gideon dead I'll as soon stay where I am and trust to fate, though looking at my brother sleeping next to me, his white-whiskered face an inch from my shoulder, his nose abloom with tiny red roads, I wonder at my faith. Perhaps like an old dog I prefer the familiar kick to the unfamiliar smile, the uncertainty of a new allegiance.

Restless, restless, my head full of whisperings I can't make out. Waking into the dark tonight, still half in my dreams, I heard the creak and boom of doors closing deep in the core of things. The lake, adjusting itself. Breaking to the wheel. Or, like me, resisting that accommodation.

He twitches his paws in his sleep, then shifts with the cold. I adjust the blanket, drawing it up around our shoulders.

III.

In the summer of 1856 the road to Kernville was little more than a dirt track, soft as talcum, and when the last rain came it raised puffs of dust like bullets all along the way. Dark little circles appeared on the wagon, the harness, the children's feet. And then stopped. The dust joined the layers already whitening the roadside brambles wagon-high and wagon-deep like blight, and stayed. We clung to the things we knew— the smell of rain, the splintered helve, the weight of slops or stone—but even these, it seemed, struggled to escape us. Nothing came easy. The corn was slow that year, barely knee-high by August.

And yet I think back on that time fondly. We all still lived in the house at Mount Airy then, Addy and Sallie making out as best they could, the children always underfoot. Christopher was barely eleven, seemingly convinced the world had gone deaf, forever climbing, like a cricket in a jar, to the top of anything handy. Josephine and Catherine were ten and inseparable. Natural mothers to man and beast, quick with the salve and the sticking plaster, they spent their days nursing what the dogs didn't kill—mainly three-legged tortoises with stars on their shells—in the hospital hard by the chicken coop. My Nannie, marshaling the younger ones—James and Susan, Patrick and Victoria—would arrange funeral services for those who succumbed to her sisters' ministrations, as well as for the parade of cat-killed moles and newborn possums left each night like vestal offerings on the doorstep or the parlor rug.

By the time we awoke, the procession would be winding its way through the locust trees and past the sheds to the bald spot by the garden. There the deceased would be laid to rest with appropriate solemnity (unless one of the dogs happened to make off with him, which would change the spirit of the proceedings considerably) under a cross of twigs tied together with twine. Everyone had a role. James would always dig, I remember; Susan would cover; Patrick or Victoria would drop the sweaty little handfuls of violets or phlox. And saddened but virtuous, they'd make their way home. What sweet days those were. I've never had tomatoes like the ones that grew there, trellising themselves on the children's crosses, bearing them down with the weight of their fruit.

Hindsight is the Almighty's compensation for brittle bones and shattered sleep. We grow crisp and crotchety, fully half our organs ignore our commands—whistling to themselves, as it were, while we struggle to bring them to attention—but to balance the ledger we are allowed to dwell on the past, revisit the sites of our old humiliations, reread (without the aid of spectacles) our own misjudgments. And we do, believing that it was there, in our past, that our last best chance for happiness lay hidden; that somewhere in that thicket, now dense with self-recrimination and foolishness, trickled a freshet of joy powerful enough to redeem us.

It's been fifty-eight years since Chee-kou died, but I can still feel the warmth of the feathers in the hollow of her back, see the place on the bank of the Meklong where we taught her to hop on one leg and quack for food and walk across a wire—her wings out like a tightrope walker—straight into my arms. Sitting here I can see the saplings to which we tied the wire. I can smell the mud, the fish rotting in the roots, feel the sun like a fevered hand resting on the back of our necks.

And there!—like a quick stab, so sudden, so unutterably familiar—our mother's voice, calling us back to the boat and home. I can see her glance up from her work —*Where are they?*—unaware that her boys are doddering old men sitting before a fire a lifetime away, who, dreaming their old men's dreams, suddenly hear her calling their names.

IV.

We'd had no rain to speak of since May that year. The livestock barely moved, the flies were unbearable. My brother was untroubled. Divine dispensation, he said, looking at the rows of bolted lettuce in the garden. I could hardly argue. The Lord in His Whimsy had apparently decided to cook us all, sinners and saved alike.

Our morning sessions on the porch had begun by then, and twice a week and once on Sundays we would repair outside, my brother to study the wisdom of God, I to contemplate the many roads to damnation, as he so neatly put it. There was little help for it. I can still see us there, like clerks behind the old dining-room table, he quietly mumbling his way through Deuteronomy, I trying to calculate approximately how long it might take him, having pushed off from Egypt, so to speak, to reach the land of Canaan. In the first hour he turned the page once, I swear, then turned it back, apparently having missed something. Eventually Aunt Grace would waddle out and ask if there was anything we'd be wanting. "Deliverance," I would say. My brother would say nothing, secure in my torment.

A summer of nights, as I remember it now. Everything that happened that season seemed to happen between dusk and dawn. Our slaves, laboring under the overseer's less-than-vigilant eye, topped and suckered the tobacco at dawn, scraped the rows by lantern light. On Sunday nights we would allow them to go down to the sandy little beach that used to lie just below the bluff before the floods erased it in '62. Even on the darkest nights you could see it from the rise—a wide, sharp tooth, floating in the dark. The women would lay out the food on the bank (you could see the watermelons like a clutch of great, dark eggs, cooling in the mud), then wade slowly into the current with the smaller children on their hips, their dresses momentarily blossoming around them, then trailing off downstream. They walked with a slow, pushing motion, their arms swinging in a loose arc as if sowing the river with the corn-bread or honey cake they offered now and again to the babes on their sides. If you watched from the trees, as Eng and I did, early on, you would suddenly notice one of the older men standing waist-deep and still, a seam opening in the river just below his hips, staring off toward the opposite shore. Lost in the shadows, holding his hat to his chest like a supplicant, he would look just like an old, half-flooded stump, only the smear of pipe smoke lifting away from the current giving him away.

I wonder what they thought about out there. Were they remember-ing some woman in a cornfield after dark? Or the children they'd lost? Were they coming again to a particular crossroads, half a cen-tury back—willing their feet to turn, turn now, while they still had the chance? Or did the road seem straight as a shovel handle to them—men born slaves—pruned of all possibility? Standing there, the current gently pushing at their legs, did they find themselves marveling at the speed with which the cards had been dealt and played? Or were they thinking instead of how expertly the deck had been rigged before they ever entered the game?

Useless questions. Were one of them to appear before the fire tonight—ugly and knowing as a terrapin, running his hand over his scarred and crinkled scalp—perhaps I'd ask him.

V.

What can I say about him now? What can any father say about his son?

I could say that we understood one another, *knew* each other, in a way that had nothing to do with our daily lives, but ran beneath that landscape like a vein of iron ore. Or that his smile was as familiar to me as anything I'll ever know. I could say that he was my first—the world made right, whole-limbed and single. But these things cannot begin to sum him. On the night he was born he looked at me through his watery, reddened eyes and I felt some small, furious thing inside me suddenly still. He was my peace, my understanding, my key. He was my answer to questions I barely understood. He was beautiful.

Though I punished him enough, God knows, I was loath to disappoint him. Or stand in his way. Not that it would have been that easy, necessarily. More than anyone else I ever knew, Christopher had his own mind, and quietly obeyed its dictates. Defiance—for its own sake, at least—had nothing to do with it; he would accommodate me when possible. Having made up his mind to do something, however, nothing would move him. He would go his way. I could wear out my arm—and had, more than once—to little effect.

I still remember my surprise the first time I saw him there among them. He couldn't have been more than eleven at the time. A strange sight, my boy among all those blacks—I don't know that I ever got quite used to it. Yet I let it go. The late nights by the river didn't hurt him; his lessons were as strong the next day, his chores completed no more slowly than usual. When I noticed that he had struck up a friendship with Lewis's son, Moses, I did not discourage it. They were friends for years. I can still see them leaping down the grass slope to the stream, or coming out of the corn, the rope between them heavy with whiskery bullheads. Once, when we came across them wrestling in the dust, tearing their clothes and cursing in ways we hadn't known they knew, we quietly backed off and left them to it. I might have felt differently had it been someone else.

We'd bought Lewis, his father, in Richmond for six hundred dollars. Fourth on the block that still, sultry morning, after two sickly looking boys and a comely wench in a blue dress, there was something about him (though he had to be held up by two men, having recently been beaten) that caught my attention. A certain look. Eng, though skeptical, allowed himself to be convinced, and after assuring ourselves that no permanent damage had been done and that his general state of health was good, we bought him from a bulgy, uncooked-looking individual who claimed to have seen us in a show, years earlier. He'd thought we were fake, he said.

"Did you?" I remember my brother asking.

"I sure did," he said. "There was a little midget there too, quick as a cat. Figured he was real enough. And a woman, big as a house." He slapped at a horsefly that had lit on his neck, crushed it between his fingers without looking at it, and tossed it in the dirt. He scratched the reddened bite. "I seen the Living Skeleton too. Arms no bigger round 'n this," he said, extending a finger with a long, untrimmed nail. "They had to bring him out in a chair." He nodded, remembering. "Well, good luck with the nigger," he said. "Glad to be shut of him, myself." And with that he left.

.   .   .

We brought him back in irons, I remember, lying on a bed of straw we spread over the boards of the wagon. An hour or two into our journey I turned around to find him sitting up with his back against the sideboard, watching the country pass. He didn't move. Though I knew he must have seen me turn (he was looking almost directly past me), he refused to even glance my way, but just sat there, his head lolling slightly on his neck with every jolt and roll of the wagon, staring out across those hot Virginia fields as if acknowledging my presence wasn't worth the effort required to turn his head.

I waited. Nothing. I stared at him, willing him to turn. A bluebottle lit on his face, just below the split lip. Nothing. I watched it walk up to the edge of the cut. And suddenly I knew, with absolute certainty, that he would never turn so long as I wanted him to, that we could circumnavigate the globe a dozen times over, my poor oblivious brother at the helm, and, unless something interfered, remain precisely as we were, a sculpture in flesh and bone, a study in stubbornness: *Chang Contemplating the Bust of a Slave.*

His pride—if that was what it was—infuriated me. It seemed almost contrary to nature, like a mole chattering at a mastiff, or a rabbit showing its teeth. Yet there was something fascinating in it as well. Trapped by circumstance, a slave for life, he would defend his collection of invisible dignities to the death, stake his claim to a pebble in the ditch—not that one, this one—and obstinately refuse to budge. I had heard of condemned men refusing to eat their last meal without a napkin, or stubbornly refusing to duck their heads into the noose. This was no different. It made things difficult. It changed nothing.

And then it came to me. I would give him his napkin, so to speak, let him place his own head in the noose. I would speak first. "Are you thirsty?" I remember saying to him.

He turned to me then as though seeing me for the first time, his face swollen, his head wobbling only slightly. Something—some inscrutable Negro mixture of surprise and disdain—passed across his face. And in that moment, though I had the distinct urge to strike him across the face,

I knew we understood each other—that we had found a ground on which we could both exist.

He nodded, and I dipped a ladleful of water from the barrel we kept in the back of the wagon, and he drank.

He married Berry late that fall—a steady, yellow-skinned wench we'd acquired some years before. Moses, if I remember rightly, was born the following summer. Perhaps the natural fear of losing his family played a part. In any case, his nature changed. Whatever rage he may have had left he turned, with admirable success, to work. He became a steadying force, a decent husband, a good father to his son.

No one was better at sniffing out a game trail or reading the dogs. No one was better at pushing the bucks out of the briar thickets on a drive, or finding the places where the does bedded down in the heat. When Moses and Christopher were old enough to feel for catfish in the dead-falls at night, it was Lewis who taught them, who showed them how to keep from winding up like Toner Hugg who, three years earlier, had lost his hand in the craw of a big-river blue as big as a sow; a fish with a head the size of a horse, whiskers thick as a man's thumb.

That same summer, when Christopher, feeling about between the sunken boards and branches, pulled his arm out of the river with a twenty-pound flathead attached to the end of it, it was Lewis who moved before anyone knew what was happening, who jammed a stick through its gills before it could wrench the boy's arm out of its socket, who stuck a knife through its skull while it thrashed about in the dark without cutting through to the small hand inside its mouth.

Christopher lived off that fish all year. As I did later. For whenever I tried to tally all the happy moments of his boyhood, as I did sometimes in the years that followed—counting them over in the small hours of my nights as though by counting, and counting again, I might arrive by some miracle at a different sum—that long-gone catfish ran high on the list.

That summer no other boy could come close to him. Lewis hacked off the big whiskery head and laid it on an anthill by the back orchard and when the bones were clean, gave it to Christopher, who hung it on a nail in the tobacco barn after first trying to hang it over the doorsill to the main house. It was a thing they had between them. It hung there for twelve years, I remember, long after either of them was there to see it.

VI.

The summer wore on. The boys squabbled and fought; bruises appeared and disappeared; cuts scabbed and healed over. One of Matlack Benner's slaves, in the middle of a row, put his head to the ground as if looking for something very small and died.

It was that summer that we got into the habit, after everyone had retired, of walking the mile along the river to Gideon's for a drink, our double shadow, on moonlit nights, running on ahead. Gideon's house, with its west-facing porch, was perfectly placed to catch whatever breeze there was to be had, though that summer, as I recall, even the wind seemed to be dying. We sweat sitting still.

I can still see us there on the good doctor's porch, three slightly drunken watchmen, no longer young, watching over what couldn't be saved, keeping each other company. No lamp would be lit, not because of the mosquitoes, which seemed to do equally well with or without our help and guidance, but because that August, for its own particular reasons, nature had decided to produce an extra generation of moths, a harvest of biblical proportions.

Drawn by the lamp, they'd come fluttering in from the fields, the forests, from under the shaggy, flaking skin of the locust trees, and by ten there'd be a thousand, maybe more, tracing tiny parabolas and vast, far-flung orbits, drawing tighter to that central sun. We ignored them for a time, waving away the ones that brushed against our faces, laughing when Gideon's hounds snapped and smacked their lips at them, jumping whenever a junebug cracked against the glass. And yet, though we tried to ignore it, there was something ghastly in their rush to the flame, something vaguely obscene in their eagerness to die. There was nothing to be done. We sat at the far edges of the storm, the small, burnt bodies piling against the wick, until the night a huge, dark beauty half again the size of a swallow fluttered over the rail, turned once about the porch and then, as though knowing precisely where it was going, stuffed itself carefully down the throat of the lamp. Too late to move, we saw it momentarily block the light, the hieroglyphs of its wings magnified against the walls, then burst into flame.

For a short while, no one spoke. Inside the smoking lamp, two bits of wing still burned, tipped together like cards, or the walls of a house. Leaning over, Gideon gently tapped his pipe against the glass. The cards crumbled. "Not a feather falls," he said, quietly. And with one small breath he put out the light.

We sat in the dark after that, I remember, listening to the thin quavering in our ears, the rhythmic scratching in the thick, knotted grass, the high invisible armies sawing back and forth over the fields . . . But even after the moths had gone, the lamp remained unlit. We had grown to like it that way. On particularly dark nights, I'd feel my way to tobacco or table, bottle or glass, listening to the small adjustments of our bodies, the creak of the doctor's chair against the wall, and there was a comfort in this business of knowing without seeing that the lamp would have taken away.

We talked. My God, how we talked. Gideon had the gift of seeing the world the way another man might see a stone or a root; if the stone was smooth he didn't imagine it otherwise; if the root was misshapen he didn't wish it straight. Neither callous nor complacent, he simply had, as he explained it, a high regard for his own insignificance, a firm belief that, despite his best efforts, the sun would rise and foolishness reign. In any other man, this kind of fatalism would have been insufferable; in

Gideon, tempered as it was by the energy and solicitude that he brought to his daily round, sweetened by the heart he tried, and failed, to keep hid behind the wall of his gruffness, it was somehow charming. We completed each other, he and I, we fought like cats in a bag; we drove each other mad. I loved him like a brother—no, more than my own brother, who would become a stranger to me as the years came on and Jesus came between us. In Gideon's company I could be wholly myself, a thing made possible, somehow, by the fact that he never attempted to overlook our peculiar condition, as Barnum used to call it.

"Welcome, my hyphenated friends," he would call from the porch as we approached the house, looking every inch the doctor in his crumpled suit (though with his white hair and beard and his beak of a nose he could as easily have passed for some battle-weary general, and actually resembled, though we could hardly have known it then, a slightly stooped Bobby Lee), "welcome to our airless abode."

By mid-August we had bonfires going all night to draw the moths. Though the heat was fierce for those who had to tend the flames, there was no help for it. Without them, the cotton would have been gone in a week. From Gideon's porch the fires set along the edges of our fields appeared strangely alive, as though burning inside a blizzard; every now and again a man-shaped space would block out the flames like a woodcut out of Dante, send a gust of sparks soaring into the night, and quickly disappear.

A fever in the land. I believe that if we had stopped and listened, we could have felt it growing. That was the year that John Brown, God singing in his ears, reduced the proslavery population along Pottawatomie Creek by five.

VII.

The truth is I'd never thought about slavery much. It was a fact of life in the country we had come to—a necessary evil, as benign or brutal as the individuals involved in it. If the majority of blacks bore their burden with relative equanimity, it seemed to me, perhaps it was because they instinctively recognized the necessity of their situation. We were all slaves to something, after all—to time, to love. Perhaps the reason Barnum's crowds had never tired of coming to stare was because our "band of union," as Dr. Bolton had always called it, had made visible a universal condition. We were the word made flesh.

When I said this to Gideon one night he raised a glass to my eloquence, then suggested that I consider offering my services to the *Charleston Mercury*. If a stump could be found large enough to accommodate us, he said, we could arrange to debate Mr. Wendell Phillips, trope for trope and verse for verse. We'd have the abolitionists on their knees in no time, he said; our sable brethren would cheer. He swiped at the dark in front of his face, then took a long, meditative sip. "Slavery is slavery," he said. "You can call it necessary. You can call it a blessing and move to Charleston. You can call it God's will from every pulpit in America, for all I care, but you can't call it natural."

I said nothing, as I recall. Neither did my brother. We knew enough by then to stay out of the way on those occasions when Gideon caught the spirit. And though I would not allow myself to admit it at the time, I knew he had a point. I had seen enough in my life to know that we were all, in our way, creatures of our condition.

Had the king's physicians succeeded in persuading our mother to have us sawed apart at birth, after all, would I still have believed as I did? Had I been able to walk the streets of Paris with Sophia that winter in 1830 a single man, or to leap from the loveseat on which my brother and I now sat and run off down the road, or to sit on the steps with my son, unattended, would I have been as eager to argue with Mr. Phillips and his fellow abolitionists? To speak for the principle of universal bondage? Or would I have stoutly declared freedom the universal truth, and any attempt to thwart it an offense to man and God?

I held my peace. It hadn't been that long, after all, since Eng and I had inquired, for the tenth time at least, about the possibility of having ourselves separated, of having the good doctor rend asunder, so to speak, what God in His Wisdom had seen fit to join. Gideon had answered, as he always did, that separating us was hardly the problem. The divorce could be realized in a matter of minutes, he said. Any idiot possessed of a sharp saw and a strong stomach could do it. The problem, he said, was that he'd grown accustomed to our company, which was why he was willing to defer the fame that a scientific description of our condition would bring until such time as we grew either so dull or so annoying that fulfilling our wish began to seem like a good idea.

"And besides," he'd asked us, "what could you possibly do apart that you haven't already done together?"

"Nothing," I'd answered. "But we could do it alone."

"And this appeals to you? After almost fifty years of living and breathing together? After all you've been through?"

"Utterly," I said, more out of habit than conviction.

He looked at Eng. "And you too?"

We'd been this way before. It was a kind of game we played, my brother and I. Like children who cling to the notion of a particular present long after any real wish for it has faded, who have memorized their

reasons for wanting it and reel them off, in order, at the slightest suggestion, we pretended we truly desired to be separated, dreamed of it daily,
while in truth no longer even imagining the thing could come to pass.

He never answered. Looking down at the glass he held against his
stomach, my brother scratched at some imagined roughness with his
thumbnail, then looked off across the fields to where the fires still gusted
and flared against the dark.

VIII.

Samuel was barely two months old when he died. A tiny, listless little thing, he had barely been here at all, and then he was gone. I remember Gideon nearly living at Mount Airy those last two weeks—he was there that much—and then he was standing in front of the bedroom door, shaking his head, and I was swinging a pick at the ground as if to kill something only I could see.

Addy bore the blow better than I did. I threw myself at whatever offered, dragging my brother from task to task, afraid to stop. In less than a week we had fixed a quarter-mile of split-rail fence, begun the new tobacco shed. The sun meant nothing to me. Eng, never a weak man, slogged on beside me, hour after hour, day after day. We worked by lamplight when we couldn't see, slept like the dead, and began again. Addy came to our bed that week, but though we pleased each other, sweating in the darkness, neither of us took much comfort in the thing. It was a weapon, nothing more—something to wield against the grief—and both of us knew it.

Whether it was because Eng, affected by my loss, had curbed his growing dissatisfaction with me or because I, too distracted by my own thoughts, had simply failed to take notice of his feelings, I don't know, but I remember that the trouble that had been growing between my brother and myself seemed to recede during those weeks. The flood tide fell, revealing by degrees the familiar landscape of our life together. We grew close again, retiring and rising without argument, working long hours side by side—handing each other tools, anticipating each other's needs—with something like the correspondence of mind and body we had for so long taken for granted.

Late that summer, as we did at the midpoint of every month, we loaded the wagon and made the move to Eng's house, traveling late this time to avoid the heat of the day. Josephine, Christopher, and Stephen went ahead with their mothers, the boys to handle the horses, Josephine to help with the younger children. We followed about an hour later, my Nannie and Victoria sitting in the back with Catherine and Julia; James and Patrick sitting next to their father, taking turns at the reins.

At that time I still enjoyed returning to Eng's farm. It was a good house, comfortable and well placed. Addy gladly relinquished control to her sister for the fortnight, and I for one didn't mind the change. The children for their part had grown quite used to the routine, their pangs of regret over the animals they left behind balanced by their joy at renewing acquaintance with those that had been waiting for them. I never ceased being amazed by how the younger ones simply accepted as natural the fact that they should live for two weeks in their father's house and two weeks in their uncle's.

A still, hot night. I remember passing Stoneman's place, looking well tended and neat even in the dark, the light from a pair of lanterns drawing stripes in the dark where the tobacco sheds were—Stoneman and his sons fixing racks, likely as not. Gideon and Mary were out on their porch. From the road we could barely make out the paleness of his light-colored suit and her dress, rocking together in the dark like two spirits playing at being human. We had hardly passed the entrance to their drive when Gideon's voice came out of the dark. I had thought he might let it go this time, given the lateness of the hour, but Gideon, more than most, had an appreciation for the materials from which children build their worlds.

"Hark, who goes there?" he called. "Friend or foe?"

"Friends," came a chorus of voices from the back of the wagon.

"What name do ye go by?"

"Bunker."

"The Bunkers of Mount Airy? Of the court of Gideon the Wise?"

"The same."

"Then greetings, Bunkers all. Greetings, Bunkers large and small. May luck be with you on your journey."

"May we pass?" called the happy voices at our backs, though we hadn't slowed and were, in fact, now well past the house.

"Pass on," came the reply, followed by a few inaudible words and Mary's low laugh. And then again, more quietly this time, as though speaking to himself, "Pass on, my friends."

A huge, swollen moon, round as a slice of orange, had risen over the drying corn to the east. We rode on through the hot air smelling of field and horse and honeysuckle, James still holding the reins, Patrick, two years younger, asleep against his father's arm.

"This one always was a sleeper," said Eng. Slipping his arm around him, he let him tilt into the jerk and shift of the wagon, then pulled him, floppy as a shirt, onto his lap. "Get his legs."

Boys' bare feet in August: soft and dry as cowskin; each pad a small shell, thumbnail-hard. A few strands of clover stuck out from between the small toes of his right foot as though hoping to take root there. I looked at him sleeping, his mouth open and his head tilted back across his father's leg, his left arm dangling loose to the floorboards.

"Wish I could sleep like that," said Eng.

"You do," I said.

Eng smiled. "Tired?" he said, turning to James.

"No, sir."

"Think you can take us all the way home?"

"I know I can."

Eng nodded. "All right, then." And then, to me: "Can you get that end?" and together, working from either side, we began fixing Patrick's misbuttoned shirt. A moment of peace—unbidden, unexpected, fragile as a scent.

At one point in our journey, hearing the children call, we looked back over our shoulders. A wagon-thick wall of dust, like a castle battlement, rose behind us, unspooling with every turn of the wheels. We built it as we went along, separating cornfield from cornfield, neighbor from neighbor, farm from farm. A strange and ghostly sight: though made of air, it seemed so substantial I half expected it to be there still when, a fortnight later, we made the journey back.

Eventually, of course, the dust settled as dust always will, or a breeze from some new quarter simply erased it like a dream. Our real world, I remember thinking—our days and deeds, our pasture walls—are as like to the gods; on certain nights you could almost fancy you could hear them laughing as they passed in their celestial wagons.

Dust to the gods, perhaps, but not to us. As we turned at the cross-roads and the house came into view—the twin lights in the parlor windows looking so fragile against the dark mass of the oaks—I was reminded, again, that nothing had changed. Though my own grief was fresh that summer, it was small compared to his. I had hardly had a chance to know Samuel, after all. Rosalyn, on the other hand, had been nearly two—had made a space for herself in his and Sallie's hearts. Though it had been nearly two years, I could see he still berated himself for having left her that morning with a girl he'd bought only a month before. I could tell by how quiet he became as we approached the farm, sinking deeper into himself with every dust-softened clop of the horses' hooves as though grief were a place rather than a sickness—an unrelenting cramp in the heart.

I know now that my brother's return to the church began that cold, blue morning in '52 when the earth rang like an anvil and Rosalyn toddled into the fire, that the sheer unspeakableness of that horror (the way her little back had lifted off with the poultice like the skin on a pot of boiled milk) had hurled him headlong into the arms of God and away from me who would never, after all, have taken her away from him, and who mourned her more than any Heavenly Father ever could. But justice had nothing to do with it. No, like a small stone deflected off a larger one, my brother had spun off toward the Almighty, though to my mind the events of that morning could just as well have cast him the other way.

IX.

The rains arrived that September, storm after storm pulling across the sky, though by that late date their only purpose seemed to be to wash away the cinders. "The Lord shall make the rain of thy land powder and dust," my brother had observed at the height of our troubles. I anticipated a new verse shortly.

We continued to make our regular pilgrimage to Gideon's porch, the air suddenly sharp and cidery with fall. I recall one night in particular— deep and blue and beautiful. Stoneman's pond lay still and dark as water in a bucket. As we passed I saw a single ring spread against the deepening sky, reminding me for some reason of an evening in Scotland when, cramped and sore from the road, we had persuaded the driver, an old man with a small, dangling mole on the side of his neck that I kept wanting to pluck, to stop the carriage so that we might stretch our legs. We had stepped out onto a rough country lane, somewhere outside Edinburgh. There had been a pond there. And an evening star. And another fall coming on. My God, how young we had been then. And how very fast the wheel did turn.

I remember that Gideon, whose literary tastes tended to the ponderous if not downright inscrutable, had been reading a novel by a man named Melville, whose descriptions of his own amorous adventures in the South Seas a few years earlier had caused such a fuss and set the Reverend Seward and his brethren to clucking and fluffing their feathers. The new novel, I gathered now, was not nearly as amusing. No caressing breezes. No Marquesan maidens climbing naked up the chains, their jet-black tresses dripping with brine. Mr. Melville had apparently traded debauchery for Descartes, the lovely Fayaway's charms for Mr. Ralph Waldo Emerson's, and produced a tome whose sheer weight gladdened the good doctor's heart.

He had been thinking, he said, about a passage in which the author described the dead as setting forth from this world like travelers reduced to a single carpetbag, free of all their worldly possessions. He paused, taking his time. I can still see him leaning over without uncrossing his legs, opening the tobacco pouch lying by his side, carefully stuffing the bowl of his pipe. He placed the stem between his teeth. "What would you put in that carpetbag?" he said, tilting the lamp glass with one hand, with the other holding a splinter to the flame. "If you had one thing, one memory, to take into the afterlife—assuming, for a moment, there is one—what would it be?"

An absurd, two-o'clock-in-the-morning kind of question. Only humans, I thought, would torment themselves with choices that would never be asked of them. And yet, for whatever reason, the memory that flew into my mind was not, as I would have expected, of some still and blazing moment from childhood before the cholera came to Meklong, or of Sophia's face that February evening we walked past the snow-covered walls and gabled ends of Montparnasse, but of Christopher as a child, that April afternoon by the stream.

It had been a late spring. The hills, where they showed through the trees, looked furred, soft as a pelt. We could see him peering down into the water where the crawdads gusted up and back in small puffs of silt, the tea-clear current breaking into bubbles around his legs. To the right, on the gently tilting bank, Sallie and Addy were laying out a picnic in the shade.

"Now that's something we haven't seen in a while," my brother said at one point, pointing downstream with the stem of his pipe. A veritable flurry of orange butterflies was coming down the stream alley—

dipping, floating, doubling back. Here and there one would pass through an invisible ray of light coming through the leaves and flare into color.

Eng chuckled. "You'd almost think they were coming for him," he said. I glanced at Christopher, who was no more than three at the time. The boy had seen them coming, and had stretched out his arms as though he were a tree. I remember I felt a pang, anticipating his disappointment, aware that the world doesn't come when we wish it. And then a butterfly settled on his arm. Another on his shoulder. A third on his head. They were all over him, tipping this way and that, climbing awkwardly up his arms. I remember one sat contentedly on the white tip of his ear, fanning slowly like a living flower. A smile of such happiness was on his face that I was struck with the thought that the boy had been born lucky.

I would take the look on his face, I remember thinking, to remind me of all I'd loved.

Moon and whiskey had both descended a good way that night before the conversation, wandering about like a dog in no hurry from crops to neighbors to politics, stopped, for a moment, on the subject of photography, which Gideon believed—with the passion of the converted— would some day prove as important an invention as the printing press or the steam engine. He had paid a visit to Henninger's studio on Cooper Street, and had left full of enthusiasm for glass plates and silver iodide. Within a few years, he said, we would all have our own library of photographs, not just of the Taj Mahal or the Egyptian pyramids, but of our parents, our children. Nothing would be too small.

We argued, I recall. I said that I had no use for such tinkering. That I could see the past clearly enough already. That I didn't need the evidence of my losses hanging on my wall.

Gideon was unconvinced. He said I had a brooding soul, and that brooding, like the mythological snake, not only feeds on itself but grows larger in the process.

"This is your professional opinion?" I remember asking him. Mary had long since gone to bed. Gideon was leaning back in his chair, one leg over the other, the bottle by his side like a dog waiting to be scratched. It was, he said. He was offering it to me free of charge. I said I supposed that next he'd be wanting to bleed me for my dark humors. He said it would be appropriate, given my scientific views.

"And to replace the loss?" I asked.

He would prescribe a restorative of some kind, he said, carefully pouring us each a fingerful. Something to neutralize the accumulation of bile.

We were silent for a moment. "Science is a wonderful thing, Gideon," I said.

"It is indeed," he said. He raised his glass. "To science, my friends. And fate, which Mr. Melville here"—he patted the fat book on the table beside him—"tells us always deals the featuring blow."

X.

We had emerged, after that long and suffocating season, into a cleansed world, and like travelers who walk into the bruised light after the storm has passed, and who breathe in great lungfuls of air and look about themselves like people recalling, not without tenderness, some small foolishness of their youth, we felt utterly, joyously alive.

Any final tally of happiness in my life would have to include that blessed month. Death, for a time, had been banished from the garden. We were—every one of us—strong and well. Food tasted better than it ever had before, or ever would again. Laughter came easily. We went out into the air every morning like kings, or children, and strode across our land, looking with pleasure at the things our lives had given us. The world came when we whistled and lay at our feet.

Perfection. Even the weather played its part. Following the turn of the season, Nature poured out a stream of sunny, smiling days so still, so deep, so perfectly poised on the sweet edge of sadness, that it seemed as though somewhere, wherever it is that beauty is minted and happiness struck, the workers had discovered an endless supply of gold and, throwing out the baser, cloudier metals, had dedicated themselves to stamping out one shining day after another.

In the mornings the mist stayed on in the bottomlands till late, covering the ponds and the low-lying fields in thick billowy pillows of cloud from which a bull might emerge like Zeus come to earth to seduce some wide-hipped servant girl, or a flock of geese stream as though pulled along on a string. There were no middle hours; we'd look up from our work and the day would already be leaving. And yet there was no feeling of loss, of things having passed too quickly. To the contrary, the hours felt full and appropriate. There was a silence to those days—the bark of a dog or the lowing of a cow made small by something other than distance—as though the world were waiting, listening for an old lover sure to come.

The harvest, such as it was that Year of Our Temperamental Lord, 1856, was largely in by then. Our fifty acres of corn had brought in hardly a hundred bushels. The Irish and sweet potatoes, cowpeas, and beans had all done poorly, as had the cotton: hardly fourteen bales for the eighty acres we had planted. And yet what ought to have been a ruinous year was hardly that. The bright leaf tobacco saved us. In the Richmond papers that fall, demand and prices were high, as few farmers had had the nerve to try it. Between the tobacco and the livestock, we knew we'd do fine, and maybe considerably better than that.

But it wasn't just the harvest. Quarrels with neighbors died before the seed could set. Stoneman, his four sons behind him, appeared on our porch for the first time in nine years to ask about the bright leaf we'd planted, listened politely, then cleared his throat and offered us the use of his reaper—the only one to be had in those parts—then nodded once, as though agreeing with himself, again to the four hulking boys waiting hat-to-stomach by the door, and left.

And so it went. Though my brother had returned to his devotions, I hardly minded. Aunt Grace had made her plum cake, whose recipe called for a glass of brandy. Compensation enough. And so, while Eng struggled on toward the land of milk and honey, the bodies piling in the margins, I dwelt contentedly in a Canaan worth struggling for, a Canaan in which plum cakes so light they fluttered the hearts of the heavenly seraphim had long ago been voted in, under threat of secession, as the only proper food for the soul.

Nor was it just the soul that received its due that season. Now that the air lifting the curtains made the blanket welcome once more, Addy and Sallie had begun spending the nights with us again; Addy in particular, whose interest in sharing our bed had declined in recent years almost as fast as her sister's, seemed to have recently stumbled across some minor springlet of Ponce de León's fountain of youth behind the garden.

We had never been particularly conversant in matters of love. Though she had adjusted easily enough to our situation at first, our desire for each other had begun to gutter and fade almost as soon as it was lit. I was made to understand, by slow degrees—a general lack of interest, a hand gently moved—that any attempt on my part to bring some variety into our lives would not be welcome. Recognizing her many virtues, I did my best to uphold the vows I had taken on the day we were married, though here again, if truth be told, my best grew better as the years came on, and my memory of the love I had once known and lost gradually came to matter less.

And now, suddenly, a whisper after dinner, a smile over cards. A willingness, if not to be pleased, then at least to humor my desires. I was relieved to learn that, despite the fallow periods that had extended, by slow degrees, from weeks to months, I had not grown enfeebled in the act of love, and though Eng's face, where I could make it out in the moonlight, invariably carried the expression of a man waiting for a carriage, Addy's look of surprise at my youthful vigor (the effect of her pleasure diluted, somewhat, by the tonic of her amusement) more than made up for it. On a particularly dark night, in the midst of our passion, I felt both her hands suddenly press into my backside, pulling me down to her. And though it later occurred to me that she might simply have intended to accelerate the crisis and have an end (which was precisely what happened), I'd never known such boldness in our marriage, and basked in the glow of it for days.

Weather doesn't come from the west, Gideon liked to say; it comes from the bedroom. And though I recall arguing the point—unhappy days can cloud the mind—I knew even then it was true, having sensed for myself how very sweet a drizzling March in Paris might be. The general calm that spread from the bedroom now seemed to cover the entirety of our days.

In the evenings after supper the younger children would gather around (Nannie almost always on my lap, Christopher, though quite a big boy now, tight against my shoulder), and Eng and I would spin tales of Siam: of ageless tortoises and man-thick pythons whose skin flashed blue as a butterfly's wing, of raging typhoons on the Andaman Sea and the light that shone from the skin of the Emerald Buddha the day we were brought—a fishmonger's sons—to meet Rama III in the Audience Hall in Bangkok, and on and on with only the clock in the parlor keeping the time until half the children were sleeping and the others on their way. At some point, often toward the end of a story, Addy and I would look at each other across the heads of our children and our look would hold for a moment, and then the king would clap his pudgy hands, the tiger vanish in the ruined wall, and the four of us would carry them off, one by one, to bed.

XI.

I still see him in the big dirt square between the barn and the smoke-house, pushing a wheelbarrow heaped high with wood. From around the corner of the shed comes the short sharp crack of a log being cleaved in two, followed by the double thump of the halves falling to the dirt.

"Good morning, Lewis," said my brother that morning. "Firewood's coming along, I see."

"We're *makin'* it come along, suh," he said. "It don't want to go."

My brother smiled. "I'm sure it doesn't. How much have you got?"

"Three walls to the eave, 'nother half done." He ran the sleeve of his shirt over his gleaming forehead. "I got to watch them boys, Mistah Eng," he said, not smiling. "They get up a good head of steam, they won't be a tree left standin' 'tween here 'n' Richmond." As though to make the point, two axes now came down at once, followed by a third. Behind them, I remember, I could hear the dry whip, whip, whip of the women threshing the oats. A baby started crying. The sound of thresh-ing, steady as crickets, diminished slightly. An axe struck and hit.

Raising the barrow, his forearms ridged and hard, he leaned his weight into it and the wheel began to turn. We watched him pilot his burden across the broken ground, then disappear—first barrow and wood, then straight back and bent knees, then flapping left shoe—

around the edge of the tobacco shed he had built the season before. Less than three weeks later he was dead.

It would be unfair to say that our troubles began that November, or that Lewis's death, in one blow, destroyed the understanding my brother and I had built up over a lifetime. But it wouldn't be wrong, either. Though it left the house standing, it exposed the crack beneath the rug, the weakened joists and rotten beams we had always known were there, forced a reckoning that might otherwise never have come.

It was our fault, mine most of all. With most of the cotton ginned and pressed and the tobacco safe in the sheds for a week, we had felt, when we heard Price still had half his crop in the field and only six slaves to cut and rack it, that we could safely loan him Lewis for a time. It was already late in the season. We'd had fires in the parlor for a week. Every morning I expected one of the children to come running in with a thin pane of ice from the trough.

I had always disliked Price. A big man saddled with a small man's soul, still uneasy with himself at an age when most men have grown comfortable with their shortcomings, he had compensated by cultivating an array of tics and mannerisms that always appeared, with amazing consistency, just slightly off the mark. Leaning in a doorway, he'd appear to be imitating how other men leaned; bursting into laughter, he would give the impression of practicing something he had admired in someone else. Trapped by his own character, he'd lash out when nothing called for it, just as a dog with three legs will bite before a whole one does. He had cheated us twice. More competent than some, hardly a fool, he knew how to ingratiate himself with others, stroke and salve—and cut from below as necessary.

If it had been up to me, I would have let him sink. It was Eng who noted that nearly everyone—Smythe, Stoneman, even poor, hapless Benner—was offering to send a slave of their own to help; Eng who pointed out that Seward had mentioned Price that very Sunday in his sermon on Christian charity; Eng who reminded me, finally, that it hadn't been that long since the citizens of Wilkes County had smashed all the windows in Judge Yates's house on hearing that his daughters were engaged to a pair of carnival freaks from the Orient. Doing nothing, he argued, would hurt us, not Price.

But though the initial arguments were Eng's, I was the one who suggested sending Lewis—the one man, by his nature, least capable of enduring what would come his way. Having made the decision, I felt we might as well offer the best we had. No one could help noticing that we'd sent the best; Price, having stolen from us, would feel the sting of our generosity the most. As for Lewis, I hardly gave him a thought. I might as well have hung him myself from the cross beam in the barn.

We found him and Moses that Sunday afternoon squatting in the small dirt yard between the cabins, whittling new legs for the three broken chairs that stood leaning against the wall under a half-opened window. It was a fine day, yellow and soft, redolent with fall. A slight breeze, the timid forerunner of winter's gales, moved now and again through the thinning grass.

I could see them talking as we approached, looking up from their hands for a moment or two, then back with a shrug or a nod, Lewis gesturing with the hand that held the knife as if cutting the world into bits of field and wagon and wall. Even at that distance you could tell they were father and son, and I remember wondering, idly, what it was that made that link so obvious, and how odd it was that with some—a man and wife, for example—the bond was visible at fifty yards, while with others you could talk all evening and never know.

A woman's laughter cut off as we entered the yard.

They both stood when they saw us coming, swatting at the shavings that clung to their pants like bits of curling paper. We explained our business. Lewis said nothing. Behind him the wind ruffled through red-tipped ivy crawling along the sill.

It was only for three or four days at most, we told him. We had spoken to Price. He would be treated well, as one of ours.

"I know Mr. Price," he said.

"You should get along just fine, then," said my brother, misunderstanding.

He nodded slowly, then turned to his son. "Go on, boy," he said, nodding his head toward the cabin. "I'll be in in a spell."

He waited till Moses had gone, then spoke as calmly as if he were telling us how much work had been done, or asking for boards to fix his roof.

"I won't be beat no more. I'm too old for it."

"No one's going to beat you, Lewis," I said, slightly taken aback by the weariness in his voice. "You have my word."

He left the next morning at dawn. We never saw him again. I don't count the shape we found bleeding in the dirt by the drying racks. No, the last time I saw him he was squatting against a peeling wall with his son on a November afternoon, talking, as a woman's laughter carried from one of the back cabins.

XII.

We never knew what happened at Bellefonte that night. In the weeks that followed we learned a few things—bits, pieces—not enough. We learned that Price had been driving his slaves ragged trying to make up for his own stupidity. That two had been whipped the week before— Ben, a big, quiet mulatto, just a day earlier. We learned that late that Tuesday night a fight broke out in the clearing behind the drying racks between two big men—Lewis and one of Price's slaves, a big buck named Joah. That the fight erupted with such ferocity and was over so quickly that Mason, Price's overseer, hardly knew what was happening before it was done. That Lewis, bleeding from the face, shattered his left arm blocking a short, hard swing with a shovel, and the next thing any-one knew Joah was walking in little squares in the dirt, holding his neck with both hands as if trying to hide Lewis's tobacco knife buried in his throat. Before anyone had time to react or think, Price was there with the shotgun.

Lewis had tried to run for home. It was this that troubled me most, I think. That this man, whom I had never known to be afraid of anything, had tried to run. How very afraid he must have been those last few moments, seeing the world unraveling, realizing all he would leave behind.

I had told him he would be treated well. I'd lied. Holding his useless arm as if cradling a child, Lewis ran for the dark. He'd nearly made it to the edge of the clearing when the buckshot caught him and opened up the back of his head.

Gideon woke us just before midnight. Even before we climbed off the wagon we could see them in the lamplight, the two of them lying side by side on a gray blanket, Lewis's arm bent wrong at the elbow, Joah's head turned to the side as though whispering something to the man who had just killed him. A short distance across the dirt, between the sheds, stood a group of slaves. I recognized the mulatto, Ben. Price was sitting in a rocker on the porch, the gun across his lap.

"A bad business, Bunker," he called out. He pointed with the gun. "Your nigger there killed one of my slaves."

We squatted down by Lewis's side. Taking him by the legs and shoulders, we rolled him toward us. I raised the lamp. The entire back of his head—or what should have been the back of his head—was now a sticky mass of dirt and sawdust. His colorless shirt had been pulled halfway down his back; a dozen pink craters in the black skin of his neck, already dried, marked the edge of the pattern. I couldn't move, or think. I just sat there staring at him, mindlessly stroking his leg as though he were a child in need of comforting. My brother, with some effort, slipped his fingers under Lewis's head. Turning it slightly, he began to brush at the dirt as though looking for something.

Embarrassed at this show of emotion, Price rocked in his chair for a few moments, then stood and walked down the porch steps. "He's dead, Bunker," he said. "No use in that."

"What happened here?" said my brother.

"Look for yourself. Stuck a knife in his throat. I tried to aim low, but . . ."

My brother grasped Lewis's woolly hair, turned the back of his head to Price. "You took his head off at thirty feet."

I could feel the blood pounding in my head like ocean surf. Lewis's pant leg had pulled up from the shoe. I could see the skin of his calf against the dirt.

Price smiled. "Don't think I don't know what you're trying to do, Bunker."

"You owe us two thousand dollars," said Eng evenly.

Price laughed. "I'll see you in hell first, you little yellow bastards."

"And an apology."

Squatting twenty feet away, the shotgun cradled in the crook of his arm, Price turned to Gideon. "You listening to this?" he asked.

"Every word," said Gideon.

Price shook his head, pretending to control himself. "I'm not an unreasonable man," he said, standing. "We're neighbors, after all. And I'll be the first to say it: Lending me your nigger was a downright Christian thing to do. But look here, Bunker. There's two niggers dead and we're even."

"Is that right?" said my brother, and in that moment I knew where we were headed.

"Not a court in the land would see it different. You know that. Hell, at least one of you has to have some sense."

Taking a handkerchief out of my pocket I reached over and slipped it, as best I could, under Lewis's face. We stood up. My hands were shaking so badly I had to make a show of dusting the dirt off my pants.

"Maybe so," said Eng, nodding. We started walking toward Price. I could see Gideon straighten from where he'd been leaning against the shed. The slaves, I noticed, were still standing, like so many silhouettes, in the shadow between the sheds. Mason, the overseer, was nowhere to be seen.

"I'm glad you see it that way," said Price uncertainly. "I'm sorry for it, but there it is."

"There it is," said Eng, extending his hand.

In all our life together my brother only beat me to a punch once, and this was not that time. A split second before his right landed on Price's left cheekbone, its twin, my left, landed on his right. He fell like an ox. I kicked the gun, which he'd been holding high on the stock, off to the side, saw Gideon, out of the corner of my eye, stroll over to pick it up.

We fought as we always had, swinging from the outside, using our inner arms up close to grab or hold or block. Tougher men had fought us and lost. Price, however, was a problem. Scratching and slapping, he tried to claw his way free, then turned and fought like a woman, gouging at our eyes and throats, tearing at our hair, trying to drive a boot or knee between our legs. At one point, hearing my brother scream, I turned to see that Price, with a strange, mewling whine, had sunk his teeth like a dog into my brother's shoulder. Forcing his head down to keep him from pulling away, I grabbed the spongy mess of his broken nose and he let go. A few seconds later, my brother's fist took out the teeth that had bitten him.

It was while we were on the ground that I felt the sudden blow to the back of my head. The world grew silent, as though I were being submerged under water. Clawing my way back to the surface, unable to turn around, I fought on as best I could. A second blow never came.

I'm not sure we would have stopped had it not been for Gideon. Price hadn't moved in a while when, as in a dream, I heard a voice saying, "That might do, gentlemen. All good things must end."

A hand came down and grabbed me by the elbow. My brother and I staggered to our feet. I felt a strong arm around my waist. Mason, the overseer, was lying on the ground, a piece of stovewood by his side. Gideon's face drifted briefly into view.

The porch tilted crazily, then righted itself. My brother, I realized, was holding me up from the other side. "Walk," he said.

Lewis and Joah were lying where we'd left them.

"We can't . . ." I began.

"We can," said Gideon.

"No."

"All right," I heard him sigh. "Just get in the goddamn wagon. I'll get him."

It was Gideon who lifted Lewis into the back of the wagon that night with the help of one of the slaves: the same wagon we'd laid him down in twelve years earlier. And fully awake now, the blood and the salt stinging our eyes, we drove him home.

XIII.

I gave Moses a white-handled Barlow knife. I couldn't think of anything else to do. He thanked me nicely enough—he and his mother were in the house by then—and put it away in his overalls pocket.

He would carry it until May of 1864, when it worked its way through a tear in his pocket and fell, unnoticed, into the corpse-fed grass of the old Chancellorsville battlefield. Finding it missing, he tried looking for it—a white-handled knife would be easy to spot—but found the huge, sweet-smelling field his company had slept on so thickly sown with the dead, the yellowing bones of their toes and their knuckles peeping from the grass, the circlets of their spines protruding from the dirt like half-buried bracelets or burrowing snakes (as though that thousand-acre field were the very coatroom of death), that he gave it up for lost. That afternoon his unit of Grant's army entered the Wilderness.

XIV.

Like the silt that keeps a footprint where the water is slow, the world holds our shape for a time. For days after he died I kept seeing him walking back from the fields or disappearing between the drying sheds. Lewis, it seemed, had occupied more space than I'd known.

The world is full of omens. Reason blinds us all. The day before he died we had let the hogs into the corn on a still, lowering afternoon just as the sun, disappearing under a lid of clouds, turned the fields of broken stalks, the fence rails, the western walls of the sheds a strange, unearthly orange. The hogs went through the downed corn like fire—rooting, grunting, squealing. I'd seen it before, yet this time—perhaps because of that strange light—there was a madness in it, in the sight of pigs as big as men rooting out moles and mouse nests, crushing tortoises hidden in the stalks, snorting and snuffing through the broken shells . . . One of the sows grabbed a snake. We watched as she tossed it left and right to break its spine, the snake flailing in her mouth like a long black rope. And I knew—as mother claimed she knew, as the blacks said they knew—that something bad had wormed its way up into the visible world, and would make its presence known.

A week after we returned home, though I knew it would leave us short in the field, I brought Berry and Moses into the house. My brother argued. We had already lost our best worker, he said. To lose two more was madness. I refused to give in. We argued on, just as we had twice as children, when, unable to walk away from one another, our anger fueled by our proximity, we had fought until we couldn't move from sheer exhaustion and just lay side by side, sobbing, until we found the strength to stand and walk home.

"They're not coming into my house," my brother said.

"I know that," I answered. "They're coming into mine."

Without our being aware of it, a train of events had been set in motion, though it would sometimes seem to me, in the years to come, that the train had actually departed the station on the day we were born, that it had been there all along, running on invisible rails over seabeds and continents, and that the events of those days had simply made it visible to us. It hardly mattered. Predestined or newly born, our fate came rushing out of our past and hurtled by, leaving us standing, like twin travelers on the prairie, watching the lantern in its final car disappear into the dark.

We had topped a rise, and begun the long descent to war.

PART TWO

I.

Muang Tai, or Siam to a *farang* like me, is a dream now. The brown Meklong, turgid and ripe. The sun. The particular rankness—the essence of childhood, and not unpleasant—of water and waste and things drowned in the roots. The palm-thatched houseboats, tied each to each along the banks. The warm smell of the bamboo mats; the seething of the rain. We swam in the river a thousand times, laughing at the old women who assured us that Akuna would drag us down by our skinny ankles to join the company of the dead he kept under the shelves of rock, their mouths forever open like fish and their eyes as white as clouds; when we were older we grew bolder still, diving under the fishing boats as they came upstream, swimming smooth and fast as eels. Our father told us not to, but we didn't listen.

Muang Tai was fish on the drying racks and the sweet smooth flesh of the lamyai scooped with a fingertip from a hard brown shell. It was the familiar outline of the branches of the shoreline trees at dusk—a pig's head on a stick, a laughing man with a broken arm, a sad man with twigs in his hair; it was a trunk along the river path, a wrinkled old boll like an elephant's eye.

Muang Tai was the great, lumbering beetles we tied to strips of river grass and fought against each other in the dirt. They had great purple jaws like scimitars and we would play with them for hours, or so it seemed, listening to the minute clicking of their jaws, moving them this way and that, lifting them up into the air like puppets whenever they seemed about to get a real hold. Though of the same tribe they hated each other instinctively (though it occurs to me now that it might have been as much their predicament as their nature that made them what they were), and we would fight them on and off for days sometimes, keeping them in crude cricket cages we made ourselves, feeding them bits of fish and fruit, until the day Eng's beetle, a slightly smaller variety, closed its jaws on mine and neatly scissored off its long, whiplike antennae. Hardly an oversensitive child, I crushed it with a stick to allay its suffering, but the image of it blundering around, turning in small circles, stayed with me, and I never played the game again.

And then there was the sadness of the leaf cups, each with its little candle, sent down the river on Loy Krathong. And the heavy, head-shaking walk of the buffalo in the paddies. And the day my father saw a half-grown python looped like a small tree around something on the riverbank. When we threw sticks at it, it vomited up the small dog it had almost swallowed, and slipped, as though through a crack, into the water, a reticulated chain of velvety black and brown and yellow that gleamed a pure peacock blue where it passed through the sun. Left behind in the mud, covered in a smooth, unctuous cream, the dog looked like something that had been born too early, or had long ago drowned in milk. I did not feel sorry for it.

It's been sixty-three years now since we stepped aboard the *Sachem* with hardly more than Mr. Melville's carpetbag to our names. Nearly a lifetime. We received little news of our mother or our brother Nai: a letter a year, if that, less as the seasons passed. And just as the time came when the language of home grew wooden and strange in our mouths, when we had to work to remember the names of the most common things and finally gave up trying, so it was with those we had left behind. Year by year, as if by some chemic process inexorable as the rusting of steel or the greening of bronze, their touch, their anger, their familiar essence faded, until those we had known as intimately as we knew our own skin had been reduced to little more than a name, an occasional sorrow, and a small collection of hardened memories, unrecognizable under the verdigris of the years.

We didn't intend it that way. We would have had it otherwise. But the plantain-leaf boats we released on Loy Krathong went each their way. Some, pushed out too hard by their eager owners, or swamped by the waves from a fisherman's boat, winked out early. Some, caught by an invisible loop of current, came back around. And some—a relative few, admittedly—just kept going, receding farther and farther into the dark, their tiny flames bobbing precariously on the black water until they had disappeared from view. And we from theirs, I suppose.

I would have stayed. As would Eng, though he would never admit it. But Hunter, behind his Scots reserve, was as ruthless as Barnum would ever be, and Coffin, despite his Presbyterian posturing, could hear the ring of bullion at ten miles. Hunter knew he'd spotted a goldmine the afternoon he saw us, as he put it, swimming in the Meklong River like some strange animal with two heads and four arms, and Coffin, having wheedled the affections of King Rama III, knew how to grease the path whether it wanted greasing or not. The king's permission was secured. We were promised a salary and a chance to see the world. My mother, who would be losing not only her two oldest sons but their income as well, was offered three hundred pounds. She did not say no.

When I think of her now I see her as she was then, as though time had simply stopped in Meklong when we left it. And more and more, I find myself remembering not the person I once knew in life but the one I came to know in dreams. I'd seen her in my sleep, talked with her, scores of times over the years, but it wasn't until after her death that I realized that those ghostly meetings—without the ballast of flesh and blood to balance them—had quietly taken over the territory of the past. Now, when I thought of her, I found it easier to recall the person I'd seen standing in the moonlight by the tobacco sheds in a dream than I did the distant figure crying on the pier in Bangkok in 1829 as the boat carrying her two boys and their pet python moved off into the harbor.

If someone had told us we would never see her again, we would not have believed them. But then, how many of us, stopped by some Elijah on the pier when we were young, would have believed that our lives would take the turns they did?

When she was five or six, my Nannie began asking about her grandparents, as children will. She wanted to know about her grandmother in particular—what she looked like, whether she got mad at us when we were boys—and Eng and I did our best. We dusted off the old anecdotes, untangled their strings, made them jump about. We described the Grand Palace in Bangkok, with its blue-and-orange tiled ceilings and gold mosaic walls. We told the tale of King Trailok's beloved boatman who, upon running his lord's barge aground on one of the bars of the river, insisted, over his lord's offers of leniency, on being put to death. We repeated again the threadbare tale of how our mother, a fishmonger's wife, sent away the king's physicians who wanted to separate us at birth, how this quietest of women, who often smiled but seldom spoke, had stood at the door of our houseboat, a stick she'd taken from the fire in one hand and the knife my father used for cleaning fish in the other, and told them to leave.

Nannie's curiosity was limitless; not so my inventiveness. Strangely touched by her interest in a woman she had never met, aware as well of how much it would have meant to our mother to know that a daughter of ours would one day ask about her, I struggled on, filling in the chinks as necessary, tidying up the thatching, feeling all the while that my memory—our memory, for Eng remembered even less than I—had betrayed us all. This was not our mother. In the age-old battle between language and time, I thought to myself, neither wins. Time hurries off with its prizes; our words are all that's left us.

But then something unexpected happened. As we continued to tell our tales over the course of those two weeks, the inadequacy of our words became less troubling, their failure to capture the truth less obvious. They came to seem, if not true, then good approximations of the truth, and so, our consciences partially salved, we sailed on; we offered them to the children who gathered in the parlor by the old double chair every evening to listen—stories that had never really happened, about people who had never quite lived—and they, by some miracle of transubstantiation greater than all the breads and fishes, took the stories we told and fashioned them into something very much like truth. After listening for the twentieth time to the story of our mother and the king's physicians—a story so much deeper, sadder, and more beautiful than I could ever begin to tell—Nannie turned to us one winter night as we chunked up the fire and said, simply, "Grandmother was very brave." And there it was: a nugget of truth in the gravel of our tales.

"She was that," I said, blinking away the tears that had suddenly come to my eyes. "She was that, child. The bravest woman I ever knew."

We were born with our heads between each other's legs (and not up our asses, as Gideon once informed us in the heat of an argument) on a hard bamboo mat on a houseboat tied to the shore of the Meklong River in ancient Siam, the exotic Orient, land of tigers and peacocks and little yellow people very much like us. Like little Tom Thumb and Anna Swan and Mr. Nellis, the Armless Wonder, we'd been blessed by God's inattention, undercooked or too well done, a pinch of dough forgotten or triple what was asked for, a batch half-divided and sent on its way. Unlike them, we had the added blessing of our place of birth to be thankful for, which in the minds of our newly adopted countrymen, as old Phineas Barnum well knew, called up a wonderful hash of pagodas and harems, child kings and barbarian hordes. Ancient Siam, made visible in the cast of our skin and the shape of our eyes, was as far from State Street as you could get. It was sin and opium smoke. It was elephants with diamond collars and dark-eyed beauties with rubies in their navels. Siam was everything unfamiliar, everything our God-drunk countrymen feared and desired, and we were its exotic export, otherness distilled and hyperdistilled. And so they came in droves to stare and poke and prod. And pay. And pay again. We made nothing. We grew nothing. We were like priests, offering absolution for sins we had never known and could barely understand. For six years, like whores in the marketplace, we peddled the wares of God.

It might have been otherwise.

I can see our birth—I was there, after all—the small, tilting room with the bamboo mat, the smell of the water and our mother's sweat, the women's excited chatter when we gushed at last into this world, tight as a doubled nut slipping its shell. Twins. And two little buds in the mass of slippery legs and arms. Sons. For the first ten seconds of our lives, we were good fortune. And then the growing silence, the confusion as they attempted first to untangle us, the cries of fear at the band of flesh, suddenly visible, that grew between us like some unnatural plant.

They ran. Ran from a band of skin hardly two fingers wide at the time, ran—these women who had known my mother for years, and who would know her for years to come—as from something unclean. Our mother, as she always had and always would, did what was necessary. Left alone on a mat with a pair of unwashed twins crying between her legs, she pulled herself over to the knife the women had dropped in their rush, cut the twin ends of the blue, ropy cord that bound us to her, then tied off the ugly little tails that remained with a bit of string she found on the floor. Seeing how things were, she carefully untwisted us so we could lie head to head and settled herself to wait for the afterbirth. The rain began, hissing in the palm fronds, turning the shoreline outside the windows a pale, watery gray. By the time my father came home (no one had had the courage to get him), she had washed and suckled us and put us to bed.

I wonder what they talked about that night. From all I know, they took our birth for the fact it was and went on with their lives. They had three children already. Now they had two more. In many ways, the peculiar nature of our birth was like the weather: One might wish it to be different, but typhoons would be born in the Bay of Bengal and the river would flood when the monsoon came whether one wished it or not. Our father, I suspect—though I hardly remember him at all— shook his head over our common bond, noted that we looked healthy and strong, let us grasp a finger each, and returned to his selling table outside our door.

Others were less sanguine. News of our birth reached Bangkok almost before my father's boat had bumped against the house that May afternoon, and like any new event, whether celestial or earthly, it had to be worked into the tissue of superstitions that made the people feel secure. The learned men of the royal court put their heads together and lo! there was light. If an unnatural birth was a bad omen, they reasoned, a birth such as ours, of such surpassing strangeness, could only prophesy the end of the world. The sun would turn black in the sky. Rama II himself, the Lord of Life, decreed it: We would have to be separated or put to death.

We were neither.

They came three weeks later in a pouring rain, their sandals slap-slapping in the mud: a group of five men, three holding vermilion umbrellas with gold tassels—a thing never before seen in our village—and two in the yellow robes of the Buddhist priests. They stopped on the shore at the foot of the walk to our house. The gaggle of soaked villagers who had been leading them pointed up the plank and stepped away. "We have come to see the marvel," said one to my mother, who, all unsuspecting, wordless with astonishment at this august delegation standing before our houseboat, invited them in. My father was out fishing.

I can see her running ahead, shame quickly outstripping amazement at the thought of her clothes, the smallness of the rooms. Our poverty, I imagine, must never have been as visible to her as it was in those few moments. The room where we lay sleeping on a mat by the wall, despite the open windows, smelled hot and rank. We had shat ourselves. Quickly drawing the soiled cloth from under us, she wiped us with a clean edge, slipped a fresh cloth under our bottoms and ran out the back door just as the boat gave a telltale heave and the group stepped aboard. Anyone watching from the opposite bank would have seen our mother burst out the side door as though the boat were under pressure, make two quick swipes with the cloth in the river, drop it on the plank in the rain, and rush back in. By the time the men had filed into the main room, led, no doubt, by our screaming (they were prepared for the ill manners of the peasants, and the stunned awe their own appearance could provoke), she was there to greet them in a fresh skirt, her head bowed low between her raised arms in the *wai* she had been too startled to offer earlier. A bowl of bright red ngáw fruit sat on the table.

They wasted little time. Ignoring the fruit she offered them, they walked over to where we lay crying under the faded yellow cloth we had succeeded in pulling over ourselves. One of them, a small, wizened-looking man with a pointy beard, asked my mother to remove the cloth.

A shocked murmur greeted our appearance. This was ghastly, an evil omen indeed. One of them, bolder than the rest, ran his smooth finger across our bridge, then flipped us over. We screamed. My mother began to step forward—though whether to stop them or help them is unclear—then paused. Consensus was immediate. We would have to be separated. If we lived, a case could be made that the threat had been forestalled; if we died, the king's decree would have been carried out.

But if the desired end was undebatable, the means by which to achieve it were not. Something of an argument ensued among the three physicians, during which my mother at first stood awkwardly off to the side like a young girl hoping to catch the boys' attention, and then, perhaps unable to think of anything else to do, went to the fire. One maintained the bond between us was dead flesh, or very nearly so, and therefore susceptible to sawing or burning. The second, reaching for a piece of fruit, disagreed. Sawing through the flesh would be too crude; the ligament, he pointed out, squatting by our side, was of considerable thickness. It might link us more vitally than his colleague assumed. A clean incision was therefore of the utmost importance, and while the idea of burning had some merit, the operation would have to be performed as swiftly as possible. A hot wire applied here and here, he believed, running a long fingernail down the twin bases of our bridge where it attached to our fist-sized chests, would have the greatest chance of success. The monks in their yellow robes had said nothing. The rain had increased.

Nonsense, interrupted the one with the pointy beard. To do as his colleagues suggested they might as well put us in a sack with a good-sized stone and throw us in the river. We were much too young to survive such extreme measures. No, to have any hope of success the thing would have to be done by degrees. He paused strategically, then pointed at us, still wailing on the mat. Notice how they are of approximately the same size and weight. Hang them over a fine gut cord, one on either side. Take them off only to bathe and feed them. Within a few weeks their weight will force the cord up through the ligament, successfully separating them, but the process will have been so slow that the wound will have had time to . . .

They turned as one toward the strange, almost inhuman sound coming from the other side of the room. Our mother stood with her back to the fire. In her left hand, hanging by her side, was the blackened stick with which she had been prodding the flames. In her right she held my father's cleaning knife, its point at her throat. The steel, they could see, had already pierced the skin; a thin, dark stream was winding its way down her throat and into her shirt. She seemed unaware of the sound that came from her—a perfect joining of rage and despair, a monotonous internal whine like the sound one might hear from a child tormented by bullies in some empty schoolyard, tormented beyond fear, beyond tears, past caring for its own preservation. It didn't stop.

One of the men began to say something, then stopped. Instinctively, faced with this thing, the group began to back away. The sound still coming from her throat, her lips pressed so unnaturally tight she appeared to be straining to keep something from escaping her mouth, my mother began to move toward them. By the time she had passed the mat on which we still lay screaming, her head had tilted back involuntarily and the point of the knife had gone deeper into the soft skin of her throat. The stream had thickened into a dark stem. On her soiled blouse, over her left breast, a dark blossom was opening.

They backed out of our house into the rain, forgetting, in their haste, the vermilion umbrellas they had left inside the door. When, two years later, no one had returned to claim them, my father quietly sold them for a hundred baht each in the marketplace.

In some ways, hardly a heroic tale.

And yet, nothing if not that. Shy by nature, incapable of even speaking to these men from the capital who suddenly appeared in her house-boat like divine beings, carrying with them the air of the royal court, my mother could not even begin to conceive of resisting them. They were like gods. We were nothing. They spoke daily with King Rama II, who took his meals and listened to music on an island in the Garden of Night in the Royal Compound. We were a bit of dirt under the fingernails, a scattering of fish scales on the edge of a rack.

His power was unlimited. His blood could not be shed. For the funeral of his father, he had commissioned a golden coach forty feet high and weighing over ten tons. One hundred and sixty men had been required to move it, another one hundred and thirty-five had been needed to act as brakes. No one outside the immediate royal family and his own inner circle was allowed to look at him. His own councillors were not allowed to touch him. His every whim had the gravity of law. Within three days of his succession to the throne, he had had the son of King Taksin, a celestial prince, beaten to death with a scented sandalwood club.

For my mother to act as she did toward the royal physicians therefore must have seemed—to herself as well as to them—not only mad but unimaginable. One might as well attack a typhoon with a candle.

And yet that, in a sense, was precisely what she had done. Leaning into the gale, she had done the only thing she could: She had held the candle to her clothes, watched as the flames paused, then leaped up her sleeves. A gesture born of utter despair. The wind died. The palms righted themselves. On the horizon over Bangkok, a star appeared through a rent in the clouds. Then another.

The king's physicians never returned. Busy collaborating with the court poets on a translation of the Hindu epic *Ramayana*, King Rama II forgot that he had sentenced us to death to avert the end of the world. An artist by nature, a man who insisted on personally sculpting the decorations for the buildings he commissioned, he lost himself in the adventures of Ramachandra and Sita and let us live.

The world, as is so often the case, did not end. Our mother's and father's fears, like the terror that cramps the heart before dawn but win-nows to a joke by breakfast, came to nothing. We lived, we grew, we wrapped our arms around each other and rolled laughing down the hills above the river, the sky and the grass spinning round our heads like the years. In a word, we survived. The sentence of death was extended, the full stop changed, as in most men's lives, to a comma. The only mark it left on the visible world was a small, dark scar in the skin of our mother's throat.

II.

Perhaps it comes down to this: our mother squatting before the fire, our brothers laughing from somewhere outside, the taste of rice and fish. Perhaps it's the number of times our father pulled our ears or touched our faces, or the days (how many weeks or months would they make, added all together?) the three of us spent knee-deep in the sun-warm river, bent over the drying racks. What makes a home? Was it the familiar bump of our father's boat when he returned in the afternoons? Or the way the floor would tip ever so slightly when he stepped aboard? He would strip his shirt and wash his arms in the basin, then cup his hands and gently pat water on his face and head. Was it the sound of the water raining down into the bowl?

I barely remember those early years now. Our lives were not easy. Even if they had wanted to, my parents could not have made them so, and they showed no signs of wanting to. We were never coddled. We crawled, we walked, we ran. We fought other boys our age and older in the dirt where the market used to be. We learned to swim. With the possible exception of climbing trees, we could do anything anyone else could do, only better, since there were two of us. When the floating theater came to Meklong we went to see it, and though a lifetime has come between that night and this one, though the storytellers we listened to are all long dead, and the tumblers and the jugglers as well, I remember them all. We watched as a strong young man in fantastic dress fought invisible demons with a flaming sword, thrusting, parrying, the blade streaming sparks against the dark until suddenly, tilting back his head, he raised his arm and in one smooth movement swallowed the burning steel to the hilt. The crowd gasped. A number of women screamed. We had just started to cry when he drew the extinguished blade out of his throat, tossed his hair and plunged it quivering into the wooden stage.

But these—the floating theatre, the giant *pla buk* that somehow made its way up the Meklong and tore up my father's net, the purification fires burning on the eve of Songkran—these are the few boulders that rise above the river. The rest—the familiar voices, the songs, the thousand victories and humiliations of childhood—have sunk beneath the surface. I can hear them sometimes when the evening is still, quietly knocking against each other in the current. The small bones of memory.

But my point is this: Our childhood was hardly different from anyone else's in the world we knew, and a good deal happier than most. Our father was Chinese, and, like all the Chinese sons of Piatac, the soldier who long ago had rallied the conquered Siamese army and driven the Burmese out of Muang Tai, he enjoyed without qualm all the privileges to which his birth entitled him. Exempt from having to work in the rice paddies every year, able to buy his way out of military conscription with a small tax, he seized the opportunity offered him and prospered.

His success alone, however—measured by a new net, a bit of cloth for my mother—would hardly have been enough to explain our happiness. Our parents, as far as we could know, seem to have had a genuine regard for each other. My father, though hardly a gentle man by nature, always treated our mother kindly, praising the food she prepared or the way she kept our house, discussing his business affairs with her as though she were a man, taking her side when she had been cheated in the marketplace rather than blaming her, as most men would have, for her inattention. In their years together, he never struck her.

Our mother, for her part, quietly bore him nine children, working from the first muzzy gray of dawn to the deep mahogany light of dusk—sleep to sleep and season to season—without complaint or criticism. When Lun Li and the other women spoke of their husbands' laziness while sweeping the planks in the mornings, she would nod in sympathy but refuse to join in, and they, noting that she did this without putting on airs or gloating, ascribed her reticence to fear and welcomed their timid sister back to the fold.

A noisy, happy home, all in all. There was always a good deal of talk in the evenings, and more than a little laughter. Quiet in the company of others, our mother would grow almost lively in ours, and though he had never hesitated in letting us know the weight of his hand when it was necessary, my father could joke and smile when he wanted. On good nights, our brother told us, he would imitate Chong Lu getting caught in his own net, or Luang Bhirasi the day he almost stepped on a baby cobra, dancing like a man possessed before falling into the *klong*.

Father. Where has he gone, I wonder. I imagine him leaning back, perhaps putting his hands behind his head as I do, as Christopher used to, as *his* son surely would have. I can almost see him, chuckling at the seven of us holding our stomachs from laughing, the little one wriggling on the mat, even my mother, the baby at her breast, smiling quietly into her hand. A man content. It's dark outside. The still air moves, bringing the sounds of familiar voices, the creak of wood, the smell of fruit and mud and heat. He sighs, reaches for his cup. The moment passes.

The cholera came to Meklong when we were eight. It came like a wave, a darkness. It came out of nothing—a small pain in the side, a sudden dizziness at the nets—and ate us alive. As in a dream, the small familiar figure in the market turned—and sank her teeth in our throats.

Our younger sister Song was the first, followed by the two babies. I remember my father holding her head, trying to get her to sip from a cup. The young ones went quickly, held over buckets, retching. Zuo, our brother, who was two years younger than us, came next. He shat himself raw, cried quietly, and then was still. Our parents, disbelieving, rushed from room to room—washing, holding, emptying the pots of brown liquid, thin as river water, that flowed out of their children, listening as their babies one by one emptied themselves with small barking noises, slumped into whimpering sleep, and died. Li came next. And then our father, a strange look on his face, bent in the middle and started to shake.

I don't remember him dying. Our mother claimed, years later, that he talked to us almost to the end, reassuring us, comforting us, cleaning himself as best he could until he couldn't raise his head or his arms and asked my mother not to let us in the room anymore. He was a strong man, and disrespectful of death.

I killed the week it took him to die. I killed him too. Killed him retching over the pot, then shaking his head and trying to smile. Killed him making his little jokes while holding the wall to keep from slumping off the bucket. I buried him so deep that a full thirty years would pass before I saw him again.

On a night in America, as far from Muang Tai as I would ever come, I woke in a house my brother and I would come to call our own to the talk of far-off thunder in a dream and, waking, couldn't tell whether it was mumbling over the hills at our back or over the giant steps of the rice paddies thirty years ago. The rain never came, so perhaps the thunder I heard really was over Bangkok.

I remember thinking how strange it was that I should dream of him after so many years. I couldn't remember his face or his voice, and yet he had seemed so familiar, so utterly and completely alive, that I was struck with the thought that death is less than we make of it, that perhaps we simply live on—singing, arguing, swatting at flies—in other people's dreams.

It was night in Meklong. My brother and I were children again. We were in our houseboat. I could see a baby sleeping on a bamboo mat, our brother Nai eating jun fruit out of a wooden bowl. I could hear a baby crying, a man arguing with his wife. That must be Wei-Ling, I remember saying to myself. His houseboat is next to ours.

Mother was in the dream, scooping pieces of fish and rice into the clay pot with her fingers. "Your father will be home soon," she said to the fire, and I wondered to myself by what accident we had found ourselves home again. Just then the house rocked slightly and he walked in. I knew him instantly—his wide, kind face, his eyes, his movements. His familiarity broke my heart. He bent down to touch his sweating fore-head to ours and I could smell the river. I looked past the netting. On the outside selling table, gleaming in the moonlight, was a small mountain of silvery fish.

We sat down at the table. I looked at my father's hands and started to cry. They were fisherman's hands, with constellations of thin white cuts and miniature crosses and puckered scars. A fresh cut on the knuckle of his thumb was bleeding.

"What is it?" he said to me. He noticed the cut. "This?" He began to suck on it.

"I'm afraid," I said.

He put down his bowl and smiled. "There's nothing to be afraid of," he said.

I looked out the door. Past the selling table, I could see vast rice pad-dies, striped with water. Mountain terraces dropped down to a long, narrow valley. A fire burned on the horizon. My father saw it too, and put down his food. He turned to my mother. "I'm sorry," he said.

And then we were in the paddies. The houseboat was gone. I could see the dark spears of the rice plants, like rents in the sky. The stars wavered and blurred and were still. In the distance the fire still burned, larger now.

I tried to say something, but tears choked my throat. "I have to go," he said. He smiled. "A nuisance is all it is," he said, tipping his head toward the fire gusting up in the darkness, and his courage gripped my chest like a giant fist. "My brave boys," he said, looking at us, then touched our faces, turned quickly, and started off, pushing hard through the knee-deep water, scattering stars. The night sky closed seamlessly behind him.

I woke crying from my dreams for the first time in my life. Eng was awake. "Would you like to get some water?" he asked.

"I'm fine," I said. "I had a dream about Father."

He was silent.

"Do you remember him?" I asked.

"Hardly at all."

"Anything?"

I felt him shrug. "I remember swimming in the river. And the time he got angry at Li."

"That's all?" My brother, I realized, had buried him too.

"I remember when he died," he said quietly.

But he didn't really. He remembered—as I did now—the smell that filled the rooms when the cholera came. He remembered how very quickly they all went—our brother, our sisters, entire families—how the living, too weak to bury the dead, had thrown their bodies into the river where the current slowly turned them like huge fish, soft with mold. He remembered my mother washing and cleaning for days, mechanically. When our father died she took the small sack of baht and anything else worth money and went to the temple priest. In the name of the bodhisattva he took it all.

To see him dying would have burned a hole in our hearts. But even if neither of us could bear to look at his death directly, enough years had passed that we could at least see the ghastly light it had shed around it. Lying in the dark next to my brother, I remembered now how high our father's coffin had seemed to me on its wooden bier beneath the white canopy woven through with dying flowers, how distant the flutes and drums and gongs had sounded in the thick, scented air. I remembered the Buddhist priest reading a prayer, and the crimson cloth that was taken from the head of our father's coffin and cut into five pieces—one for each of us left. I could see again the lighted tapers, flickering against the green of the jungle, the strange coolness of my mother's hand.

The priests took the coffin inside the temple. When at last they brought out our father's body, washed and purified, and laid him on the wood, it wasn't him at all, but someone much smaller and thinner, and when the priest lit the taper and the mourners set the wood ablaze, the vague dark mass at the center of the flames no longer seemed human at all but a crude effigy, nothing more, set there by the priests to fool us all.

The year was 1819. The *uparaja,* the king's brother, had died two years earlier. Across the river from the carved gold gables and the serpentining *nagas* of the Grand Palace, the Wat Arun—the Temple of the Dawn—was rising out of the earth as steadily as the event it was named for. We neither knew nor cared. Had someone come up to us as we stood by our father's selling table in the weeks following his death—our hands slick with fish and smelling of the *blachang* we sold for ten baht a bowl—and told us that the king, who had designed the temple himself, had less than five years to live, or that *Wat Arun* would be completed only after his death by his son, it would have meant nothing to us. The capital, less than three days' journey down the river, was a separate world: remote as the stars, vaguely mythical, as indifferent to our fate as a tiger to the snail beneath his paws. The earth spun, kings died, stomachs rumbled.

That was the year we went to work. We never stopped. Our mother, desperate to feed the four of us who had survived, had first tried extracting oil from coconuts. Finding the labor hopelessly slow and unprofitable, she began gathering broken earthenware, fixing it as best she could, and selling it for a few baht in the marketplace. It came to nothing. And then Ha Lung, who had been a friend of our father's, and who had lost two of his own children, hired us to help him with his catch, and our fortunes changed. Eng and I worked well together, pulling or lifting nearly as much as a grown man, able to clean two fish at a time. A year later, we bought our own boat with the small amount of money we had saved and went out on the river alone. The other men, amused at the sight of us double-poling up the *khlong,* made room for us to pass. Our income increased.

It was Eng, who had always had a nose for money, who first suggested we use our boat to buy cheap goods up along the river, then ferry them down to the floating marketplace. He had seen the other merchants selling their wares for a profit and saw no reason why we couldn't do the same. People would be curious about us, my brother claimed, and give us their business. I agreed. And so, by slow degrees, we began to learn the delicate art of selling ourselves.

It was just as my brother had said it would be. Curious to see the double boys, people crowded around our boat. And we obliged them, clowning for some, remaining stoic with others, helpfully pulling up our shirts (but not so often as to cheapen the effect), making them pay for their sympathy with baht, their revulsion with baht, their staring eyes and open mouths with baht. Soon we were saving a respectable amount every week. Returning home, we would give our mother the small sum we had made and she would take it, as she had once taken the money our father made, and add it to the small pile hidden beneath the floorboard in the bedroom.

The credit, I'll readily admit, was my brother's. Shrewd as Poor Richard, he sensed our value long before I did, and nurtured it well; years later, he would bargain our fees in New York with Barnum as coldly, as successfully, as he had once bargained for embroidered cloth or wooden bowls in the floating market in Meklong. But his, too, was the blame. More flexible than his stupid brother, he gave away too much, bent to the needs of others too easily, resisted the staring world and its dollars and pounds too little.

I didn't know this at the time. I worked alongside him. I smiled and clowned and turned handstands on the deck, and when faced with a stubborn customer, would pretend to be jerked just slightly off balance by my brother's movements, so as to bring her attention back to our plight. Because of our condition, the government classed us with cripples and idiots and charged us no tax; I accepted this as our due, and happily pocketed the profit.

We traded on the Meklong for three years, tying up our boat in the evenings with the other merchants, listening to them talk about women and war as they ate from their bowls in the evenings, sleeping lightly to protect our wares from thieves. In the morning the creak of wood and the sound of ropes uncoiling would wake us in the dark and we would be off, poling in the warm rain as the jungle slowly appeared around us; though no more than boys, together we almost made a man.

Five years had passed since the cholera came to Meklong. My brother had saved us. Long before the death of King Rama II, we were no longer hungry.

III.

The facts are these: Robert Hunter never found us, never discovered us, never rescued us, as he liked to claim for the benefit of those fresh-faced newspapermen who clustered around him, eager for our story, and who kept his ever-hungry purse well fed and fat. We found *him* that steaming afternoon in 1824, stumbling along the bank of the Meklong like some exotic fool, his face like a sundial and his skin as damp and freckled and pale as a flower.

The descendant of a British merchant ignominiously kicked out of Virginia after the Revolutionary War, Hunter had ground ashore in Muang Tai. Hardheaded and arrogant beneath his dour Scots reserve, he could be persuasive, even charming when he wanted to be. In no time at all he had acquired a warehouse across the river from Bangkok, established contacts in the Royal Palace, and begun scouring the countryside for goods and artifacts with which he hoped to resuscitate his flagging export business.

We would be his finest export, his salvation, his passage from the obscurity to which his fate and his talents had consigned him.

We were thirteen years old. We had gone for a swim in the river that afternoon and were climbing back on board our boat when we heard someone call and turned just in time to see a tall dark figure, hurrying toward us down the bank, catch his toe on a root and pitch forward into the grass. It was his manner of falling—as though someone had nailed his feet to the earth and at the same time given him a violent shove in the back—that impressed us. In a moment he was up again, wiping haplessly at the mud on his clothes, waving his arms, rushing on as though nothing had happened. When he came to the marshy edge of the water he beckoned to us to come nearer. We had never seen a Westerner before. Against our better judgment, we poled closer, thinking we could always hit him on the head if he tried to board the boat.

Would that we had.

What could he have been thinking, I wonder, stumbling about the country in that dark suit and high collar as though taking a late September stroll through Edinburgh. Standing on the shore, he called out all manner of impertinent questions, gesticulating wildly, drawing pictures in the air to supplement his ignorance of our language. In short order he learned that we were merchants, that we had a sister and brother, that we lived with our mother on a houseboat in the village of Meklong just around the bend. He asked if he could come visit. We didn't know what to say. To refuse someone hospitality, in our culture, was wrong, and yet the thought of bringing this creature, even now standing up to his ankles in the mud (for we had not failed to notice that he had quietly moved forward as he spoke, as though creeping up on a wild animal), into our home, seemed less than appealing.

Seeing us hesitate—we must have seemed the bird of fortune to him, insecurely limed and poised to lift off the branch—he suddenly rushed forward, straight into the Meklong. The man was insane. We gripped out poles to push away, fully intending to make his eyes bulge with a knock to the head if he succeeded in reaching the boat, when he began waving something in his right hand, calling "Baht, baht, baht" like a parrot, and we stopped, though still wary, and let the madman, stumbling waist-deep in the current, fill our hands with money. His face above the collar was distended, a mass of swollen bites. Standing by the boat, pimpled and staring, he suddenly put me in mind of some large, exotic fish, come to inquire about the upper world. I whispered to my brother and we began to laugh.

Unabashed, Robert Hunter asked again if he might come and visit.

He came the next week, and the week following, and the week after that, bringing gifts: a new brass pot and a pair of red embroidered slippers for our mother, a gilded cricket cage he claimed had come all the way from Singapore, thin-skinned plums that burst in our mouths. Sitting awkwardly in our houseboat, he showed us coins with unfamiliar symbols, spun strange, broken tales of the sea and of foreign lands larger and grander than we could ever imagine, countries where ordinary men could live like kings and unimaginable wealth was to be had for the asking. We knew nothing. Though we wondered why a man would ever leave such a place to traffic in bowls and folding boxes (and worried, for a time, that he must have been guilty of some odious crime, for which the leaders of these countries had expelled him), we listened nonetheless, and gradually found ourselves taken in.

Starched and stiff as a shirt, Hunter was enough of a man of the world to know that every paradise, to be appealing, must have its serpents; being who he was, he made certain the serpents did his bidding. The women of these lands, he told us one day as the three of us walked down the bank to check our dipping basket, were often as scandalously obliging as they were beautiful, willing to allow the most shocking liberties to their person by anyone who took their fancy. They were not at all like the women we knew. He watched as we levered the dripping basket out of the river and swung it toward the shore, the trapped fish flopping in the mesh. He hadn't wanted to mention these things in front of our mother, he said, but he had noticed that we were almost men, and therefore old enough to be warned of the ways of the world.

We saw none of this. We liked Robert Hunter. Boys ourselves, we were flattered to have a grown man—and a foreigner at that, a thing quite literally unknown in those parts—visiting our houseboat, calling our names, bringing gifts. And Hunter, for his part, was smart enough to move slowly, to prepare the soil, to nurse his seedlings and wait—for years if necessary—for the harvest that would be his. Any doubts we might have harbored about his motives faded as the monsoons came and went and Robert Hunter continued to appear at our home, a small, tight smile on his face and a gaudy gift in his hands.

We had no way of knowing, as he did, that securing our mother's permission was only the first, and smallest, hurdle. Like all the people of Muang Tai, we were the monarch's personal possessions; to take us abroad, he would need the king's permission as well. And so that is what he set out to get. For months and then years—indefatigable, patient as death—he wormed his way into the bureaucracy that was Bangkok, doing favors, probing for weaknesses, studying the vast and intricate foundation of deference and loyalty on which the monarchy was built as though it were a language. For three years he studied its syntactical arrangements, its tonal shades. For three years, everything he did was judged as worth his time, or not, by whether it would further his goal; for three years, his every deed and gesture was balanced and calibrated to a single target. He would tunnel, with the help of Almighty God who watches over Presbyterians in heathen lands, into the Royal Palace. In another man, at another time, with a different goal, I suppose this kind of mad determination would have been almost admirable.

As it was, we got there first.

Ironically enough, Robert Hunter, with his subterranean machinations and squirrelings, may have been responsible for our turn of fortune. A whisper among the servants, overheard perhaps by one of the royal consorts, rose like a bubble in a vat through the hierarchy of consuls and courtiers and ministers until at last, days or weeks or months later, it reached the royal ear. Rama III was in the royal garden, offering squares of plum and snail meat to the palace tortoises, watching them stretch their wrinkled velvet necks, then bend their wizened heads to his outstretched palm. Curious, the king inquired about us, and the tortoises, solemn as sages whose worries had cast them under a spell, raised their leathery heads as though listening as well. Bring them to me, he said, slowly stroking the soft skin of a long neck with the back of his fingers.

He had been on the throne just over a year. A hard man with a soft heart, he had no interest in ballet or the theatre, but devoted himself, instead, to the art of war. Whereas Rama II would sit on an island in the Garden of Night, listening to the poets reciting their verses, contemplating the doubled reflections of the candle boats drifting past the Chinese pagodas and European pavilions he himself had designed, his successor drew most of his pleasure from conquest. Within months of ascending the throne, he had invaded the Lao territory to the north, subdued part of Cambodia, sent his armies down the Malay Peninsula. A devout Buddhist, he devoted a good deal of time to denouncing the Protestant missionaries who, with Robert Hunter-like tenacity, persevered in trying to save our souls despite having failed to win a single convert in eighteen years. But aside from feeding his tortoises and heaping mud on the sweating sons of Martin Luther, his pleasures outside of war were few, his curiosity limited. Word of us, however, had apparently been enough to break through the crust of royal indifference.

Our mother received the summons, delivered by an official emissary of the royal court to our houseboat in Meklong, while we were on the river. Believing, at first, that the new monarch had decided, after fourteen years, to revive the sentence of death, she could hardly bring herself to speak. The messenger, seeing her trembling, assured her this was not so. His majesty was intrigued, nothing more.

Within minutes of his departure, grown men, confederates of our father, had been sent out on the river; they found us a half-day away, bargaining with a shrunken old man for a pair of ducks with which to expand our egg-laying business. Four men whisked us on board a long, thin boat; another jumped on ours—he would follow in due course. Late that night we were home, our houseboat riding low in the water with the weight of excited, chattering neighbors. Nothing remotely like this had ever happened in our village. If it hadn't been for the witnesses who had seen the royal emissary actually walk up the plank to our boat, leaving the two powerful men who were with him waiting on the shore, we would have thought our own mother mad.

We were prepared for the royal audience, lectured on proper behavior and deportment by Fang Chu, one of our neighbors in Meklong, whose father, it was said, had once worked for a man who had sold slaves to the palace under Rama II. Our mother, with the help and advice of the village women, sewed beautiful new jackets with a concealed rent below the armpit to accommodate our condition. She bought us new shoes. Four days later, on the morning of our departure, she combed our hair and braided it into long Chinese queues.

It was my brother who, despite everything going on around us, had the presence of mind and the nerve to insist on bringing the duck eggs. We had been doing very well with them. Dipped in a mixture of clay and salt, then covered with ashes, they would keep their freshness for up to three years. The royal visit, my brother argued coolly, might gain us nothing; at the marketplace in Bangkok, however, we could sell our eggs at a considerable profit, then use the money to buy goods only found in the capital. These we could then sell on our return home. If worst came to the worst, we would at least make enough to expand our business. We might never have another chance.

And so my brother and I set out to meet the official junk, already waiting like a beached whale at the predetermined point an hour down the river, dressed in emerald-green jackets, our hair in queues, and pulling a cart of preserved duck eggs: an example of how, in life as in nature, small things attach themselves to large ones. We had expected resistance, prepared arguments and entreaties. The officials chosen to escort us to the Royal Palace, however, had only one thing in mind: to deliver us, unharmed, into the king's presence at the appointed hour. It was not their place to question us. We had been summoned; that was enough. The duck eggs might represent some small part of our appeal. We watched in amazement as two men brought them onto the boat as delicately as newborn kittens and stacked them in an inner room where no harm could come to them. Had we appeared on the shore that morning with twenty quacking ducks and a pair of oxen, I'm convinced they would have taken them as well.

The capacity for wonder shrivels with age as surely as muscles grow soft. We were fourteen years old; nothing could have prepared us for the things we would see. The river widened as though it would cover the earth. Gleaming rice paddies appeared, so vast we could barely make out the workers stooped far out over the water. Herds of black buffalo, their massive shoulders hunched, walked along the roads, driven by men with sticks. We passed so close we could hear the slap-whip of their tails against their sides.

Approaching the city, we felt as though we were sailing into the seething heart of some giant hive or anthill. The river seemed narrower here. Houseboats and floating shops by the hundreds crowded in from the shore. Men in vessels of every size and description poled this way and that, making way for us as we passed. In the crowds along the shore, scattered like flowers in a field, we could see the bright yellow robes of the monks. A thousand voices, shouting, laughing, arguing at once, many speaking in languages unfamiliar to us, were crying their wares: We recognized the call for *blachang* and dried fish, clothing and earthenware, as well as the names of what sounded like medicinal herbs—words unfamiliar to us. My brother pointed. There, rising high above the clustered houses, like something out of a dream, was a slim golden spire, glinting in the sun.

The landscape drifted by, revealing, by degrees, the magnificent temple below it. Further off we could now see another, very much like it, then another, grander still. Gathering up our courage, we asked the fatherly-looking man who had welcomed us that morning, and who now stood, expressionless, a short distance away, watching the river pass, whether this was the Royal Palace. He didn't laugh at us. He didn't smile. Bending down deferentially, he explained: These temples, though beautiful, were very much like each other. There was nothing like the Royal Palace—in this world or the next.

From the moment our boat was met by representatives of the king, who presented us with a gift of fruit and tea, then quickly covered us with a silken tent and hurried us away, explaining that none might see us before the king had satisfied his royal curiosity, we walked and spoke as in a dream. A dream of unimaginable splendor; of worlds within worlds; of rooms so vast and silent one could not be certain whether the figure sitting by the carved door on the other side was human or not, yet could hear the hissing of the flame at his side. A dream of power so profound, so quiet, the closing of an eye in frustration or boredom could close a life.

That night we were instructed in how many obeisances to make to the throne, how to address the monarch, how to answer, should he deign to ask us questions. We practiced bowing our heads to the floor under the watchful eyes of no less than a dozen men who patiently corrected us if we prostrated ourselves too quickly or rose too soon, who explained the importance of bowing in perfect unison, who demonstrated, again and again, the precise timbre and pitch our voices would have to assume when we addressed the king himself, who listened as we recited, for the sixth, the tenth, the fifteenth time: "Exalted Lord, Sovereign of many Princes, let the Lord of Lives tread upon his slaves' heads, who here, prostrate, receive the dust of His golden feet," then nodded and said, "Again." To remonstrate with them was unthinkable. Everything about them—their dress, their manner, the quiet steel beneath the civility of their voices when they said, "And again"—reinforced one essential and incontrovertible truth: This was a world, for all its scented rooms and gilded spires, in which a man's head could be separated from his body as easily as a bloom is cut from the stem.

In the morning we were led to a twelve-oared barge. Oarsmen in scarlet uniforms rowed us along the walls to the outer gate of the palace. Four powerful men carried us in a net hammock attached to long red poles across a courtyard nearly as broad as our village, passed through a second gate guarded by soldiers, then carried us down a wide avenue. We passed an open expanse where a dozen elephants were being taught to kneel by their keepers. Passing through a third gate, we were set down on the ground. Before us, soaring above the inner wall, rose the spires of the Royal Palace. We were informed that the king was in the Audience Hall, and almost ready to see us.

It wasn't until a month later that those few moments in the Audience Hall came back to us; at the time, all we saw was a towering room, its walls and ceiling painted vermilion, its cornices blazing with gold, and a row of columns leading to a throne high above the ground. As we approached I could hear the doubled drum of our hearts, beating as though to burst through the cages of our chests. And then the throne was above us, covered in golden plates. On it, shielded on three sides by gauzy curtains, under a canopy of gold umbrellas, sat King Rama III. He had a calm, round face. He pulled on his gown, then absentmindedly touched his neck with his right hand, small as a child's.

Afterwards, the courtiers told us that we had conducted ourselves appropriately; that the king had been well pleased with us. They said we had answered all of his questions about ourselves to his satisfaction, and even, at one point, brought a small smile to His Highness's lips. We remembered nothing. All we knew was that suddenly a gong like a crash of thunder sounded from somewhere in the audience hall and with a single, deafening shout the courtiers around us threw themselves to the ground. When we looked up the curtain had closed around the throne like a door. The king had disappeared. Our audience with Rama III was over.

And yet our day had hardly begun. Standing outside the Audience Hall, trying our best to answer the questions of the courtiers who now crowded around us, we were informed by the court officer assigned to us that we would be allowed to view some of the wonders of the palace until His Majesty's wishes concerning us were made known. The Temple of Gautama, the royal stables, all these—with the exception of the sacred white elephants—would be shown to us. He clicked his fingers. The crowd of courtiers dispersed. But first—it was His Majesty's express wish—we would be introduced to the king's wives and consorts in the Royal Palace. They had heard of us well in advance of our visit and had been clamoring for an audience of their own.

A lifetime later, it is not the ponies from Yu-nau Province in China that I remember, or the paintings depicting the adventures of Rama. Or, more accurately, though I remember them, they have absorbed the shadow, the essence, of what preceded them in precisely the same way the taste of raspberries can contain a lover's face, or the scent of jasmine blooming in a schoolyard return the taste of blood to our mouths. The woodwork in the Temple of Gautama, the ruby-eyed statues of demons and men, of eight-legged tigers with human faces and long-necked birds with the wide, flat heads of serpents, these now come to me freighted with a meaning, a significance, no one else could know. Twenty years later, the hollow behind a woman's knee would remind me of the slide of rubbed and oiled teak beneath my thumb, and even today—so old I remind myself of an elm or an oak, half its branches sapless and dead, waiting for the next good wind—I cannot recall the translucent skin of the Emerald Buddha, which we saw that afternoon in the Temple of Gautama, without a quick shock of shame and excitement.

We were taken by the court officer and three courtiers to the Royal Palace, led down hallways lined with statuary, past sumptuous tapestries and swelling, priapic columns studded with gems. At some point the courtiers stopped. The three of us continued on. Another hallway, another room, and the court officer handed us over to a pair of soft-looking men standing in front of a massive doorway, turned and left. Leaning their weight into it, they swung open the carved wooden portal and beckoned us in. The door closed slowly behind us like a stone rolling into place.

The room we found ourselves in was nearly as large as the Audience Hall, a great, cavernous space with gold ceilings and gleaming walls. A quick murmur of excitement greeted our entrance. Everywhere we looked, small groups of women (there might have been fifty or more in all), all of them young, lay about on divans and cushions, talking, laughing, fixing one another's hair, busying themselves with some form of needlework we had never seen before. Even in my dazed state I could see they were exquisite—each one, though subtly different from the others, lovely in her own right.

One of the women, greeting us, called to us to come forward. We could hear laughter, whispers. Walking uncertainly toward the center of the room, we noticed four or five women leaving by side doors hidden in the wall. The others, rising to their feet, quickly formed a circle behind us.

Every feminine allurement multiplied a thousandfold: bare feet with toes as delicate and perfect as gems; eyes so beautiful they froze the heart. Without even leaving the country, we seemed to have found ourselves in the paradise that Robert Hunter had warned us of. But that was not how it felt. Not at all.

They wanted to know how we moved, how we slept. They asked us to squat, then stand. Could we hug one another? Could we stand back to back? They wanted to see the bond between us. We took off our jackets, then peeled down our shirts. They gasped. Did it hurt? Was it strong? Could they touch it? I could feel my brother trembling. Out of the corner of my eye I could see more women streaming through the side doors, a never-ending flow. The room was almost half full, the circle pressing in, the din of young female voices and laughter everywhere around us. A thousand hands, it seemed, were touching our bond—the hard upper edge, the underside, the soft indentations where it met our ribs. Could we feel this? And this?

The questions changed. A strange sort of fever, reckless and frightening, seemed to be coming over the room. Were we strong? How strong? Could we lift a table? Could we lift her? Or her? Do it! Show us! A woman with a blood-red blossom in her hair, her lips slightly pursed as though taunting us, stepped out of the crowd. "Lift me, double boys. Show me how strong you are. Do it!" She lay in our arms and we lifted her up. I could smell her hair. She put her strong, pale arms around my neck. I could feel the softness of her pushed against my chest. And suddenly, shamefully, I felt myself reacting as any boy my age might be expected to react. I set her down, holding her carefully away from my body, praying no one would notice.

She knew immediately, from the tension in my body, the way I set her down. She looked about the circle of faces that seemed to have grown a mile deep around us. "Shall we see if they are men?" she asked, then turned in the roar of laughing and clapping women, but already hands were upon us, pulling down our clothes, jerking them over our hips. I could feel my brother stagger. Any moment one of the king's courtiers might enter, might see. I jumped when a woman's hand closed around me as brazenly as any courtesan's ever would. "This one shows promise," she laughed, pulling me forward like a dog by a rope. "But see, they *are* different. This one's not quite cooked yet." I glanced at my brother's face. He was staring straight ahead between the wall of laughing faces, his lips pressed tight like a man determined to ignore the rack. Tears were running down his face. And then, shriveled by fear, he began to dribble himself.

The woman screamed, a number burst into laughter.

"That will do." The circle suddenly widened around us, then parted. A woman seemingly older than the rest, with a full, curved body and a calm, knowing face, appeared before us. She glanced at us standing there with our clothes around our ankles. The shadow of a smile passed across her face. "You may get dressed," she said. We hastily pulled up our clothes. Raising her right arm, she bent her wrist as though indicating something on top of her head. Three women stepped into the space next to her, laden with colorful parcels. "Thank you for coming to visit us," she said.

I glanced at my brother as we were led back through the Royal Palace, then reunited with our guide. He had wiped his face. Nothing had happened. We moved on, the three courtiers, carrying our gifts, walking behind us. I wanted to say something, but couldn't. In the king's stables, one of the stud ponies was tossing his coarse black mane and neighing. The men behind us laughed among themselves, pointing to the fifth leg that hung, dark as an intestine, nearly to the ground. My brother, though born and raised in the country, said nothing. Everything shamed him now.

That afternoon, in the Temple of Gautama, surrounded by the menagerie of imaginary creatures the royal sculptors had released from the wood, we were shown the Emerald Buddha. Speaking in tones adjusted to the silence, our guide informed us we could approach the altar.

Nearly transparent, the Buddha's skin appeared thin as a soap bubble one moment, solid as stone the next. Contained and apart, settled deep in the heart of things, he seemed to give off a cool heat, an eternal, measured radiance. For two thousand years, I remember thinking, he had been watching the lives of men wax and wane. A hundred generations had passed before him. Children had grown old and died and others had taken their place and grown old in turn. Ten thousand voices, a million dreams, each particular to the dreamer—gone. And though each of them, in passing, had taken a part of the world with them, the Buddha remained unchanged, undiminished.

And for a moment, standing there beside my brother, staring into that light that now seemed to pulse, gently, like a heart at rest, I thought that if only I could remember this, absorb into myself some part of this vast, oceanic acceptance of the world and its ways, nothing would ever touch me again. And I would be happy.

Quite possibly I was right. But I never managed it. I spent my days as my nature demanded, thrown this way and that, too close to life. Acceptance, I came to believe, was for statues and monsters and gods. I gave up trying to see anything larger than a man. My brother never did.

IV.

We returned to Meklong laden with gifts, our pockets filled with the money we had made selling eggs in the vast marketplace outside the palace; my brother, typically, had refused to leave Bangkok without carrying out his plan. Everything we made, everything we were given—with the single exception of a miniature jade Buddha, no larger than my thumb, that would remain with us the rest of our lives and that sits, even now, in its niche in the wall above our bed—we turned into ducks. By the river near our houseboat we built a huge fenced enclosure with a pond, filled it with quacking and feathers. Twice a week we poled down the river to the Gulf of Siam to catch shellfish with which to feed our flock. They grew fat as Chaucer's friars and set themselves to begetting long lines of offspring that followed them about the yard like miniature quacking trains.

Within a few months of our return from the capital, we had begun to prosper. We hired Ha Lung, the man who had given us work after our father's death, to help us haul the vats of salt and clay, and to bring our goods to market. With his short bandy legs and boxer's crouch, Ha Lung worked like an ox. Unlike some of the other villagers, who resented our good fortune and mumbled jealously among themselves, he seemed untroubled by the way the tables had turned or by the fact that he should find himself working for mere boys; if it ever occurred to him that we were only a year older than the son and daughter he had lost to the cholera, he never said a word. A widower now, living with the one child—a daughter—who had survived, he seemed cheerful enough but rarely spoke during the long hours we worked alongside one another, plastering eggs or hauling crates. Only one time, I remember, did he stop in the middle of the path to the river. It was early in the morning. We had had a good week. The air smelled of grass and mud; the shadows seemed painted on the green water. On the boats, tied side by side, the crates were already piled thigh-deep.

As we came up behind him, carrying our load, my brother asked him what was the matter. "Your father would have been pleased," he said, without turning to us, and suddenly the back of his bristly head blurred and ran, then cleared. "He would have been pleased," he said again, and walked on.

Day by day and week by week, the miracle of our visit to the royal court receded like a shrine at the end of a long, straight road. Our lives resumed something of a normal pattern. Twice a week we brought our eggs to the floating market. Worried that a thief could find our savings underneath the floorboard and take everything we had, our mother began sneaking out in the darkness and secreting a portion of our money in a short piece of bamboo under some loose thatching. If we saved carefully, my brother and I believed, within a year's time we would be able to build a second enclosure and expand still further.

In our dreams we saw ourselves trading in duck eggs all the way down the river, saw our boats, which by now had multiplied into a grand armada, sailing daily into Bangkok, saw ourselves, in fine clothes made to accommodate our condition, living in a house in the capital with a view of the Royal Palace. The king himself, hearing of our success, would request another audience. We laughed when we said these things to each other as though to say, "It's all a joke, no more, a bit of harmless foolishness to pass the time," wary, I suppose, of offending the gods of fortune with our presumptuousness. But oh, the dreams we dreamed squatting in the dirt by the Meklong, our bare feet slippered with the runny green waste of the duck yard, our hands white-gloved to the wrists with drying clay and salt. Those, it seems to me now, were among the sweetest times we knew in Siam. How absurd we are, to ask of dreams that they fulfill themselves. As though the shadow, diminished and pale, could ever live up to the thing itself.

But we were not the only ones dreaming. Though momentarily stunned by our success, Robert Hunter had resumed his attentions. Like a horsefly, or a suitor who appears at the door day after day even though he knows his intended would just as soon throw herself into the river with a stone around her neck as marry him, he seemed to have made up his mind to get what he wanted or annoy us to death, one or the other. Week after week he appeared, uninvited, bringing gifts we did not need, doggedly telling stories that had long ago lost their charm, laughing at things no one else thought amusing. Week after week we would find him sitting on a bamboo mat in our house, sweating into his collar. Like a dog he would follow us as we went about our business. We didn't know what to do. We began to feel sorry for him and, like most human beings, hated him for it.

We were too young to know the power of tenacity, the extent to which pressure, applied with enough single-mindedness of purpose, for good or ill, can shape the world around it. We were too young, too arrogant. Seething inside like a vat forever about to boil, Robert Hunter hunted us. He had no shame, no sense of reticence. Frustrated at one point, he would try another. Losing the trail, he would double back and begin again. If ten years had been needed to petition the king to allow us to emigrate, he would have given it ten years. If twenty, twenty.

But he didn't need twenty years to tunnel into the Audience Hall. Or even ten. Less than two years after our return from Bangkok, Robert Hunter broke through the palace floor, so to speak, and caught the attention of a well-placed merchant who periodically spoke to one of the councillors to the king. A month later—mirabile dictu—he was granted an audience.

I like to imagine him before the throne, making his obeisances to the heathen king, his forehead leaving a damp stain on the stones at the monarch's feet. I like to imagine him reciting, as we had: "Exalted Lord, Sovereign of many Princes, let the Lord of Lives tread upon his slave's head . . ." It amuses me. It's an interesting picture. But of course he would have had no difficulty doing whatever was asked of him. He had been prostrating himself for two years. He would have cleaned the floor of the royal stables with his tongue if that had been what was required to get us out of Muang Tai.

He was told to rise. With his eyes cast down from the royal presence, his mind racing madly, Robert Hunter made his request. He was Robert Hunter, a merchant, the citizen of a distant empire of unparalleled power called Great Britain. He had been fortunate enough to make the acquaintance of two subjects of His Majesty, the so-called double boys from the village of Meklong, who had entertained his Royal Highness two years earlier, and so forth and so on. They were indeed one of the rare fruits of the world, a living symbol of the many wonders of the empire, et cetera, et cetera.

He had no idea what the king was doing, or thinking. Dimly aware that he was going on too long, he rushed to the point. He, Robert Hunter, humbly wished to ask His Majesty's permission to take his subjects abroad—for a short time only and under his constant supervision—in order to exhibit these human wonders to the rest of the world.

Oh, the joy of it! The monarch, who had been looking at a spot on the floor a few feet to Robert Hunter's left the entire time, inclined his head slightly to the right, at the same time raising his chin. He seemed concerned, even troubled. On his forehead a network of tiny creases had appeared, like miniature streams. A river of concern split the royal brow. Instantly, one of the official courtiers was at his side, his ear to the royal lips. The monarch was worried about one of the royal tortoises. It hadn't been eating as it should. They must try something else. Immediately. Or perhaps it had come to His Eminence's attention that the stone to the Westerner's left was unsightly and discolored.

A great gong sounded. With a shout, the assembled courtiers threw themselves to the ground. The royal audience was over. The monarch had not deigned to reply.

. . .

A pair of sandals and a boulder in Tartarus would have been preferable to this. At least the son of old Aeolus, justly punished for his trickery, had known the will of the gods. But Robert Hunter, unlike Sisyphus, knew nothing. Returned to the base of the hill for no reason he could discern, he did the only thing he could. With hardly a glance at the flowering world about him (which must have seemed, by this point, as barren and dark as Hades itself), he began up the slope again. Perhaps he was an American and not a Scotsman. Only in America did we ever encounter a zeal so refined, a God-driven avarice so pure. Only in the bubbling caldron of the New World could the basest motives have combined with the highest justifications to produce a disrespect—toward time, toward fate, toward the finite measure of our days—so perfect and profound.

Nearly three years had passed since Robert Hunter had first seen us swimming in the river. We were sixteen years old. He had gained nothing. To the contrary, he had been deposited outside the palace walls like a rejected parcel of goods, sent ignominiously packing without even the courtesy of a reply to his petition. He set his feet, began to push. The next time the monarch would listen.

And yet, though Robert Hunter would never know it (mercifully, for even he might have been staggered by the way his every effort seemed destined to pass him by and illuminate *us*) Rama III *had* heard him, or had heard enough, at any rate, to be reminded of our existence. Preoccupied with making plans to send a diplomatic mission to Cochin China for the purpose of regulating trade between the two nations, the monarch now determined that we should accompany it. We were a rare product, he pointed out, like a fruit; a living symbol of the wonders of his empire. The king of Cochin China would surely be diverted, as he himself had been, by our presence.

And so, for the second time in the span of our short lives, the royal emissary appeared in Meklong. We had been offered a great honor. King Rama III wished for us to accompany his diplomatic mission to Cochin China. When the time came, we would be sent for.

V.

We sailed into the Gulf of Siam aboard a five-hundred-ton Siamese junk of marbao and teakwood. From the moment we stepped onto the hard and polished deck, we knew we had entered a new kind of world, a world of salt and wind, of horizons straight and sharp as a strip of bamboo. We watched the crew drag up the anchor like a great barnacle-encrusted beast. The canvas, receiving the wind, snapped impatiently, then bellied out. The beams under our feet groaned mightily. And Bangkok began to grow smaller in our eyes. We stayed on the bow that entire first day as clouds covered up the sky, not even realizing how the wind quietly flayed our unaccustomed skin. That evening we watched the taper-thin horizon glow orange as though somewhere, beyond the edge of the earth, the sea were on fire. Perhaps it was.

For six weeks we sailed south, stopping for days at a time in ports along the Cambodian coast. At Vung Tau, a rocky promontory jutting like a stubborn chin into the gulf, we headed up a vast and muddy river. Huge and boiling, it hissed against the banks. Whirlpools sucked at the air; unseen currents formed whorls in the brown water, then vanished. A week later we dropped anchor below the city of Saigon. News of our arrival had preceded us. Fourteen elephants, sent by the governor of the district of Kamboja to transport us further, stood in the warm, hard rain, their massive heads bent like supplicants to the royal court. We were hoisted, with some difficulty, upon a broad, blanket-covered back, and tipping and swaying like a small craft in heavy seas, our outer legs hanging over the side, we began to move.

There were no premonitions, no prophetic dreams. If everything seems dark to me now as I see that caravan, once again, winding through the hissing rain toward Saigon, it is only because I know now what awaited us. At the time, I am convinced, my brother and I noticed nothing, neither the tension in the straight backs of the men in front of us nor our ambassador's suddenly careful, measured formality.

When wolves are afraid, so the saying goes, the wise man bars the door. We should have noticed. A gray-haired nobleman admired for his easy grace and impeccable manners, a direct confidant of Rama III, our ambassador had bantered with us twice on the deck, genially listening to our sixteen-year-olds' nonsense while his personal guard stood impassively by, apparently accustomed to his ways. We had taken to him immediately. And yet even we could not help sensing, under the pleasant exterior, a soul of exceptional temper and strength. He had been a warrior during the reign of Rama II. The king himself, we had heard, at times deferred to his judgment. We had heard he was fearless. It wasn't true.

Of course, it's possible that our ambassador himself—that none of them, in fact—knew what manner of world we were entering; that they walked carefully, like a cat in the open, simply because they felt exposed, uncertain, because the rain fell so relentlessly or because the servants in their drenched, elaborate costumes responded to the barked commands of their leader with an alacrity that seemed inspired by something more persuasive than duty or obedience. There was nothing obvious. The *wai* which had greeted the representatives of our king, though of the proper depth, had seemed just slightly hurried, as though such things were unimportant, a mere formality. Coming from underlings, there was something disconcerting in this obeisance without respect, and though our ambassador's smile remained in place, I fancy I remember his eyes slowly taking in the soldiers with their hard, impassive faces, waiting stolidly in the rain. There was something wrong here. An empire, he knew, drew its nourishment from the imperial root. He had caught, I suspect, the first faint suggestion of rot.

For an hour or more we moved through the rain. Just beyond my knee I could see our elephant's left eye, recessed far back in the thick, wrinkled skin, blinking at the rivulets streaming down between the small, stiff hairs that covered its head. It appeared sentient, terrified, and for a moment I felt as though I were looking at a human being trapped inside a tree, peering out from a knothole in the bark.

I found myself counting the number of times it blinked. I had reached fifty-six—for some reason I still remember this—when the dripping curtain of the jungle slipped back as if pulled aside by invisible hands and we were on a wide avenue lined with shops and stalls and small wooden buildings. People were coming out of the buildings to stare, the rain, rushing off their peasant hats, nearly veiling their faces. Within minutes we were passing through a milling, pushing crowd. Here and there, below the sea of straw, behind the ropes of water, I would catch a quick glimpse of a glistening chin, a stubbled jaw, a long tooth in a gaping mouth.

A horizontal forest of thin arms, streaming water, reached out to us; I could hear a thousand voices, shouting something we couldn't understand.

"What do they want?" my brother yelled to me above the roar. I didn't have time to answer. Our elephant had stopped in front of a huge wooden edifice. Soldiers appeared out of nowhere, beating back the crowd with small rattan whips. Strong arms reached for us, dragged us off the elephant's back. The crowd surged forward. I saw men and women beaten to the ground, kicked between the legs. One after another they curled up like snails into a shell of arms and knees. I saw a girl, struck in the throat, suddenly jar to a stop, a look of utter surprise on her face, then fall. A woman with a huge, welling cut from her nose to her jaw was stumbling about the thinning crowd holding her hands beneath her chin to catch the blood, looking for her hat.

.   .   .

This was our entrance into Saigon. That afternoon, a guard of a hundred soldiers was posted around us for our protection. They were to be with us for the rest of our stay. For three days they followed us everywhere. They surrounded us as we walked through Saigon's main bazaar while the official delegation was conducting its business. They waited, eight deep, just outside the door of the governor's residence as we prostrated ourselves, touching our brow to the cool stone floor. Slovenly and undisciplined, with the dull, uncomprehending eyes I had seen before only in the perennially malnourished or preternaturally stupid, they seemed to wake from their lethargy only to strike, to give pain, and having knocked off the hat and elicited the screams of the man or woman deemed to have approached too close, they slipped back into sleep. It did no good to argue with them. They didn't understand a word we said, and wouldn't have listened if they had. Instinctively stepping forward one afternoon to interfere in the beating of an old man who was crawling about on all fours in the road, too foolish or gone in the head to beg for mercy or to protect himself, we were faced with raised arms and blank, expressionless faces. At any moment, one felt, the guard could turn inward and devour its own.

When we turned to our ambassador for help, describing to him what we had seen, he explained that there was nothing he could do. We were in a foreign land. We must control ourselves at all costs. As emissaries of the king, we must see our mission through to its conclusion. He sighed. These are not your people, he said. The fates of foreigners should not concern you.

But they did concern us.

For nearly a week we pretended to be ill, so as not to have to go outside. I knew my brother. For days I had been watching him grow quieter and quieter. For days—almost since our arrival—I had been following the change in him; bit by bit, the fat was disappearing from his gestures, the ease from his voice. By the fourth or fifth day in Saigon he hardly spoke; slept without moving. Every movement now was a small violence. I knew what would happen. Like water in a sealed drum, his anger would freeze until it burst.

If he went, I'd go with him. And we would both go down. And so I proposed feigning illness until the message our ambassador had sent on to Hue, requesting an audience with the king, had been answered. For six days we lay side by side in a big bed, complaining of headaches and stomach pains for the benefit of the physicians, downing the bitter potions they prescribed for our nonexistent malady, whispering quietly to pass the hours. We played memory games, trying to remember every detail of some event years gone. We searched for shapes in the wood above our heads. We talked endlessly of what we would do on our return home. We slept. In some ways it was like being children again, except that everything outside us had grown dark and wrong: Our mother and father had been replaced by strangers; what had once been a sanctuary was now a steel-tongued trap. We could hear the guards on the street below our window: long silences punctuated by a single word, the hawking spit of betel, the creak of a board.

Many years later, when a journalist from the *Hartford Courant,* apropos of nothing, asked us if we had ever been in prison, I answered yes, and my brother did not correct me.

On the seventh day, having heard that a message had come from the Royal Palace in Hue, we emerged from our rooms. We had been instructed to embark for Touran, a village up the coast, there to await His Eminence's further instructions. We left Saigon two hours later.

The marketplace, when we passed through it later that May afternoon, was nearly deserted; swarms of flies sparked about the shaded stalls. The sun, after days of rain, had emerged. Everywhere we looked the palm-thatched roofs of the city smoldered as if the world were about to burst into flame. Steam rose from the dirt of the roads; carts passed, trailing smoke like censers. Led and flanked by a small army of soldiers—absurdly, for no crowds appeared—our elephants walked past the shops selling Chinese silks and porcelain. Toward the end of the avenue, I remember, we passed a small stall shaded by strips of cloth strung over poles. Inside I could see a man carefully flaying a python with a small, curved knife. Winding the skin in a thick bandage about his arm as he worked, he made a quick cut, loosened it from around his fingers, and tossed it on a pile in the sun. It fell like a fat ribbon on a pile of ribbons just like it, and the jungle closed around us.

Five days later we reached the port of Touran in a driving rain. A message from the King informed us that a mandarin would be arriving the following day with four galleys to take us on to Hue.

The galleys we boarded the next morning, though a hundred feet long, were more like spears than boats. Forty men waited at the oars of each one. When all had been made comfortable on the cushions piled amidships, four men stood in the stern of each boat, each holding aloft two lengths of bamboo. A cry went up. One hundred and sixty oars emerged from the water, hovered, poised. At the sound of the bamboo cracking together, the boats leaped forward. At the end of the stroke, the bamboo cracked again. The oars reached for more, caught and surged. Less than twenty-four hours later we were at the mouth of the river Hue, our boats cutting past the fort, in which we could see lines of soldiers watching us pass. A few hours after that, we were in the capital.

A high-ranking mandarin with a retinue of soldiers conducted us to a house that had been prepared for our arrival. No sooner had we entered the magnificent wooden structure with its curved banisters and ornate furniture than we heard barricades sliding into place. The doors, we were told, had been blocked, all entrances secured. Though free to leave the territory of Cochin China at any time, we would, for the duration of our stay, be considered prisoners of the king: a precautionary measure only, we were assured, a formality of sorts, designed to prevent any possible misunderstanding with the populace. The people were unfamiliar with foreigners and might respond in unexpected ways. We looked outside. Soldiers surrounded the building.

The mandarin smiled. Our every wish would be answered, he said. His Eminence would grant our ambassador and two senior diplomats an audience in due course. In the meantime, entertainment would be provided to compensate us for our long journey. Entertainment, he felt certain, unlike any we had ever known.

I find it amusing now, sixty years later, to think that one of the great horrors of my life should have been presented to me as entertainment. That it should have been offered, like a glistening monstrosity on a silver platter, as legitimate compensation for our weariness. The world, it would seem, loves a good joke.

The original performance planned for us, we soon discovered, had unexpectedly fallen through. Only a week before our arrival—fortuitously enough—the king's forces had suppressed an armed rebellion in the provinces—a minor affair, we were assured. The leader of the uprising, a former general in the military, had been captured alive. We were to be honored guests at his execution. As representatives of Rama III, whose recent military successes in Cambodia and down the length of the Malay Peninsula had not gone unnoticed, we would surely appreciate the rigor with which an equally great empire enforced the lesson of obedience to the throne.

The unnamed traitor, we learned, was to have entertained us in the traditional manner. In the first act, securely trussed but free to scream, he would be lowered on ropes, feet first, into a vat of boiling water. The descent would be stopped at the knees. In the second act, still fully conscious (the criminal must be aware of himself throughout, must feel the weight of his crimes), he would be seated on a sharp steel pike. His own weight, and time, would kill him, driving home the metaphorical point—so essential for the people—that his own deeds had been responsible for his fate.

But it was not to be. To the fury of all concerned, apparently, the prisoner had somehow managed to poison himself in his cell. The performance had to be canceled. Informed of these developments while sitting in the plushly appointed meeting room downstairs, our ambassador, as usual, betrayed nothing, neither the weakness of disgust nor the cravenness of feigned disappointment. Flicking a speck of dust off his lap, he strolled out across the chasm, walking the line between sympathy and disinterest so confidently that he seemed at one and the same time to be commiserating with his hosts and trying his best to keep from being bored by their troubles.

But our hosts would not be deterred so easily. At mid-afternoon of the next day we were escorted to a garrisoned fort a short distance away from the official quarter in which we had been housed. Guards ushered us in. Walking up a flight of dark steps, we came to a bare inner hallway that seemed to run the entire circumference of the building, then passed through a pair of nondescript wooden doors. For a moment, the sudden brightness blinded us. Directly below us, bright as a coin in the sun, was a sandy arena, open to the sky. Around it, rising into the shadow of the vast, circular roof, were twenty or more tiers of wooden benches arranged in a semicircle. Far below, at the exact center of that vast open space, chained to a stake like the hand on a watch, was a full-grown tiger.

The great beast was lying in the sand. We were just seating ourselves, wondering whether this was the new entertainment that had been prepared for us, when the mandarins and their retinue of soldiers arrived. The man who had welcomed us the day before took his place next to our ambassador. The seats filled quickly. I could see our ambassador, sitting on a silk cushion, lean over to ask his host a question, to which the other smiled and pointed to the great block of sun filling the open gates of the fort. And then I felt them, shaking the wood on which we sat. I glanced at my brother. He sat still and unbreathing, a study in disbelief.

They came through that gate in four ranks of fifteen, regally adorned, ridden by keepers in uniforms that sparked in the sun. Still not understanding, believing that we would be shown some pantomime of battle, some rehearsed and bloodless allegory of terror vanquished by monarchical strength, we found ourselves looking at the tiger below us. Why didn't it snarl? we wondered. Or lash its tail? Or pace about?

Always slightly quicker than my brother to credit a horror, I understood a split second before he did. A great spasm of sympathy gripped my chest. It didn't move much because its claws had been torn from their sheaths; it didn't snarl because its jaws had been sewn shut, leaving only enough room, presumably, for food to be thrust between its teeth with a stick. It could barely move, much less fight. It took a few steps, its whiskered chin glistening with drool, then began to rub the side of its head in the dirt. From all around us now came a rising chorus of angry voices. Why didn't it do something? Why didn't it move? Men were standing up. Someone threw a whip into the arena. It fell to the sand like a shot bird.

I looked at Eng. Tears were running down his face. For some minutes I'd been aware of a muffled trembling coming through our bond, deep as a fever. There was nothing I could do. "It will be all right," I said nonsensically. "Don't look." And reaching over with both hands I pushed gently on his back and head. Like a child he allowed himself to be bent over.

I tried to look down with him, but couldn't. Raising my head, I could see the ranks of behemoths, each as big as a small house. Their keepers, looking like toy soldiers beside their hulking charges, now stood beside them. Thirty yards away, the tiger still hadn't moved. Standing square like an old dog, its great skull sunk down between its shoulders, it suddenly heaved a thin rope of vomit onto the dirt and sat down.

It was at that moment that one of the bull elephants, a giant with great, brown-yellow tusks, broke ranks. Trumpeting wildly, it began to back up. Ignoring the lilliputian keeper running alongside it screaming orders and beating its sides with a rattan whip, it started around the perimeter of the circle.

It all seemed to happen at once: the elephant, headed off by three others, was brought under control. The keeper was kneeling in the dirt. A man was standing to his side. I heard someone laugh and glanced to my right. A sound like a blade splitting a gourd. I glanced back. Something dark was rolling in the dirt like a ball of rags. I couldn't see what I was seeing. A soldier was doing something; another was kicking dirt over a welling scratch in the sand; two others, ahead of him, were dragging the keeper's headless body to the side. And then my stomach heaved and I was quietly ill on the boards between my legs.

It fought. Impossibly, even absurdly, out of some deep well of instinct, it fought. One by one they were made to charge the stumbling cat throwing itself about like a hooked fish at the end of its chain. And as they came on, it threw itself against them, batting at their faces with plate-sized paws that should have held and raked to the bone, pushing its useless jaws against their necks, spinning and turning in the air each time it was thrown yet somehow managing, again and again, to roll from under the legs, thick and heavy as Doric columns, that sought to trample out the little life it had left.

The arena was weirdly silent; no one moved. It was as though the battle were taking place at the end of a long, dark tunnel, and I was the only one watching this cat, somehow grown beautiful again, quietly throwing itself at a moving wall. And suddenly, for just a moment, the gears seemed to stall, to hesitate, and in that moment I caught a glimpse of the impossible like some shy forest creature at the edge of a clearing at dusk. And then it was gone. The gears meshed. The tenth or twelfth or twentieth giant, wrapping a python trunk around the tiger's neck, threw it high into the sun and it fell, with a horrible tearing sound, onto an upturned tusk. A slick white point thrust obscenely out its back. The battle was won.

Trumpeting wildly, flinging its head from side to side like a dog with a rat, the elephant slid the cat from its tusk and slowly trampled it to a crushed brown mat of blood and bone and fur. My brother wept. But I had seen something. With my own tears still stinging my eyes and the acid taste of vomit in my throat, I understood, for the first time, that resistance—when our defeat has been predestined and the gods themselves are thundering in our ears, baying for our blood—is as close to the sacred as we are permitted to come in this life. And I thought then (but I was a child still, and fear had made me brave), that though we all—each and every one of us—came into the world with our mouths sewn shut and our claws pulled out, I for one would never give in. I would never accept the rock simply because it was harder than flesh, never capitulate to the laws of necessity simply because they were irrefutable, never cravenly bow to reason (or its whispering kissing-cousin, fate), merely because they could not be avoided. I would run out the length of my chain, by God. I would split my jaws on the world's thick hide. And I have.

VI.

And so we returned to Meklong—an odd, inverted journey under a leaden, gathering sky, first down the Hue to the port of Touran, now dry and still, then on to Saigon for an interminable week of discussions of which we were not a part, then back down the Saigon River, around the chin at Vung Tau, and finally, like Orestes fleeing the Furies to Patmos, up the endless green of the Cambodian coast to Bangkok. Two days later we were home.

Nothing had changed. Ha Lung had reinforced one of the enclosures, begun building a second. Everyone we knew, it seemed, was well. Our mother welcomed us with tears of relief in her eyes, and that evening gave us an accounting of the money Ha Lung had made while we were gone. We had done well. When neighbors came by to hear of our journey we put them off, explaining we were tired. We didn't speak about what we'd seen. We let it stay inside, like a bullet lodged too deep to touch, hoping time would absorb it, too young to know that though the bandage drops away and the scar fades, every buried thing becomes a seed.

That night, lying on our mats in the dark, we talked over our plans. A warm wind moved through the thatching over our heads. From the houseboats next to ours came bits of conversation, words and phrases like leaves torn from a branch: "still," "more," "he said to me," "never again," followed by a low, uncertain laugh. Unable to sleep, we chattered on late into the night. We had been timid too long, we both agreed. We would raise our sights, adjust the scale of our ambition. We would strike now, while we were still fresh from our journey, before the old habits of behavior and belief had had a chance to reassert themselves.

"What about Ha Lung?" my brother asked, feigning concern. "He is old and set in his ways. He might not see it our way." A small wave rocked the houseboat like a cradle.

"Then we have to explain it to him so that he does see it," I said. "And if he still doesn't," I continued, like a boy trying to reinforce his new voice before it breaks, "we'll give him the choice of taking his share and going his way."

"Ha Lung can be stubborn."

I laughed, riding my own bravado. "I can be stubborn, too," I said, and then, covering up the discomfort my own words had begun to cause me: "I'm not saying he doesn't mean well. But we're not children anymore. He's held us down long enough."

It was agreed. The demand for duck eggs was boundless. Every week we were forced to turn people away. We would take the money we had, all of it, and triple the size of our flock. We would buy a second boat. It would be hard at first, but within a few weeks, maybe less, we would have enough to hire an extra worker. Or two, should Ha Lung decide to go his way. By June we would be bringing in three times what we made now. By the time we were twenty-two we would be living in Bangkok.

In two days, we had found a boat that suited us. By the end of the week we had accumulated the supplies we needed—extra barrels of salt, a small mountain of clay wrapped in wet sacks and stored in the shade. We had hired two little boys to collect ashes from the village cooking fires. We had arranged to rent the land on either side of our property, and begun work on the additional enclosures. Ha Lung was invaluable. Though initially unhappy with our decision, when given the choice to stay or go he had thrown in his lot with us, coming to our door with a small, carved box full of money. Nor was there anything half-hearted about his work; now that the decision had been made, he would do everything in his power to see things through, to make our enterprise a success. Despite our brave words, we were glad to have him.

We worked from dawn to dusk that first week, building well up from the river, securing the fences against the monsoon, stopping only when our mother, who had not opposed us, brought us our food. I remember how nice our boats looked, riding side by side in the current. Three of the pens were finished and filled. Groups of sleek, close-feathered ducks were waddling about or sleeping or exploring the low shelters and egg-laying boxes we had carefully set out for them. The rest of the pens would be finished within a week's time. We sat on the hill and ate. Our lives lay before us like a broad, smooth path. Just ahead, its spires glinting in the sun, lay Bangkok. I felt a rush of tenderness for the village I had known since birth. We would come back here. We would not forget this place when our fortunes changed. And looking about me with brimming eyes I heard our sister calling something, saw a black bird wing slowly up the current with something in its beak, saw Wei-Ling's wife arguing with her neighbor in the houseboat next to hers, waving her arms like a marionette whose strings were attached to the swaying branches overhead, and knew, with utter certainty, that though we might one day have a fine house in Bangkok, this would always be our home. A hot, wet breeze tousled our hair and died.

In my mind the events that followed were as abrupt—and linked—as the two-part concussion of a thunderclap. Robert Hunter, who arrived that morning looking as though he had just run from Bangkok (the reason my sister had been calling) was the first part, the ominous mumble that slowly tightens the world, then grudgingly subsides, fretting and turning interminably, into silence. He had been gone less than ten hours—striding angrily out of Meklong with his coat flapping in the rising wind like some wild-eyed prophet bent for the wilderness—when the second hit us, a ripping crack that seemed to tear the stone of heaven in half.

"I have secured it!" he cried out to us when we were still some distance away. "I have secured it. The king himself has given me permission to take you abroad, to see the West."

It was tremendous news, he said. Unprecedented. A turn of fortune such as he had never expected. He had everything worked out. He had met a man named Abel Coffin—a merchant—who had connections in the Royal Palace. When Hunter told him about us, Coffin had grown very excited. And why *shouldn't* he be excited? He was a man of the world, after all, as well as a man of God, a shrewd businessman with a keen eye who had made a living for twenty years plying his trade in difficult latitudes. He had seen the possibilities immediately. The two had agreed to form a partnership. And suddenly, less than two months later, the thing was done. He could hardly believe it himself.

Hunter rushed on, oblivious to everything around him. In six weeks time Coffin's ship, the *Sachem,* would be anchored in the port of Bangkok. We must be on it, as eight months or more might pass before Coffin returned to Siam. He, Hunter, was already working toward bringing his various business affairs in Siam to an appropriate conclusion, so that he might sail for the West with a clear conscience and an untroubled heart. He most heartily advised us to do the same. "Think of it," he said, almost shouting, giddy as a felon handed his pardon at the prison's gates. "In three months' time you shall be strolling through Kensington, or walking the cobbles of Lisbon, or sleeping on feather pillows in Paris."

In the silence that followed I heard a board creak and turned to see Ha Lung, who had come with us to see what the excitement was about, and who had probably understood just enough from Hunter's mangling of our language to grasp the shape of the conversation, walking back down the planks to the shore. I had absolutely no doubt where he was going. There were enclosures to finish, pens to clean. The monsoon would be upon us at any moment.

We had never seen him angry. He spit, he raged, he fumed like a child. He wheedled and cajoled one moment, whining for our understanding, threatened us the next. Had we lost our senses? The West would make us rich. Our mother would be given the equivalent of three hundred pounds—a princely sum, he might add, to do nothing—to compensate for our absence. We would return in a year with more than we could make in twenty peddling our damned eggs. This was outrageous. We had discussed it all beforehand. We had had an agreement, on the basis of which he had made certain irrevocable arrangements. Everything was in motion. Our refusal now would ruin him.

We rose to our feet together as always but it was my brother who spoke. We had had no agreement, he said, his voice as calm as water in a bucket. If he had already taken steps based on this misunderstanding, we were sorry, but the fault was his, not ours. We had traveled enough. We had no intention of leaving Siam. And now, if he would excuse us, we had work to do.

His eyes bulging as though an invisible hand were squeezing his gullet, Robert Hunter stared at us, spun on his heel, then turned again at the door. He waved his arm to indicate our boat. "This is what you want? This is what you aspire to? To spend your days peddling eggs and relieving yourself in the river with your fellows? Living in filth?" Out of the corner of my eye I could see our mother and sister standing by the wall. Hunter's hand had come to rest on a small figurine of the Buddha. He seemed to have lost his mind.

"We have work to do," my brother repeated.

Hunter was staring at us as though trying to remember who we were. For a terrible moment I thought he might lose control entirely: burst into tears like a slapped child, or throw himself at our throats.

"God has no mercy on heathen like you," he hissed, "and rightly so, for you deserve none."

"We have work to do," I heard my brother say again.

The words were hardly out of his mouth when the figurine smashed against the bamboo wall. "Then work and be damned, you little yellow bastards," he yelled, in his rage breaking into English, "but don't come crawling to me on your bellies when you've changed your minds!" And he was gone.

· · ·

It begins slowly. A whisper in the thatching. Small black birds, like pepper in the wind.

An hour later the trees toss and still. Toss again.

By midday the palm fronds, razor-edged and stiff, have begun to rub and scrape against each other. The sky is churning like a stirred pot. In the pauses, everything is silent. Someone coughs. A baby cries. Nothing can be secured against what is coming: no love, no sail, no roof or wall. People huddle in their rice-paper shelters under the descending boot, the mothers always, always, wrapped around their babies, pressing their heads into their laps as if to return them to the womb. The men stare at the bamboo walls, wincing like unetherized patients with every gust of wind. And the song begins.

No words can describe it. No roaring winds or cracking cheeks. Even now, a lifetime later, I can only see it slant, describe it, as one might describe the burning sun—which in the days that followed seemed turned to ashes in the sky—by the depth of its shadow, the penumbra of fear it cast around it. Perhaps it was not a typhoon at all. Perhaps it was Hunter's Calvinist God, flown down from his soul-feathered nest in Basel or Boston to smite the heathen. To stir the cup. To lay waste the land on behalf of his pimpled emissary in the East.

God would have no mercy, Robert Hunter had told us. He was true to his word.

Our sister's body was pulled from a flooded rice paddy nearly an hour downstream from our village. The last time we saw her she was lying on her side, holding the ugly wooden doll our father had made for her years ago. Our mother was lying behind her, I remember, our little brother nested tight between them. Already the wind was too loud for us to speak. I smiled at her (I was always braver for others than I was for myself) and she smiled back—quick and familiar—and for a moment it felt as though we were children again, playing at hiding from someone, some unseen other even now walking about the houseboat poking under tables, prying up the boards. I felt as though I hadn't spoken to her, seen her, in years. And then something cracked and crashed outside and I ducked my head against my brother and she was gone, erased along with half the people we'd known, the village we'd grown up in, the ridiculous landmarks—tiny mites on the world's vast girth: Praphan's garden, the double-trunked palm—by which, in dreams always unutterably lonely and lost, we would continue to try to reckon our place in the world for the rest of our lives.

In those dreams we would always come upon Ha Lung sweeping or hoeing or twisting a wire in his hard brown hands, and ask him for directions. He would look up from his work and point, as though we had not been gone for twenty or thirty or forty years, as though nothing had changed and our home were a place that could still be found in this world, its location plotted in earthly degrees of longitude and latitude; as though somewhere, just around the bend, the rows of houseboats still cut their thatch-topped shadows out of the green water of the Meklong in the long afternoons and he himself had not been found twenty feet up in a razor palm half a mile from the village, impaled on the foot-long spines of the boll.

There was nothing we could do. This was an unnecessary, spendthrift fury; a rage beyond reason. A tenth of the storm would have been enough to erase the village we had known, to adequately flay the hills, to gouge the river's curves and turns. A fraction of that prodigal fury could have crusted every south-facing thing with a rime of salt, decorated the mountains of brush and broken furniture with the dead.

A shrieking roar. As the winds rose we wrapped our arms around each other and waited, huddled under the boards we had piled over our heads until suddenly the floor began to steepen below us and we were falling down into the wall. I could feel my brother's arms around me like an iron band, his head tucked against mine. Something cracked and splintered. We were soaked. Something soft—a skirt, a sheet, a length of cloth—fell over us. We pulled it around our heads and held on, spinning in the center of that maelstrom like a doubled nut in a torrent. I found I could breathe in the space between my brother's jaw and shoulder. I breathed. Somewhere, far off, I could hear a tiny screaming.

We awoke to a world of lighthearted whimsy and death. A dog was found unharmed in a tree. The floor and one entire wall of Wei-Ling's house were found in the forest with one of his chairs still standing in the corner. Entire families had drowned like kittens. Drifted against every fallen tree, filling every crack, were dunes of small, perfect shells. In the silence we could hear them clattering faintly, shifting like sand.

For three days we burned the dead, then dug a pit in the wet, rooty ground and buried the ducks we had found piled like sodden rags against the fences. Our boats had simply disappeared. We had nothing.

We built a crude shack above the river. For two weeks our mother couldn't speak but just sat in the corner holding our brother until he squirmed out of her grasp and came outside to where we were cooking meat over a fire, ate what we gave him and returned to her arms. With the other men in the village we began pulling the bits and pieces of our future homes from the river. We found a drowned parrot in a wooden cage and a small live python, as long as my arm, twined in the thatching of a roof we dragged from the current.

Two months later, on a dark, rainless day that never seemed to fully dawn, we stepped aboard Abel Coffin's *Sachem* with nothing more than a python in a parrot cage and a small trunk of clothes which Robert Hunter had kindly bought for us in Bangkok. Our mother and brother stood on the docks. Next to them stood Ha Lung's daughter, who had appeared at our door and never left.

I remember the three of them standing back between the hills of crates and yellowed rope; the air was barnacled, sharp with resin and salt, and they looked very small to me, as though time, anticipating itself, had already begun its work. Coffin was shouting something from the captain's deck. Small, oily birds were floating in the narrow crack between the groaning continents of hull and pier. And I remember Eng saying, as quietly as though the rubbing of wood and the tightening of ropes had somehow forced his unwilling thoughts to the surface, "Thank God we're together, brother."

"Little choice there," I smiled, afraid that his fear would encourage my own. We both stared straight ahead as the ship began to move. Raising my arm to wave, I scared a gull standing on the rail. I could see the two children leaning into our mother's waist from either side, her brown, familiar arms like a pair of bandoliers tight across their chests.

We were never to see them again.

VII.

We never meant to go. We would have stayed, begun again. At seventeen life is endless.

But in 1839, from a shack on the hill above the Meklong River, three hundred pounds appeared an enormous sum; magnified by our losses— by the smell of the dead daily unburied by the rain, by the small swift streams cutting channels in the dirt beneath our beds—it was undeniable. With her grasp on the things she loved sufficiently loosened by fate, our mother gathered up what little strength she had left and sent us away. And we went. I don't blame her.

There is a violence in leaving, even when it is necessary or kindly meant. We tear ourselves loose like a plant from a pot. One good yank and there we are, lying on our side in the shade of the wall, a mass of hairy, painful roots still shaped to the shape of the world we knew.

Perhaps we'll root again. Perhaps a voice will become our new ground, or a face, or the view from a carriage at a particular crossroads. More likely we'll lie there like geraniums on a broken slate, quietly fuming that the pot should go on without us. There's nothing like leaving for acquainting us with our own unimportance, for collapsing the bladder of our self-esteem. Unless we're young, that is, in which case the bladder may simply inflate with the romance of our leaving, and float us right over the spears of regret.

So it was with us. We spent little time mourning the world we had left. I was not yet the connoisseur of loss I would become with age; my brother, though distressingly sober for seventeen, could still respond to the world with enthusiasm and joy. And the storm, I suppose, had already imposed a leavetaking of sorts; by the time we arrived in Bangkok to ask Robert Hunter's forgiveness, the world we had known was no longer there. Siam had left us before we left it.

And yet, God knows, there would have been enough to regret had we had the heart for it. We didn't. Running about the sun-warm decks of the *Sachem,* we were living emblems of the fact that youth and mourning, like the lion and the lamb, were never meant to lie together; that the former, without much hesitation, will quite naturally devour the latter, woolly head to cloven hoof, then sleep the sleep of the innocent. And besides, no sadness was possible here. The huge sky would not permit it. It wheeled about our heads all day, building towering columns and ranges of cloud. We would spend hours standing in the nodding bow, listening to the water hiss against the keel, or climb high up the mast just for the pleasure of feeling the stately sway of the world—like the movement of an inverted pendulum—move through us. From above, the ship looked small and hard and beautiful, a single bolt holding down the vast shimmering cloth of the ocean.

How impossible it seems to me now that those two boys were us. That there should have been a time before Montfaucon, before Paris, before Jack Black and the room in Frying Pan Alley. Before Sophia. Looking back on us, it seems to me we were somehow pregnant with our own lives. We must have sensed them, felt them moving: the worlds we would bring into being; the language we would come to inhabit for the rest of our days.

PART THREE

I.

We had been an oddity, a phenomenon, an act of God. We had entertained kings and councillors. We had been a marvel of nature, a
prophecy, an emblem shaped, like river clay, to the needs of others. And
yet, through it all, we had remained exactly who we were, familiar to
ourselves. It was the West that made us freaks.

It was the mirror of the crowds—the spittle on the lips, the roar of
revulsion, the frantic, almost desperate reaction to a simple backflip or
handstand—that did the bulk of the work. We had never seen such
hunger. Night after night they came, filling the halls with the smell of
ale and human sweat, determined, like children poking a stick into the
carcass of a dog, to be afraid. To dirty themselves. And we let them. We
were their sin and we were their absolution. A bargain at five or six
shillings a head.

Nor was it just the common folk—the shopowners and the cloth merchants and their like—who needed us. In salons and drawing rooms
from Brussels to Boston, the wish to be appalled, though partially
masked by the accoutrements of class, was shamefully visible. At the
palace of the Tuileries (no doubt in the same room where, two years
later, little Charlie Stratton—pardon me, *General* Tom Thumb—would
pop out of a pie during a performance of *Le Petit Poucet* and slide
through the legs of a group of chorus girls), a lovely young lady hardly

older than ourselves, dressed in a deep blue damask gown, suddenly put her hand to her mouth as though she were about to be sick and burst into a fit of sustained giggling so severe that she had to be led away to recover in another room. I had been looking at her neck, at a thin blue vein that trembled, like something struggling to break free, just below the skin.

It would be some time before Professor Dumat, something of an expert on the subject of *monstres et prodiges,* would explain to us that, etymologically speaking, we were ludicrous rather than terrifying, that all freaks of nature such as ourselves traced their lineage to a single chuckling ancestor. We and our kind, he said, pausing to take a sip of wine, were *lusus naturae*—jokes of nature. He smiled. Perhaps the young lady had known Latin.

We did very well, my brother and I. Very well indeed. Robert Hunter's trade in opium, I suspect, had acquainted him with the imp of the perverse who resides, all velvet stroke and thorny goads, in all of us; who whispers to us to go ahead, to touch what we would not touch, to go where we would not go. Though ignorant of Latin, he was fluent in the language of shillings and francs; understood, as few men I have known, the grammar of human shame. Desire and fear, to Hunter, were not verbs but nouns, things to be sold like a tippet of fur or a set of butcher's steels; they were subject and object, interchangeable but linked; *he* was the verb that gave them relation, that brought them to life. Or, rather, we were.

None of this was new, of course. The world we discovered in Belfast and Dublin, Paris and Pamplona, had preceded us, had always been there, waiting, as it were, for our arrival. Keeping itself entertained in any way it could. We simply stepped into the places already reserved for us. We were the guardians of the damned in hell, the grinning gargoyles chained to the pediment. We were the monster in the looking glass, the rustle in the wilderness of realities.

And more. For Ambroise Paré, from whose sixteenth-century work the good Professor Dumat read to us at length, we had been evidence of the glory of God. And proof of his wrath. A corruption of the seed; a plant twisted by the smallness of the womb. A product of interference by demons or devils. Or the artifice of wandering beggars. You say I am being unfair? That things had surely changed since the days of Paré's speculations? That science and reason had lit the lamp, banished our fears, et cetera, et cetera? I say nothing had changed since Paré's contemporary to the north allowed Trinculo, dreaming of showing Caliban to the masses, to speak the simple truth: "When they will not give a doit to relieve a lame beggar, they will give ten to see a dead Indian." Just so. Hunter was our Presbyterian Trinculo, you see, transported to 1829. There were lame beggars aplenty to be had, as many or more as in the days when the Bard leapt the slag heaps on the way to the Globe. And we? We were the dead Indian, of course, who for a time drew them in from salon and straw yard alike, who let them finger the crinkled parchment of his drying flesh—so exotic! so red! so very much like theirs and yet not! not!—while discreetly lightening their purses.

No, if science and reason had accomplished anything, I thought, it was to make us less ashamed of poking our fingers in the wound. Whereas before we might have shivered at the sight of the extra finger, the humped spine, the male root growing from female flesh, now we could measure and describe, draw and dissect it in the name of science. Whereas before we might have gawked at the freaks who vied for our attention and our money, now we could catalogue and collect them, Latinize and label them like carnivores' teeth in locking cabinets or malignant tumors in bell jars. And perhaps this *was* progress.

I could never believe it. We had merely replaced one form of cruelty with another more brazen, a form no more capable of seeing the heartbreak behind the horror, yet less willing to be appalled by its own curiosities. Indeed, for some (invariably the whole and healthy) the bent limb was preferable to the straight. To the learned gentlemen of the *Baltimore Medical and Surgical Journal* (what would our education have been without the help of Professor Dumat?) civilization had so blinded us to the beauty of corruption that the collector had to look abroad, among ruder people, to find the treasures he sought. "For the truth is that the practiced eye kindles at the sight of a remarkable excrescence as the traveler's does at that of lofty mountains or colossal edifices; a monstrous birth, a syphilitic tongue, any and all expressions of the pathological sublime, will captivate and engage us (intellectually and, yes, gentle reader, aesthetically) more than any summer's peach. And yet we in the West, sadly, nip the most promising growths of disease in the bud; morbid growths stand no better chance among us than apples in a schoolhouse yard; they are all picked off long before they are ripe."

Even at our age, the lesson was not lost on us: adulation and revulsion could spring from the same source; excessive praise walked hand in hand with untempered condemnation. And drop by drop this thimbleful of arsenic poisoned our hearts, confused our sight. Slowly, imperceptibly, like twin shoots under a glass bowl, we began to twist and curve, to adjust ourselves to our new sky and its smooth, invisible logic. We began, for the first and only time in our lives, to grow monstrous, to the point that when true adoration crossed our path—no, not *our* path, *my* path—for the first and only time in our lives, I mistook it for its corrupted twin, and let it pass me by.

II.

She was thirty-one years old. A widow of means. A mature beauty whose charms could eclipse the newly minted radiance of women half her age (and tie the tongues of their escorts); whose less-than-perfect fingers, placed ever so lightly on an arm in praise or teasing censure, could confuse the young and remind the old of who they once had been. A woman of intelligence and playful humor, she had a touch of melancholy about her that added depth and color to all her more obvious qualities, a silence so genuine and unaffected, so apart, it quickly earned her the hatred of half the women she met.

Would they have hated her less, I wonder, had they known that what appeared to them as confidence was actually an almost complete lack of self-regard, that what seemed conceit was in fact nothing more than an absence of vanity? Or did they know this already, and hate her precisely because of it, because they understood, instinctively, how attractive a quality this could be to men of all ages and fortunes who, sensing that vacuum, would helplessly seek to fill it with themselves? But it hardly matters. Suffice it to say that before her much-discussed engagement to Guillaume Pluvier (the famously handsome patron of the arts whose father, Bernard Pluvier, had been with Napoleon in Italy) Sophia Marchant had been considered among the most desirable women in

Paris. *After* her engagement, the wags would add, she was more desirable still.

Begin with the music then: the quadrilles and the waltzes playing from the other room, the busy hubbub of human voices, the small cymbals of glass touching glass. Below these, the creak of floorboards and the hiss of flames in the hearth. Deeper still, the distant clatter of wheel and hoof, the shake of bells, the muffled shout.

Snow was falling on the rue Saint-Antoine the evening we met. I remember noticing it, like something alive, moving between the heavy blue curtains of the drawing room; and seeing our chance, we ducked along the thicket of spotted lilies nodding in the mirror, past the flames burning in the piano's wood, and pushed aside the cloth. Our first snow. The stones of the road were already marbled with it; the south-facing edges of carriages and fences, paling quickly. Snow was catching in the tangled manes of the horses standing side by side in their traces, still as confectioners' offerings in a window display.

"You have not seen snow before, I think?" said a soft female voice behind us, and suddenly it is as though I were standing again by that window, feeling the chill coming through the glass, and Emmanuel Dumat, our tutor and translator, were once again hurrying to our side, having momentarily lost sight of his charges and then noticed who it was that had boldly (and not untypically) decided to introduce herself to us. "You have not seen snow before, I think?" How like her, really, to sweep aside all convention, to cut like a knife (but gently, so gently) through the dead layers of expected things to a warmth, an intimacy of tone, as though the two of you were lovers at dusk in a dark room, looking out on the falling world through the same small window. She was right. I had not seen snow before. There were so many things I had not seen.

By the time we had turned ourselves about, my brother walking backward as I pivoted in place, wheel rim and spoke, Dumat was there, bowing, introducing, explaining: "Permettez-moi . . . de vous presenter . . ."

She stopped him with a smile. "I am very grateful, monsieur, but I believe these gentlemen and I would prefer struggling along on our own." She extended her hand to my brother. "Sophia Marchant."

A decade younger than anyone else present, lost in a sea of tailored waistcoats and silk cravats, Eng and I had been entertaining the company (in pairs and small groups) with a small, harmless act that seemed, somehow, to be expected of us. We had stumbled onto the idea quite accidentally when, at the beginning of the evening, a young woman had offered my brother her hand and I, unaware, had reached for it first. The group had laughed at this apparent competition between us, and as our host took us around, always accompanied by Dumat, we quite naturally, and almost unconsciously, expanded on our early success. Feigning innocence, pretending to be unaware of what all the laughter could be about, I would now snatch at any feminine hand that came our way and bring it to my lips, murmuring "enchanté," my eyes closed as if— like a Hottentot at a symphony—I found it all simply too intoxicating, too wonderful, while my brother, playing the role of the frustrated second, would shake his head and mumble imprecations or, better still, pretend to jerk me slightly just as my lips were about to touch the soft white skin of my latest enchantress.

None of that was possible now. I let my brother take her hand, then kissed it in turn.

"I saw you looking out the window," she said. "I did not know it was snowing."

"I have never seen . . . snow, before," I answered, since she seemed to be speaking to me.

"It is very beautiful?" she said, looking over my shoulder.

"It is," I said, unable to turn around. "Very beautiful."

She was quiet for a moment, setting the world to her own time. Far off, I could see her bare back and auburn hair in the mirror; behind her, the blue wall of the curtain, the fissure of falling snow. "As a little girl I should put out the lamp and sit by a window and watch the snow fall." She paused, then looked around the room, where a number of faces, having turned in our direction, now attempted to look away without calling attention to themselves. She seemed not to have noticed. "What can they be thinking, missing this?" she said quietly, and then, turning to Dumat, still hanging about with his hands clasped behind his back like a child afraid of spilling something: "Tell us, Monsieur Dumat, what do you think they are saying that is so very important? No, don't tell us. It would be too distressing. We do not want to know. Do you not agree?" she said, looking at me.

"I do," I said. "It would make us all very sad."

She laughed, turned to Dumat. "You see, monsieur? We speak English *très bien*. Together, I think, the three of us make almost one English person."

"Not so many, I think," said my brother, her warmth having thawed his natural reticence.

"Then we must practice until we are at least two English people."

Dumat smiled, sensitive enough to know when he was not wanted. "I will leave you to your English, my friends." He bowed. "Mademoiselle."

We watched him walk away, his hands still clinging to one another like lovers conspiring behind his back, his head and torso turning, first left, then right, as if welded from the same recalcitrant block of steel.

She waited until he'd crossed a third of the floor before she turned and looked at me, her eyes moving over my face with a familiarity neither brazen nor discomfiting, studying me as though we had known each other long ago and parted, and she was now trying to recall the features that had once been so familiar. It lasted only a moment before she looked directly into my eyes and smiled—almost as if, indeed, she *had* recognized me.

"Hello," she said quietly.

"Hello," I answered.

How strange that I should hardly remember her anymore, and yet the loss of her, the absence I felt when she had gone, should remain vivid these sixty years and more. Like a live coal thrown on the winter ice, she burned through and was gone, leaving only a dark hole, gulping at the water beneath. What did we talk about that night? It hardly matters. Snow, I suppose. And Paris. She insisted we have a glass of wine. Others joined us briefly, drifted away. We talked about going out for a walk, sweeping clean the straight, snowy ranges piling up on the fences, building a snowman, but didn't. She found my brother funnier than she did me—not surprisingly, for Eng, with his dry delivery and slightly bewildered expression, could be very amusing and, like any man, appreciated a good audience. I didn't mind. I could afford to be generous. During the course of the evening—so unobtrusively, so gradually that to this day I am unconvinced she herself was aware of it—she had aligned herself with me, turning her body so that, if not quite parallel, together we formed a wide angle on the world.

Was I nineteen? Indeed I was. Was I young and impressionable? Yes and yes again. Had the wine (and the snow and the lilies and the Persian patterns of the carpets) gone to my head? No doubt they had. And yet I did not behave like a fool. I did not grow embarrassingly loquacious, or spill my wine on the parquet floor. I did not grow taciturn and silent at some perceived shift of affections. There was no need. A great calm seemed to have settled over me. And though it is true that I wondered, more than once that evening, what was happening to me, it is equally true that what I saw and felt was as incontrovertible as the descending snow. There it was. The horses shivered themselves black, the music stopped and began again, the sleeve of her dress brushed past my arm, and then, as unbelievably as if a butterfly had suddenly settled on one of the lilies reflected in the glass, returned.

It is only fitting that others found it inconceivable. We did. She was, well, everything she was. We, on the other hand, were the curiosity du jour, no different really from the "man-monkeys" and the "missing links" who in those days so regularly caught the attention of the entertaining class. She was known throughout the capitals of Europe. We were a small joke masking an involuntary shiver. She was beautiful. The sight of us, Dumat had been told by the French authorities who had initially denied our visa, could affect the shape of the unborn, breed monsters in the womb.

And yet, incredible as it seemed to me then, as it *still* seems (even had I been one man I would not have been in danger of being called handsome), there was an immediate understanding between us, a comfort, that neither of us could deny. An hour passed, then two. We seemed to naturally take each other's side, and at some point I heard her say, in response to some question or other I have long forgotten, "We would rather not, thank you," then pause, as though her words had said too much, glance quickly over at me, then just as quickly away. Are there words to describe the intoxication of that glance? Or my emotions when, on the pretext of making room for someone passing, she moved next to me and remained standing by my side—say it!—as naturally as a wife stands beside her husband; no, more than that: as a woman stands by the man she loves? Through the fever I could see Dumat looking at us, now from between two heads, now over a bare shoulder. He seemed very far away.

Later, I would torture myself by wondering what she could have thought, that first evening. Did she stop and wonder, perhaps, at the grotesque comedy unfolding before her, the enormous joke that the gods, chuckling in their beards, seemed to have determined to make of her life? Did she appreciate the sheer impossibility of it, or ask herself, in a lighter moment, what could have been slipped in her wine that she should fall in love with a bristly-haired Bottom on this midwinter night's eve? Did she suddenly realize—from my stunned expression, my horrible dignity—that I had utterly misread her intentions and, feeling sorry for me, or not knowing how to correct matters, decide to humor my absurd presumption? Did she despise me (and herself) as I not only feared she might but believed, in the ignorant outlands of my heart, she should?

Even now I have no way of knowing what she may have thought to herself those first few hours in the drawing room. Against the flood of doubt and self-recrimination that rose the instant she was gone, I had only the words she had said when Dumat, apologizing profusely, had come for us at last: "You may call on me tomorrow at ten if you wish," she had said, holding out her hand. "I will take you for a ride in the country." And then, to Eng, "You will see. By spring we will be at least three large English persons." Light, unrevealing words, tailored to the presence of others. But later that evening, pressing my forehead to the carriage glass, and all through the night that followed, listening to the whisper of flakes on the sill, I held to them the way a drowning man clings to a splintered bit of wood, half wishing to be saved, half hoping the waters would close above his head at last and take him swiftly down.

III.

No one could have expected it to live. It was too unlikely, too delicate. The very air seemed to conspire against it.

Consider what fertile soil we were for scandal: a society beauty—elegant, cosmopolitan—inexplicably infatuated with a pair of monsters. Had she no shame, no decency, no regard for even the most minimal standards of feminine deportment? Was she determined to scandalize all of Paris, then? Or was she . . . but no (this whispered in the shocked, intimate tones reserved for only the most succulent speculations), was she, perhaps, driven by some genuine perversity of body or soul, governed by unnatural appetites?

Feeling, no doubt, that a bit of scandal could only encourage the public's interest (that all that was needed to ensure success was notoriety, as Phineas Barnum would put it some years later), Hunter and Coffin agreed to lend us the use of their carriage. And so we would arrive—the wheels slipping a bit in the wet snow that first time—at 40, rue des Nonaindières, blissfully unaware of the storm that now raged about her life. She had called it up herself, they would say, summoned it by her shamelessness. If so, it didn't take long to arrive. By the time our carriage brought us like doubled suitors to her door the next morning, though the sky had torn through over Paris and the sun now flashed like a blade on snow still clean of filth, the winds were gathering force.

Being who she was, she must have anticipated what was coming. Must have known that those who hated her for her masculine range of interests and the protection of her wealth, who had chafed for years under her irreverent humor and her disrespect for the opinions of those—like themselves—whose importance was so patently self-evident, would now gather into a force and collectively seek to bring her down. Hers was a monstrous unwillingness to acknowledge being hated, and for this, above all, they would make her suffer.

Or try. Imagine their fury when, having successfully summoned the tempest, their victim simply sat in the deluge, her wet hair streaming back in the wind, sipping tea. Glorying in the agitation of rain in her cup, the sensation of her clinging dress, the drops streaming off the nodding flowers on her hat.

Afterwards, there were some who maintained—and it is a testimonial to her strength—that there was no pretense to this, that she genuinely neither knew nor cared what others said. That she sat in the rain, so to speak, not in order to spite the spiteful, but simply because she liked it. Perhaps. But I always believed that, though this was true, there was some small part of her that reveled in the storm simply because it made her feel alive. Though I've never met a gentler soul, there was something about her that needed to live in extremis, to fight. And I loved her for it.

Of course, we knew nothing of this at first. In the mornings, the carriage would simply deposit us at her door. We would enter. There, we would spend the next three or four or five hours in much the same ways we imagined people everywhere spent theirs—talking in the huge, sunlit drawing room (how I loved it when Claudine, showing us in, would throw open the doors on that sudden brightness), playing Pope or cribbage, listening to Sophia play Beethoven on the pianoforte, attempting to read aloud, despite our laughter, the sentimental English novels she had decided would aid us in our quest to become English. We took long walks in the cold, she striding, despite her skirts, like a man (her arm in mine, or at times my brother's), blithely ignoring the turned head, the surprised second glance, the carriage slowing across a busy street. We spent an afternoon (could it have been only one?) taking turns peering through the eyepiece of a microscope into a world in which ordinary newsprint—the word "plus"—shouted like a banner (the vestigial tail at the top of the *p* alone filling half the view), and a single strand of her hair became a cord as thick as a ship's hawser.

But all this was just the visible. How do I sum up the language of gestures, the eloquence of silence? Where do I find the alphabet into which I could translate the sudden surrender in a pause, the nakedness of an answer not given? Words, like signposts on the frontier of meaning, simply mark the limits of their own domain. We spent a dozen mornings together, no more, most of them within a circle so small a ten-year-old boy could have thrown a rock from one side to the other. And yet, in that brief time, she and I . . . no, let me say it: In that brief time, *you* and I, my love, crossed half a continent together. Was it our fault that we never made it to the other side? That our journey was interrupted?

Perhaps it was, but consider the armies arrayed against us. In the mornings we sat on your divan and ate dainties off the trays that Claudine so gently set down before us. In the evenings we performed for the crowds that filled the small wooden halls that had now become our main venue, doing what was needed, playing to their expectations like the trick monkeys that we were. In the mornings we were allowed to pretend we were men like any others; by supper, we had stripped that pretense bare. You remember the bandage around my hand that morning, how awkwardly I drank my tea with my left, our unconvincing explanations of what had happened? How could we own up to the fact that I had split three knuckles on the head of a man who had claimed that we were a fraud, that our bond was nothing but a section of horse flesh daily stitched to a flesh-colored bodice, that he could tear us apart like a badly sewn shirt? How could I begin to explain that I could have clubbed him to death like a rat in a barrel *not* because he was wrong—no, not that— but because part of me wished him right? Because I myself, in the days since I had met you, had dreamed his lie was true? I ask you—how was I to bridge these worlds? Every morning you saved me, and every evening, baptized anew in the spittle of the crowd, I was reminded of our calling.

In this essential task, of course, Hunter and Coffin played their part. An appropriately severe-looking man with a long, horselike visage made even longer by the kind of side whiskers General Burnside would make popular half a century later, Captain Coffin had changed considerably since our days on the *Sachem*. Then, much to the crew's amazement, he would invite us to his stateroom, where he would try to teach us how to play chess, or show us the collection of curiosities he had collected on his travels. Now, increasingly taciturn and irritable, he hardly spoke to us at all except to demand a change in our clothing or our manner, or to mumble into his sherry about wasted days spent "dribbling over a countess."

Initially, it was Robert Hunter who came to our aid, who insisted, over Coffin's complaints, that the carriage be made available to us, who seemed the more willing of the two to give us some measure of liberty. Feeling, perhaps, some remorse for the way he had behaved in the past (or believing he could afford to be magnanimous, given how things had turned out), he genuinely appeared, from the time we stepped aboard the *Sachem*, to have nothing but our best interests in mind. More than once, where some small matter was concerned, he intervened on our behalf. Where once he had seemed oily by nature, instinctively disingenuous, he now appeared refreshingly direct, blunt to a fault. Gone, or nearly so, were the pious exclamations that had pocked his speech at every turn; gone, too, the painful mannerisms, the little flatterings and insincerities we had come to despise so much. In their place now was a businesslike matter-of-factness we could deal with and even respect.

With the four of us sitting like equals in the captain's comfortable stateroom, all dark wood and polished brass, he had explained—at length and without a hint of condescension—what we might expect in the year to come, how our business arrangements would be worked out, why, given his and Coffin's expenses, income from our appearances would be divided forty-forty-twenty, and under what future circumstances that might change in our favor. Eng, who had a head for such things, and whose ability with numbers never failed to amaze me, said that it seemed, on the face of it, a fair arrangement, and given our situation, even generous.

Had they lived up to it, it might have been both; as it was, it was neither. We were shown books and figures that made no sense, quoted sums for expenses that a child would have found absurd. When we demanded our share of the receipts, we were told they were unavailable, that they, Hunter and Coffin, had taken the liberty of investing them for us, and that, in any case, we would not receive the balance of our money, as per our contract, until such day as the partnership was dissolved. When Eng complained that we had signed no such agreement, they laughed, incredulous, and airily waved a piece of paper in our faces, a copy of which, they said, was on record with their solicitors at Evans, Lamberton.

They did not know—though they could certainly guess, they said— who could have put such notions in our heads. (Insulting, they were, damned insulting, said Coffin, taking his pipe from his mouth and promptly growing purple in the face as though a valve had been shut, while Hunter, next to him, simply shook his head, averring there must be "some misunderstanding.") Did we truly believe we were being cheated, after all they had done for us? They couldn't understand how we could think such things. Still, as it appeared we were serious, they felt it their duty to inform us that power and precedent (as well as the natural sympathy of the courts, given our, ah, respective stations in life, shall we say) were all on their side. Should their reputation as honest businessmen be challenged, they would have no choice but to defend themselves with all the means at their disposal; they could assure us that Evans, Lamberton, who played the Court of Chancery like a flute, would . . . well, there was no need to bring up unpleasantness that would surely never come to pass. The contract which we so mysteriously did not remember signing—though sign it we both most certainly had, and with pleasure—was legal and binding. In the fullness of time, if we could but curb the natural impatience of youth, we would receive our money, and a pretty sum it would be. How much? That would be hard to say.

Where could we go? Sophia, fighting on a hundred fronts, would not have been able to help us, even if we had been willing to ask her. In our desperation we turned to Dumat. He listened carefully, a worried look on his face, as Eng listed the facts of the situation—the head counts, the estimated receipts, the likely expenses we had been quoted by third parties—then promised to look into it for us. "If this is true . . . but no, I cannot believe it. Still, what you say is most troubling, my friends. I need hardly add that as a business associate of Monsieur Coffin and Monsieur Hunter, I, too . . ." Sharply tugging down the corners of his waistcoat, he seemed to snap to attention. "I shall look into this matter at once," he said, his trim little beard fairly bristling with indignation. "Rest assured, my friends, they shall not pull the cloth over the eyes of Emmanuel Dumat."

Of that I have no doubt, if only because they needed his help in pulling it over ours. A week later he was back. "You will be relieved to hear, my friends, that your fears are entirely unfounded," he announced, perching awkwardly on the edge of a chair in our cramped rooms. While Messieurs Hunter and Coffin were, admittedly, not the most sophisticated of men, he believed them to be essentially honest in their dealings with us. He had taken them to task most directly, most directly, and had left convinced that both gentlemen, while certainly not averse to making a profit, had only our best interests in mind. Though hurt by our accusations, they bore us no ill will, and, in fact, cherished an almost fatherly affection for us both; indeed, he felt compelled to add that, just as in real families, in which the strongest feelings often bespeak the strongest bonds, here, too, the harsh words, the wounded feelings, even the anger with which they had responded to our accusations, were but proof of their regard. And so on.

Though it was particularly difficult for Eng, who took great pride in his business sense, and who for well over a year now had been pacifying himself with the thought of our growing fortune, patiently trading in each indignity for its worth in coin, we neither of us let on that we knew where matters stood. We dissembled like masters (it certainly *was* a relief to us both; how simple it was to misunderstand the motives of others when far from home . . .) and immediately began collecting evidence of our own, quietly writing down dates and figures and monies received in a small, pocket-sized notebook Sophia gave us during one of our visits, preparing for the day when we should take our stab at freedom.

IV.

It was not to be. The jailers, as it turned out, would escape before their prisoners. Once before we had rejected Hunter's advances only to be forced by circumstances to beg his forgiveness. This time, however, we were not even given the chance to atone for his sins, to reinstate ourselves in his good graces. Perhaps it is just as well. He had forgiven us the first time because he had stood to gain by it. This time, we had nothing he wanted. He and Coffin had shelled the nut.

When I recall the arc of our fortunes in Europe that year I see a short, sharp peak—glorious and dizzying—followed by a long downward plunge. An Alp. A veritable Zugspitz of easy success and utter humiliation. For nearly eight months—a time so heady and disorienting we could hardly take any pleasure from it—we were entertained by heads of state, welcomed in the homes of the wealthy and the well connected, introduced to ministers and dignitaries, barons and baronesses whose names we could hardly pronounce, much less remember. In London we were presented to His Majesty King George IV (I remember a coughing, yeasty-looking man), then exhibited at the Egyptian Hall in Piccadilly before "the most eminent professors of Surgery and Medicine in the Metropolis." This august body, to whom we were introduced as we sat in the center of the stage on a red divan (Hunter leading them forward one by one, strewing the path with flatteries), collectively pronounced us not only genuine ("a wonderful caprice of nature") but assured the public that the sight of us would be quite inoffensive to even the most delicate sensibilities.

The gentlemen of the fourth estate concurred: "In their figure, countenance, manners and movements, there is nothing that can offend the delicacies of the most fastidious female," we read in *John Bull*. "Without being in the least disgusting or unpleasant, like most monstrosities," wrote the reporter for the *Universal Pamphleteer*, "these youths are certainly among the most extraordinary freaks of nature we have ever witnessed." The *Times* agreed. So did the *Mercury*. Indeed, to judge by the blizzard of letters, testaments, speculations, and scientific reports our appearance in London elicited, there was hardly a soul in England at that time, living or dead, who did not have an opinion regarding us. If living, they published it; if dead, they communicated their feelings by proxy.

Ours was, truly, the well-examined life. In a paper presented to the Royal College of Surgeons in London, Dr. Robert Buckley Bolton reported that "the tongue of Eng is at all times whiter than that of Chang, and his digestion more easily deranged by unsuitable diet. Moreover Chang, by his own testimony, has never passed a day without alimentary discharges, but the contrary has often occurred in Eng." From these humble particulars Dr. Bolton then proceeded on, by a series of daring leaps that must surely have amazed his audience, to the underlying nature of form. We had never thought of ourselves as apertures onto the hidden laws of organology.

Nor was our fame limited to the world of science. In letters to the editors of newpapers and magazines published across the length and breadth of England, men we had never met speculated about the significance of our single navel, wondered whether the appellation "monstrosity" was properly applicable to us or only "to those preternatural births that are analogous to animals," dilated on what a mournful sight it was "to behold two fellow-creatures thus fated to endure all the common evils of life, while necessarily debarred from the enjoyment of many of its chief delights."

"This link which unites them," wrote the reporter for the *Examiner*, firmly grasping the udders of pathos in his turn, "is more durable than that of the marriage tie—no separation can take place, legal or illegal—no Act of Parliament can divorce them, nor can all the power of Doctors' Commons release them from their bond. Taken, poor fellows, from their native land, doomed to pass their lives in a species of slavery, to be dragged about to all parts of the world, exposed to the painful vicissitudes of climate, can we wonder that their expressions, when we saw them on Tuesday, were less than cheerful?" We considered writing the young man to inform him that our somberness that evening had been due less to the vicissitudes of climate than to certain unmentionable alimentary concerns best understood by Dr. Robert Buckley Bolton of the Royal College of Surgeons, but refrained.

And yet, however gratifying our audiences with the crowned and nodding heads of Europe, however touching the minor avalanche of letters mourning our fate, these did not yet represent the high-water mark of our fame. Our correspondents, you see, did not limit themselves to prose; for a time, like tulips blooming under the feet of the Magi, verse—or something like it, at any rate—flowered wherever we walked. Of the dozens of poems penned on our behalf, I managed to save two, neatly folded in the small blue notebook in which we had begun to accumulate evidence of Hunter's and Coffin's crimes. Thus, to the *Sunday Times* of London, on April 4, 1830, had come the following:

> My yellow friends! and are you come,
> As some have done before,
> To show the sign of "Two to one,"
> And hang it o'er your door?
>
> How do you mean your debts to pay?
> Will one discharge the other's?
> Or shall you work by subterfuge,
> And say, "Ah, that's my brother's"?

> For well we know if one by chance
> To Fleet or Bench is sent,
> The other would an action bring
> For *false imprisonment.*

> Have you the consciences to sit,
> And when your eating's done,
> Rise up and "pay the piper," but
> Pay only as for one?

This was lovely, and in the years to come, would be a particular favorite of Gideon's, who would commit it to memory, and greet us at his door with the opening verse. Even then I admired the anvillike tread, the sonorous music of its language, those whimsical italics. Still, as *literature,* I much preferred the second, which Coffin had neatly clipped from the pages of the *Literary Gazette.*

> If in the pages of Holy Writ we find
> That man should not divide what God has joined,
> O why, with nicest skill, should science dare
> To separate this Heaven-united pair?
> United by a more than legal band,
> A wonder wrought by the Creator's hand!

A good question. Why, indeed?

From London, where we had enjoyed the sights of Covent Garden Theatre and the Baker Street Bazaar, Grosvenor Square and Grub Street, we moved on to Bath and Windsor, Reading and Oxford, Birmingham and Liverpool, then boarded a carriage to Scotland. Glasgow and Edinburgh passed in a blur of wayside lodgings and public coaches. The roads were pitted and hard as bone, then soft as rotting fruit. The scenery bumped and jolted by, the hours passed. We spent weeks, it seemed, in the wheeze and rattle of Coffin's snores, staring at his open mouth, a small, wet cave nearly obscured by the wiry thicket of his whiskers. Bored, we poked each other and whispered while Hunter, sitting ramrod straight, forever snuffing after profit like a pig after truffles, scribbled away as best he could on a makeshift desk that fit over his lap. Preceded by a man named Hale, whom Hunter had hired to secure accommodations and exhibition halls and to paper our route with billboard advertisements extolling the wonders of the "Double Siamese Boys," we had little to worry about from dawn to dark.

From Edinburgh we moved on to Dublin, from Dublin to Belfast. From Belfast we traveled to France, where our audience with King Louis Philippe (a gracious man with a disarming smile who actually listened, head bent forward in concentration, to Dumat's breathless translation of our words) generated an absolute fever of curiosity among the nobility. We skimmed the cream and moved on, from France to Belgium, from Belgium to Spain. Two months later, having allowed enough time, by Hunter's estimation, for the curiosity to revive, we returned to the city of love.

Consider the slope of our decline, the arc of our fall. For a year we had been the toast of Europe. For a year we had been among the chosen few, the elect. The Heaven-united pair. The wonder wrought by the Creator's hand.

But just as God himself had grown bored with his original pair of fools in time, and sent them packing out of Paradise, so did the good citizens of Paris. True, there were no serpents on the rue Saint-Antoine; no apples. No knowledge I would not have gladly risked Eden for, and more. And paradise was a person, not a place.

And yet, as surely as Satan sprang from the whimsy of God, so too did the tiny agents of our fall. Consider it: Who but God could have dreamed a tale so absurd and so heartless? Hand in hand and slow, we wandered out of Eden. Even now I can hear that high, stentorian laughter.

V.

And quite a joke it was. Their names were Ritta-Christina, the Sardinian Twins, and by every measure of horror and pity, they did us one better. Two curly-haired infants above, one below, they were a wonder so profound grown men wept at the sight of them. Two children, each without a flaw, had melted together like wax tapers. This was caprice of a wholly different order. Beautiful in their own right, their arms and fingers perfectly formed, they gave the impression, when the sheets had been swept back by their father, of having absorbed a sister whose equally perfect body now descended from their common chests.

Years later I would read that Dante had punished schismatics by pulling them apart as they had pulled others. In some cases, however, understanding better than anyone that frustrated hope—forever held out, forever denied—is sharper than any punishment, he had left the job unfinished. These few he condemned to strive toward doubling yet never part, to yearn for oneness yet never achieve it: "But look, Agnello, now you are neither one nor two." Ritta-Christina were Dante illustrated and come alive. But where was their sin? What could they possibly have sown, in this life or any other, that their bodies should be forced to reap such a crop?

.   .   .

And yet there they were, a bit of actual hell in Paris. Imagine, if you will, the hurricane of revulsion and curiosity this new Heaven-united pair elicited, the libraries of verse they inspired. Where was the Hottentot Venus now ("A rump she has, though strange it be/Large as a cauldron pot/And this is why men go to see/This lovely Hottentot") who fifteen years earlier had taken the town by storm? Where was the Woman with Three Teats; or Hop, the Legless Dwarf; or Prince Ramal, the Living Torso? Where, indeed, were we? In a flash, the wonder wrought by the hand of God had been swept from the stage and replaced by another, greater by far.

Let it be said in our favor that we were neither of us such monsters as to envy them their victory. I'll admit to a spark of . . . what? Jealousy? Resentment? The instinctive anger of even an unwilling competitor on finding himself suddenly on the cusp of defeat? To this much I'll confess, no more. And even this we snuffed out without a moment's hesitation.

But Ritta-Christina, uninterested in the river of faces moving slowly past their bed, gurgling contentedly or pulling at their ears in sudden rage, as babes will, were really just the final act. For weeks we had sensed the precipice. For weeks, perhaps longer, we had felt the ground beneath us tipping, ever so slowly, toward a future we couldn't discern. Day by day, negotiating Hunter's and Coffin's silences, sensing their obvious unhappiness with us and our declining ability to draw the crowds, we felt the angle of decline steepen.

They themselves rarely accompanied us now, contenting themselves with making the necessary arrangements and hiring a muscular escort (two if the venue suggested it) to ensure the safety of their investments. The scandal they had hoped would revive our fortunes (and theirs) had obviously not succeeded, and though they continued to talk and scheme, arguing late into the night as the rain coursing down the glass blurred the view, it was clear from the canceled engagements and the size of the halls we engaged (shrinking swiftly as if racing to stay ahead of the diminishing crowds) that we had very nearly drained the well.

Day by day the spaces grew smaller around us, the aisles filthier. Day by day, as though the years had somehow accelerated and aged them overnight, the planks of the stages on which we performed grew uneven and rough, the seats worn to a shine. Arriving early sometimes, we would look out at the rows of seats folded like teeth in the jaw of a shark. Poorly lit, the halls were a cavern, a dark mass. Here and there, where the matting bulged from a tear, one could see where the point of something had ripped the fabric through.

But even more telling was the change in the manner of the men whose establishments these were. Quicker than dogs to sense another's vulnerability, they now demanded what two weeks earlier they would have gladly forgone, and then, when they saw that we neither left nor threatened to strike them with our canes for their insolence, boldly asked for more. Gone were the hat in hand and the subservient smile, the fawning attitude and the will to accommodate. We were one of them now, or nearly so, and they knew it. The lights dimmed and began to flicker as though running out of oil.

But memory is merciful. In truth our descent was slower and more ambiguous, a sideways drifting—like snow, or dust. So gradually did we fall that for weeks we wondered whether our decline reflected anything more than a temporary depression in the public interest, whether the sudden dip in our fortunes wasn't just a correction to the unnatural height we had soared; whether, in fact, we were falling at all. And yet, as surely as dust eventually settles, fall we did. Bit by bit, as the winter wore on, the reality of our situation came clear. The facts were unavoidable: Though we could still draw the crowds from the ship-yards and the horse-slaughtering establishments at Montfaucon, the palaces and the drawing rooms of the aristocracy, where we had once been welcomed, were now closed to us.

Through all of this, lending our lives an air of ever-deepening unreality, we continued to pay our morning visits to Sophia. There, everything was as it had always been. There, though feeling increasingly besieged by enemies both real and imagined, I could restore my strength. Afraid of disturbing the balance of the world we had found, neither of us said a word about the troubles we faced when apart. I said nothing of our situation with Hunter and Coffin, of our rapid decline in popularity, of the fact that I had had to fight to secure the carriage that morning. I mentioned nothing—how could I?—of my brother's slight but growing lack of enthusiasm for the visits he had once looked forward to as much as I. More and more, these days, I found myself asking him to get dressed, or reminding him of the hour, and though he still backed me in my demand that we be allowed to borrow the carriage, I was not such a fool, or so besotted, as to miss the resentment growing between us.

I could hardly blame him. For weeks now, perhaps because she was too busy with her own thoughts to maintain the pretense of impartiality, or because she felt it was no longer necessary, or perhaps, even, because I encouraged it, Sophia had been giving me the larger share of her attention. When the three of us walked outside now, her arm was in mine; whenever possible, when we played games in the parlor, we made a team. It was as though we couldn't help ourselves. Perhaps if we had been able to follow our desires, if I had been able to lose my hands in her hair and tilt back her head and kiss her just beside the small smooth hollow of her throat, we would have had less need to declare our love at the cribbage board. But we couldn't, and so we excluded him as brutally as lovers in their first fire have always eclipsed those around them, reducing him to reading novels or entertaining himself by looking through colored prints while we talked and whispered in each other's ears. He had nowhere to go. Neither did we.

I knew what was happening, and I didn't care. I understood his wounded pride, his discomfort at having to be present, like a chaperon, when everyone wanted him gone. I understood the betrayal he felt when it first became clear to him that someone else had taken his place. I even understood the battle he fought to be happy for me, to behave as he thought I might have behaved had fortune chosen him instead. For years, given our different natures, we had been as easy with one another as men could be. Now, for the first time (desperate to be alone with her, if only in my mind), I reserved the moments of pleasure—so steeped in youthful shame, for what would she think of me if she knew what I imagined?—for when he was asleep. Oh, I understood how he felt—at times it was as though I would tear myself in two—and yet, I repeat, I didn't care.

There were things I didn't tell him now: promises I made to myself, dreams I dreamed of being free. There was nothing I could do. Standing beside her as she peered into the microscope one dark afternoon (what were we looking for that day? I wonder), I had noticed the curve of her, the way her body strained against the bonds of bone and cloth. Almost faint with daring, making sure my brother couldn't see, I had gently placed my arm around the smoothness of her waist. She hadn't removed it.

"Please don't think badly of me," she had whispered to me later as the three of us sat together in the parlor, my brother, beside me, reading a novel. Or pretending to. "I couldn't bear it if you were to think badly of me."

"I could never think badly of you," I had whispered back, taking her hand in mine. "Never. Never. As long as I breathe." And meant it. As God is my witness, I meant it.

Ah, but we must never underestimate the malleability of young men's opinions, or the speed with which others' changing opinions of us, real or imagined, can alter ours of them. Racked by hope, by fear, by daydreams of fulfillment and by nightmares in which I wandered like an amputated limb through cities I had never known, searching for my brother, I hardly knew what to wish for. Laughing, she would lay her head on my shoulder; taking my hand, she would trace my fingers, or stroke the skin of my palm. I loved her voice, her smell. We understood each other—utterly. I wanted her as I have never wanted anyone or anything in my life. And yet there were times, knowing it could never be, when I almost wished her gone, times when I would have given anything to have returned things to how they were before. And then, hardly would this thought enter my mind before I would be off in the other direction, wondering whether she didn't feel the same way, tormenting myself with the thought that she, too, wished we had never met. Arguing with Hunter and Coffin, I could feel my hands trembling, the heat burning behind my eyes. Perpetually exhausted, guilty of crimes I barely understood, I was dimly aware of the world coming apart around me.

An excuse for my cowardly behavior? Hardly. At best a bit of mitigating evidence, offered in my own defense by my older self.

All that fateful Monday morning I had been urging my brother along like an old horse, first cajoling him out of bed, then watching, with increasing impatience, as he moved through his morning toilet. Sophia would be expecting us at ten. At half past nine my brother had barely begun his breakfast, masticating his food with such equine deliberation that I became convinced he was trying to irritate me. I myself had been finished since a quarter past the hour. I had only to put on my coat and leave. I held my tongue, listening to him chew.

At last I could stand it no longer. "Can we go, please? It's late."

"I'm eating," he said, taking a sip of tea.

I made an effort to control myself. "I know you're eating. But I thought you might speed things up a bit, considering how late it is."

"I'll be done presently," he said, chewing.

"It's rude to be late."

"Since when did you start being so punctual?"

I said nothing. A strange, nervous tremor had started up in my stomach and gradually spread to my arms and legs. Even if we were to leave immediately, we would be at least a quarter of an hour late. I could see her walking to the window to look for our carriage. My brother shaved a thin curl off the butter with his knife and began to spread his toast.

"You're an ass," I said, quietly.

"You should know."

It was on our way down the stairs that we ran into Hunter, or his voice, at any rate. The door to the rooms he and Coffin let directly below us was open. "A word if we may, gentlemen," he said.

There was no help for it. It was now ten minutes after ten.

To my surprise—and my brother's, I still believe—we found the room occupied not only by Hunter and Coffin (already slumped like an irritable toad in a huge wingback chair by the fire) but Dumat as well. He was leaning against the mantel, dapper as a don. "And how are we this morning?" he said cheerily, trying to obscure the fact that they had been expecting us. "Well, I trust?"

"Off early, as always," said Coffin. "Wouldn't do to keep the—"

"We have *discussed* this, Abel," said Hunter.

"That's all we do is discuss, discuss—"

"Yes we do, and I would ask you kindly *not* to interfere until we have had the chance to explain our position."

"Bloody ridiculous, if you ask me."

"Thank you. Now if we may . . ."

He paused, then turned to us. "Gentlemen, I see no point in circumlocution"—here Coffin snorted derisively—"so let me address myself directly to the matter at hand. It is something of which we have spoken numerous times, something I am sure will not come as a—"

"But we are being so mysterious, Monsieur Hunter," said Dumat with a small, nervous laugh. "It is nothing so . . ."

"Monsieur Dumat, please. It is, as I say, something of which we have spoken numerous times before—regrettably, to little effect. Remonstrate with you as we may, we make no progress. We are left, therefore, in the unfortunate position of having to make our position clear in terms that allow for no misunderstanding." He cleared his throat. I was barely listening. Why couldn't we discuss whatever it was later? I glanced at the clock on the mantel.

"In short, I believe I am correct in saying that the three of us here are in agreement on one point, namely, that your visits with Mademoiselle Marchant, though excusable for a time, have not had the beneficial effect we might have expected, and may, in fact, be exerting a depressing influence on your career. Let me be frank: What was amusing once is so no longer. What was once merely diverting is now increasingly seen as scandalous, if not actually depraved." Here Hunter raised his hand, as though to forestall questions that none had raised. "I am well aware, of course, that the public is a fickle mistress." His lips thinned. "But so she is, and we must accommodate her as best we can."

"To the point, cut to the point," groaned Coffin. "For the love of God."

"Therefore, as Mister Coffin and I feel we bear some responsibility for your continued success (as well as the financial burden, I might add, of securing the carriage now used almost exclusively for your excursions), we feel we have no choice but to withdraw that privilege. In doing so, we hope to force you to see your visits to Mademoiselle Marchant for the unhealthy obsession they have become, and—"

"All we are saying," interrupted Dumat, "is that there are certain, ah, considerations that you, at your age, cannot be expected to be aware of. Youth is innocent, impressionable; as a result, the picture it makes of the world is often colored by its inexperience, and by the time the facts have come out of hiding, it may be too late."

"Precisely, precisely," agreed Hunter. "As your guardians, and not just your business associates, we feel we have erred in allowing you too much liberty for your age. For the time being, therefore—and I hasten to add that we take this step entirely for your own good—we will be revoking your traveling privileges until such time as—"

"You can't do that," I said, surprised at how shamefully close to the surface the tears already were. "You can't do that."

"We can't?" said Coffin, leaning forward like a dog about to lunge. "And who's going to stop us, eh?"

"Abel, please . . . "

"We can do whatever we bloody well please, my boy, and don't you forget it."

I looked at Hunter. "I'm afraid Mr. Coffin is right," he said.

My brother said nothing.

I stared at them all, listening to the dull drum of my heart. "We're late," I said. "We have an appointment with Mademoiselle Marchant."

"Will you listen to the little lord," laughed Coffin.

"If you'll excuse us."

My brother hadn't moved.

"There is no carriage," Hunter said quietly.

"We'll hire another," I said. "Come on."

"With what? You have no money!"

"Come on!" I said again, wrenching my brother toward the doorway. "What's the matter with you?"

"Lords don't need money," I heard Coffin say behind us. "They just use their influence, didn't you know that? Or they turn a few handsprings to earn their fare."

We were jammed in the doorway now, me pulling with all my might, my brother, like a troubled birth, presenting a shoulder to the doorframe. "Come *on!*" I cried, weeping openly now, wrenching at him. "What is the matter with you?"

"I don't want to go," said my brother.

I didn't give up until I had dragged him like a dead body all the way to the front door. Pushing off against the sides of the walls with my feet (for at some point my brother had simply let himself sink to the floor) weeping with rage and humiliation, I managed to reach the top of the staircase. Grasping the rungs of the banister and pulling myself hand over hand like a cripple, I propelled us over the edge. Half rolling, half jarring, we reached the ground floor. The bottom hallway was wider, but by grasping on to the legs of furniture or pushing, as best I could, against the polished floor, I at last reached the front door. Raising myself up on one arm, blubbering and cursing, I grasped the knob.

It was only then that the full hopelessness of the situation hit me. I couldn't, I realized, move both myself and my brother's body (passive under my cuffs and kicks and slaps) far enough to open the door. And even if I could, what then? Where would it end? Did I intend to drag him a mile and a half through the blackened snow and horse dung of the February streets? Straining to pry open the door, stopping only to beat my brother about the head, I finally collapsed like a child and wept. So undone was I at that moment, so lost and defeated, that I barely noticed it when Coffin and Dumat, raising us to our feet and draping our outer arms around their shoulders, walked us back up the stairs to the sofa by the hearth and covered us in blankets.

I let myself be still. Sitting there, listening to my brother breathing quietly beside me, I could feel the wetness drying on my face. I couldn't fight them all. I didn't want to. I could hear them talking about us, sounding strangely far off:

"Are they all right?"

"I had no idea he would take it so hard."

"I thought he might."

"Mother of God, I've never seen the like of it in all my days."

"I thought he'd kill them both, going down the stairs like that."

"She's got his head all in a muddle, the poor little bastard."

At last I opened my eyes. There was nothing else to do. Coffin was standing off to the side, looking again like the Captain Coffin we had first come to know on the *Sachem*. I could hear Dumat tending to my brother's cuts. Hunter handed me some water.

"Drink this," he said. "Go ahead. You have to drink."

I drank.

"Are you warm enough?" I nodded. He turned to Coffin: "Abel, get a glass of wine for this boy."

They seemed genuinely taken aback, concerned. And though I'm ashamed of it now, the truth is that at the time I was so broken that I allowed myself to be taken care of by them. I welcomed their clumsy, fatherlike ministrations as though they had just rescued us from some great trial rather than been the cause of it; as though, having gone through that morning's events together, we had somehow grown closer.

We stayed in their rooms late into the afternoon. Food appeared and was taken away. At some point a physician came in and examined us briefly—were we ill?—then stepped into the hallway with Hunter. "Shock to the nerves," I heard him say in response to Hunter's mumbled questions, and then: "difficult to say," "rest," "any undue exertion," "not at all," followed by the sound of his footsteps receding down the hall. I didn't care. I felt only sadness—deep, abiding—and the dumb, animal-like relief that comes to those who have gone through some great strain. Something had snapped—I knew that. We would not be going to see her that day. Or the day after. And whenever I thought of not seeing her face, or hearing her voice, the pain welled up as though a hot, swollen sponge buried in my chest were being squeezed, emptying its contents into my veins. But then, like a cold, clear wind, came forgetfulness, rest. Freedom from pain is a powerful thing. Capitulation, when one is young and afraid and exhausted, can beckon like a warm bed at the end of a hard journey.

I accepted the water; I took some food. I sat quietly beside my silent brother (it would be days, I knew, before we would speak), grateful for the blanket across our laps. I thought of nothing. It is only now that I see that absolution, even when offered by one's enemies—no, *particularly* when offered by one's enemies, by those who, an hour earlier, had their knees in our backs and our faces in the mud—can come to seem like the sweetest thing on earth, a benediction of the rarest sort. Left alone to rest, we sat in the darkening room as the reddened hearth emerged in the gathering dusk and a small, vindictive rain began to spit against the glass. Somewhere inside of me, Sophia's face—her laugh, her heart—still glowed like a dying ember; but I was too tired to revive it, and by the time they returned to find us asleep, the room was cold and the fire just a scattering of sparks across the grate.

VI.

For nearly a week I didn't answer her letters, merely sending word that we were ill and would write as soon as we were able. I didn't know that she came to our door that following Tuesday morning, intending to see us, and was politely but firmly turned away. Nor did I receive the increasingly desperate letters she wrote to me; these, I can only surmise, were intercepted by Hunter or Coffin. When, nearly two weeks later (still not having written, for what could I write?), I *did* receive a letter from her, its tone was so intemperate, so angry and confused, that it inspired in me only a perverse resistance. "I ask only this," she had said, "that you write and explain to me what is happening, that you allow me to plead our case. I ask this right, this mercy, only because you yourself, due to some weakness or misunderstanding, appear either unable or unwilling to do so."

Taking a certain pleasure in the drama of the gesture, I folded the letter—hastily written in her once-familiar, less-than-perfect hand—and threw it on the fire. As I did so, I imagined I saw a look of surprise, almost a wince, cross my brother's face. Was he growing soft now, having driven me to this in the first place? Flush with cruelty, I drove the letter home between the coals with the curved tip of the iron and watched it slowly shrivel in the heat, then flash into flame.

I knew that she had suffered at least as much as I had; risked and lost much more. I had heard of her battles: of the broken engagement, the public embarrassments, the fiancé who had denounced her. Pluvier had laughed at the notion of a duel: "At whom would I fire, monsieur? And killing one, would I then be forced to murder the other? It is too absurd! Honor is only an issue between men; I submit that my honor is no more at stake in this matter than if Mademoiselle Marchant had had her affections stolen by a pair of trick poodles or . . . or Siamese cats."

More than once I had asked myself why a woman in her position would willingly endure so much. Now I knew. Now, thanks to the good Professor Dumat, I understood how cunningly corruption can align itself with love, twist and grow into the other until the two are inseparable and the only thing left is to cut both at the base. The scales had slipped from my eyes, and if the sight that greeted me was a bitter one, well, so be it. I would embrace the truth, though it made me ill. I would wrap myself in it as the saints had wrapped themselves in the rags of lepers.

The truth. The truth. It would be years before I learned that the devil—who knows his business, after all—has gotten along so well in the world because he never fails to come dressed as the truth.

"My good friends," Dumat had said to us that cold February afternoon, "I would have preferred to put off this conversation until some later date; until you were older, perhaps, a bit wiser in the ways of the world." He smiled ruefully, then laid the pipe he had been smoking on a tray beside his chair. "But you have been thrown—quite precipitously, I'm afraid—into a complicated world. A world in which things don't always appear as they are. A world that can hurt you very badly."

He paused, picking his words carefully. "This is an ungrateful task. I know that you do not trust me, that since I failed to take your side against Monsieur Hunter and Monsieur Coffin, you feel I am not your friend. I will not try to change your mind. I will only say, in regard to that matter, that the gentlemen in question are perhaps neither as guilty as you imagine nor as innocent as I might wish." The coals crumbled in the hearth, briefly lighting up the room. "A cold day," said Dumat.

Behind him, a few dead leaves rose in a gust of wind like a small flock of sparrows, even as an actual sparrow—like a bit of cloth with a beak and legs—settled on the sill.

"But whether you trust me or not doesn't matter, really," Dumat continued. "We none of us have a choice. If you had a father"—at this I could feel my brother stiffen beside me—"I would gladly step aside and let him do his duty, though I trust and believe he would have performed it long before this. As it is . . ." He leaned forward, gentle, sincere, almost whispering: "You have been born with a gift, my friends; a gift, like great beauty, or supreme intelligence, that cannot be returned in this life. This gift sets you apart from your fellow man. It shapes the world around you. It imposes burdens and confers privileges. And there are times, I suspect—particularly now, when you are young—when those privileges seem small indeed and the burdens more than you can bear.

"I understand that. I understand—possibly better than anyone you will ever know—the burden you carry." Dumat leaned forward, his voice rising with conviction. Until now I had only been half listening, less interested in his actual words than in the apparently unconscious gestures that accompanied them like the hand music of the deaf. "I understand," he was saying now, "because Nature—or God, if you will—has seen fit to bless others as she has blessed you. Because you are not alone. Now and again Nature chooses to separate the individual from the common mold"—here his long, pale hands seemed to pull apart two invisible pieces of dough—"presses her thumb into the form while it is still wet"—a thumb turning into invisible clay—"and shapes something entirely new. A rarity. An exception. Something we in our stupidity and fear call a monstrosity. But we are wrong, my friends. You and your kind are a prodigy, a wonder"—hands expanding in helpless amazement—"the very word of God. And who are we to assume, in our ignorance, that just because that word is inscrutable to us"— squinting eyes, brow gathered in concentration—"a hieroglyphic more profound than any found on the scrolls of Alexandria, it holds no meaning, is not"—sharp white index finger pointing to the ceiling—"divine in origin?"

He sat back. "But I see by your smiles—no, don't try to deny it, I do not hold it against you—that my strong feelings on this subject are making you uncomfortable. Forgive me. Your discomfort speaks well for you; the truly superior are always discomfited by an excess of flattery." Pausing, he reached for his pipe, turned it in his hand, then set it down again.

"I must speak frankly, my friends, as a man speaks to his fellows." He sighed, then looked directly in our eyes for the first time that afternoon. "You are no longer boys. I know that." He lowered his voice conspiratorially. "I know that in the privacy of your thoughts, you imagine things—all manner of things—that bring you pleasure and make you ashamed, and this is as it should be." I could feel Eng shift uncomfortably.

Dumat cleared his throat. "What you cannot be expected to know, however, is that the members of the fairer sex—and I speak now of well-born women as well as their less fortunate sisters—not only share your thoughts but, in some circumstances, under certain peculiar conditions, turn what is natural and wholesome into something twisted and rank. In these cases, the seed, if I may, instead of emerging from corruption, instead of leaving its base origin and blossoming, in the fullness of time, into the love sanctioned by God and man alike, grows morbid and rots.

"I say again: You cannot be expected to know this. No one can hold you accountable, at your age, for failing to imagine the strange spears that can spring from this corrupted soil, the odd suckers and stipula that can grow on the fairest flower." Here again Dumat paused for a moment and looked at the ground to our right, a look of genuine sadness on his face, then rallied to the task. "But you *must* know. You must know, my friends—and I wish to merciful God there were someone else to tell you this—because your gift is of that class of things that, on occasion, and when encountered by an unhealthy soul, can corrupt the seed in its bed."

"I don't understand." Increasingly agitated, my brother had suddenly sat up straighter on the divan. These were the first words, beyond a simple yes or no, I had heard him utter in days. "I don't understand what it is you are . . ."

"Simply this: that there are certain women in the world who—"

"Are you referring to Mademoiselle Marchant?"

"I am speaking in general . . ."

"Because Mademoiselle Marchant—"

"My dear friend, calm yourself. I do not know Mademoiselle Marchant. I am speaking in general terms only. How these general truths apply to specific cases or particular individuals, that I cannot say."

"Because my brother and I will not have you speak badly of her. Do you hear? We will not have it."

My throat tightened suddenly; I resisted the temptation to look over at him. Dumat was waving both hands as though clearing a window just in front of his face. "You misunderstand me. Please. I had no intention of casting aspersions on—"

"What did you want to tell us, Monsieur Dumat?" I said quietly. Out of the corner of my eye I could see my brother glance at me in surprise. I did not look at him.

Dumat gave me a curt, tight nod. "No more than this: That there are in this world certain unfortunate women, certainly deserving of our pity, in whom the principle of attraction has been corrupted; turned, as it were, against itself. They are drawn by what repels them." Again Dumat's voice began to rise, as though beyond his control. "They seek out the morbid, the sick, even the cruel, in precisely the same way their healthy sisters seek out what is honorable and whole. They are a horror, an abomination, and yet, though they themselves often recognize the perversity of their natures, this perversity, this corruption, by Nature's cunning, is often very nearly invisible from without. Like the viper, whose coloration allows it to blend with the fallen leaves in which it lies, this taint is indistinguishable from the surrounding beauty in which—"

"No more!" We stood up abruptly. I had had enough.

"Please, my friends, you must believe—"

"That will do, sir. We will not listen to another word. Not another word."

"You are making a mistake. I say this only to spare you—"

But we were already walking toward the door. Dumat's voice pursued us into the hall: "You *will* listen. You must! It is not . . . I am not the only one who knows this. It is common knowledge. Only you in your innocence could truly believe that this . . . Please . . . Let me explain . . . Wait!"

We were halfway down the hall when he began to read. He must have had the volume there all along, that damnable page marked and waiting for its moment. "If you won't listen to me," he cried after us as we mounted the stairs, his voice, vaguely demonic now, echoing against the walls, "then at least listen to Monsieur Hugo, who lets her speak for herself." We rushed on. " 'I love you,' " he screamed up the winding stair, " 'I love you not only because you are deformed, but because you are low.' Are you listening?" I thought I heard a page turn, a sound like a slap. " 'A lover despised, mocked, grotesque, hideous' "—we were running down the hallway now—" 'exposed to laughter on that pillory called the stage' "—there was our door!—" 'has an extraordinary attraction to me. It is a taste of the fruit of hell.' "

Fumbling with the key as though an actual fiend were at our heels, I managed to find the lock just as Dumat read the lines that would continue to sound—alchemically changed to a woman's voice, wondering and cruel—years after our door had crashed shut like a full stop on a sentence: " 'I am in love with a nightmare. You are the incarnation of infernal mirth.' "

VII.

Even the seasons, that year, seemed beset by doubt: days of softening, restless wind followed by nights frozen fast as death. In the mornings, against the gray sky, the coal smoke rose like a forest of columns from the roofs of the city and the streets tinkled with broken glass. Bowed down by the course of events, strangely torpid, my brother and I took to wandering about the streets of the city, drifting farther and farther afield each day as though hoping, by this symbolic leavetaking, to somehow effect our actual escape. As if by simply walking far enough we might snap the bonds that held us.

How far did we wander those days? Ten miles? Twenty? On the days when we had an evening performance to attend, we would wind our way back to our lodgings by nightfall; on days we had none we would stay out late—till midnight or later—for it was only after dark, when the carriages had disappeared and the streets had grown silent, that we felt free. Once or twice we found ourselves in her neighborhood.

The branching of trees, the deepening blue of the evening . . . it might have been beautiful. But the mind, like the contents of a street peddler's cart, reflects its owner's preoccupations. We saw the bones beneath the faces of the sweepers, heard the consumptives' scraping cough, like coal scuttles on brick, smelled the perfume of the slaughter-houses when the spring wind was from the south.

. . .

My brother attempted to speak to me shortly after our episode with Dumat. "You must not listen," he blurted out suddenly, breaking a long silence. We were walking along a country lane lined with cherry trees just leafing into bloom. From a distance, against the dark fields, the orchards appeared touched with mold. A wet wind pushed at our faces. "You have to not listen," he said again, looking at me. I was reminded of a worried snail, testing the air with its roots.

"What are you talking about?" I said.

"Dumat. You have to not listen to him. You have to go on as if he hadn't spoken at all."

I snorted. "Why would I listen to him?"

"Because you did."

"I don't even—"

"I know," he said quietly. "I can tell."

"Tell what?" I laughed.

"All right. Suit yourself."

"No, tell me. What can you tell?"

He said nothing.

"Are you warning me, or yourself?" He walked on, back in his shell. I flicked him again, just to make sure. "It seems to me you could use some of your own advice, brother."

"Don't worry about me."

"Don't worry. I don't."

He was absolutely right, of course. His advice, though much too late, was both generous and wise. Dumat, who no longer appeared at our lodgings, had done his work. Though I didn't believe him, neither could I prove him wrong. "A lover despised, mocked, grotesque . . ." I had known the pillory of the stage. Did I believe that Sophia Marchant had loved me because I was hideous? That she had run her hand along my side that dark afternoon in her drawing room, allowed her fingers to explore where the base of my bridge rose from my ribs, because my condition attracted her? I did not. Could I say with absolute certainty

that it was *not* so? I could not. I was, after all, who I was: a penniless foreigner, a boy, neither handsome nor distinguished. I had been declared a
freak, the mere sight of whom could damage the unborn in the womb.
More than this, and making any natural union between us an impossibility, I was already indissolubly joined to another. And yet she had risked
so much, so recklessly. Why? Why? "I am in love with a nightmare."
Could I say with absolute certainty that somewhere deep in her inmost
soul she was not drawn to me the way fingers are drawn to a scab,
or eyes to a wound? "You are the incarnation of infernal mirth." I
could not.

And so we walked. At night, back in our lodgings, though hardly able to
stand, I walked the same route again in my dreams: There again was the
crow, screaming something from the top of a linden; there was the street
sweeper with the patch over his eye; there was the river, strangely silent,
its shifting whirlpools sucking at the air. The black dog we had seen disappear stiff-legged into a whorl in the current appeared on the opposite
shore. I had to get to him. He reminded me of something. I wanted to
gather him in my arms. And then we were sitting next to one another in
a room at dusk, her head resting on my shoulder. I could feel her
warmth through my clothes. I had been told I was dying. I wanted to tell
her, but knew the moment I spoke it would be true. And so on, and so
on, down streets strangely empty of carriages and horses, past darkened
buildings in which no lamp had been lit, by stubbled fields in which the
same distant figure labored behind a plow as though condemned to plow
the same furrow, keep open the wound, day after day and night after
night in my dreams.

But all was not a loss. Though speaking little French, we learned a great
deal on those long walks through Paris and its immediate environs. We
discovered, for example, that the horns of slaughtered bullocks were
turned into "tortoiseshell" combs, the bones of their legs into tooth-
brush handles and dominoes. The gathered blood went to the sugar
refiners; the fat, for lamps, or soap. There was something horribly fasci-

nating in this. Again and again we found ourselves walking in the direction of Montfaucon. It was as though we couldn't stop ourselves. Seeing us, the workers would quickly gather about, jabbering and staring (most had heard of us, many had seen us on the stage), until someone in a position of authority noticed the disruption and came to see what was happening. Ordering the others back to their places, he would then, often as not, offer us a guided tour.

Most of what we saw was forgotten. Some was not. I remember, for some reason, the slim figure of an artist, seated against a pile of bales, sketching the flaying of a horse. A romantic character, dark-haired and mustached, he worked at a furious pace, intent on capturing the waves of exposed muscle before they too went under the knife. At Montfaucon one cold day we watched a gaunt jobber whose face seemed permanently darkened by shadow, and whose work it was to gather the entrails for the feeding of pigs and poultry, reach into a mass of steaming offal and draw out the intestinal canal of a freshly slaughtered mare. Wrapping it like a long, dark rope open-palm-to-elbow, he made thirteen full revolutions before the tail end emerged out of the pile at his feet and snaked up his leg.

The skin, we were made to understand, would be sold to a tanner; the tendons, fresh or dried, to the gluemakers. Even the putrid flesh would be used. Covered with a pile of hay or straw, it would soon attract flies; within a week it would be rich with maggots. These would then be gathered and sold as food for domestic fowls, or as baits for fish. Nor was this all. We had noticed, no doubt, the unfortunate number of rats. Once a fortnight, we were told, the carcass of a horse was placed in a room with special openings in the walls and floor designed to allow the rats free access. At night, these openings were closed, trapping the rats inside, and the ferrets released. In one room, over a period of less than four weeks, they had killed more than sixteen thousand rats. Our guide smiled happily. "Think of it, monsieur," he said, addressing me. "The furriers in Paris pay four francs for one hundred skins. And it costs us nothing!"

Why did we go? And why did we return, though the smell that lin-

gered in our clothing alone was almost enough to make us ill? Feeling
corrupted inside, did I search out corruption in the hope of finding some
kind of equilibrium? Or did I seek out the rough precincts of death
intending to split myself against its hardness, to rub my nose against it
until, like a serpent scraping and scraping against the edges of rocks, I
felt the old skin sliding back across my eyes and crawled, reborn, from
out of myself? And what of my brother? Did he say nothing because he
felt some responsibility, some complicity for my state, or did he, too,
feel some small measure of attraction for that fallen place?

It was in this state of mind, at any rate, that we found ourselves one evening in a deserted, ill-lighted district extending along the edge of a small
canal. There seemed to be hardly anyone about. We walked on, watching our step, for the stones of the street were in ill repair. Now and again
a man emerged from the darkness of the side streets and hurried by. We
heard what sounded like a woman's laugh, or a quick, gasping cry, then
a man's voice yelling something we could not understand. Here and
there, high above the street, a candle flickered in a dark window.

But let me be clear. We were hardly so naive as not to know where
we had found ourselves. We had spent years, after all, in the company
of older men. From the banks of the Meklong to the decks of the
Sachem we had listened to their tales, grinned knowingly at their jokes.
And yet who could be surprised, given the difficulties presented by our
condition, that at the age of twenty we still knew nothing? It was an
ignorance my brother—though no less driven than I, to judge by the
frequency of his late-night whimperings and shudderings—bore with
maddening fortitude. He had always been more reticent, more con-
stricted; it was only after our experience with the concubines in the
Royal Palace, however, that his natural timidity had flared into morbid
shyness.

At times it seemed he would be willing to endure the burden of our
innocence forever. Not that I was uniformly willing to shed it. When
Coffin, only a week earlier, had hinted about the possibility of finding
female companionship for us—hoping, in this crude way, to compen-

sate us for our recent troubles—we had *both* turned down his offer. My brother, you see, was afraid, hence the tone of offended dignity, the vehement denials of any need or desire. And I? I was in love.

Perhaps we were simply tired that night. Or perhaps, given the strange, dreamlike existence we had been leading, what happened that night seemed no more or less real than a painter sketching a flayed horse, or the dreamed warmth of Sophia's hip against my side, the rustling slip of her dress. Perhaps. More likely modesty and love, undermined by pain, simply went down under the gentle pressure of opportunity, the sweet tyranny of the moment.

What was she like? She was pretty enough, with pale round arms and calves and a wealth of creamy bosom that she framed in lace like a painting of a winter scene. Ten years older than us, perhaps more, she had none of the dissipated look of so many of her sisters; slightly plump, with knowing eyes and a fine, slim neck like the stem on a cherry, she seemed to have escaped many of the ravages of her trade. We knew none of this at first. We couldn't see her. It was her voice, which addressed us from the dark of a shuttered storefront, that made us slow our step: low, almost coarse, it had about it a warmth, a teasing humor, that bespoke both curiosity and acceptance.

In spite of ourselves, we stopped, cringing inwardly at what we knew was to come—the involuntary backward step, the hand over the mouth, the small gasp of shock. No doubt she had thought we were two men walking side by side. Yet when she saw how things were with us, she seemed neither terrified nor unduly surprised. She had heard of us, apparently. A friend had seen us, she explained, painting a stage with her hands, then curtsying nicely to the canal by way of explanation. "Let's go," said my brother.

"Je suis Corinne," she said, touching a spot directly below her throat, watching us.

"Chang," I said, indicating myself.

"Chang," she repeated.

"And this is my—"

"Let's go," said my brother.

"This is Eng," I said, pointing.

"Enchantée," she said, looking at him.

"I said let's go."

"No."

Stepping forward suddenly she placed her hand directly against our bridge. My brother flinched as if he had just been bitten by a wasp, jerking me violently to the left. "Don't . . ." he began, and then, to me: "Come *on*!" Before we could move she reached up and touched the back of her gloved fingers to the side of his face, then laid them against his mouth. "Shhhh," she whispered. I could hear the canal gurgling quietly to itself in the darkness. A short cry came from somewhere above our heads. She smiled and rolled her eyes.

It would speak better for me if I could say that I struggled and argued with myself as we followed her up the narrow stairs and watched her slip the key into the lock. But alas, that was not the case. I felt dazed, drunk. I felt no remorse for what I was about to do at all. I drank in the slow shift of her skirts as she walked up the steps ahead of us, counted the dark curls that had escaped her pin. If I thought of anything at all, it was that there had been no talk of money. "We have four francs," Eng whispered to me when, with a quick smile and an explanation we couldn't understand, she stepped out into the hall, leaving us alone in the small, neat room. For a moment we both thought of escaping the way we had come. Before we could come to a decision, she was back.

Ah, the shamelessness of the innocent! Having no experience, we assumed that whatever came to pass was simply the way of things, and therefore watched, amazed but not surprised, as she first undressed us, slowly, tenderly—only the quickening rate of her breathing giving away her emotions—then unlaced and unbound herself, layer by layer, until she lay before us on the bed, shockingly naked, white as an almond slipped from its skin.

She seemed fascinated by our arms, our hips, by the muscled smoothness of our bridge, running her hands over us as though to confirm what her eyes showed. Nothing surprised her. Whatever we assayed, she understood. When, wondering, unable to resist, I touched the taut softness of her breast with my fingers, she slipped her hand behind my head and gently pressed me down, then pushed herself between my lips. When she felt my brother, in an agony of shame, helplessly pressing himself against her side, she took him gently in her hand and caressed him, all the while gentling him like a nervous horse. And when, with a strange groan, he suddenly spilled his seed across her hip and stomach, she laughed with pleasure and kissed him full on the mouth.

We had climbed, with some awkwardness, onto the bed with her. Trying as best I could to support my weight on my arms I hovered above her body, my brother, forever next to me, pressed tight against her side. Still kissing him, her arm around his neck, she reached around my back and quickly, firmly, pressed me down and into her.

The rest—the increasingly unbridled urgings of her hips, the strangled music of her cries, the reception of my crisis by the expectant, frozen look on her features—all this was a blur to me. I could feel the ecstatic rubbing of her hands across our bridge and then it was there—announced by a quick gasp, a receiving stillness—and for the space of a few moments the two of us joined in the sweet, sudden breaking of walls that had stood too long. Lost in that lovely wreckage, I could feel her placing a necklace of kisses along my collarbone.

But all was not done. Disturbed by the activities, my brother, it seemed, had been resurrected. Hardly had I returned to myself before I felt her gently easing me to the side. Unprotesting, I slipped off, thereby pulling my brother onto her. This, it seemed, was precisely what she had intended. Still half dazed, running my hand almost absentmindedly along her side, I watched as, raising her hips slightly and guiding his luckless explorations with her hand, she proceeded to give him the exact duplicate of what she had just given me. It was a gift my brother, no longer protesting, quite enthusiastically accepted—a fact I would have occasion to remind him of, more than once, in the years to come.

.　　.　　.

Do I blame us for the pleasure we took that evening? No, I do not. Life offered itself, and knowing that, for such as ourselves, another opportunity might never come, we took it. Do I blame her for tainting it? For wanting us because we were the way we were? Because the fact of our doubleness excited her? No, I do not.

I do not blame her even though at some point that night, hearing an odd scuffling as of mice in the walls, I looked up and found the doorway full of wondering women's faces and understood why she had stepped into the hallway when we had first arrived. Yet again we had been seen as nothing more than freaks on a stage. Thrusting her away, ignoring her frantic entreaties and explanations, we lurched out of bed—boys that we were—and ran half-dressed down those narrow stairs and out into the darkness, where, catching my toe on an upturned stone, I tripped, bringing us crashing heavily to the cobbles.

Would that I had known then what I do now: that the heart is large, large—enough to house all manner of contradictions. That sinner and saint sleep in adjoining rooms there, and walk hand in hand through its gardens. We might have stayed. Put off our lives for an hour. Asked them, simply, to close the door.

We were what we were, after all. How absurd, it seems to me now, to want to be desired for something you're not! Or to blame someone for wanting you for what you are, when all the world over generations of men and women have lived and died dreaming of precisely that.

And yet that is what I did. Perhaps because I didn't want to admit who I was, would never admit the justice of it. But she was not at fault. Better, infinitely better, to blame the Maker for having made me as I was. Or Sophia, for having shown me a love I could never have, a love so all-consuming I would want it for my own.

VIII.

Paris was ending for us. We knew that. The petals had browned and dropped; the bloom was off the rose. With Ritta-Christina there to draw off the few who might still have come to see us, we watched our situation grow more desperate by the week. One day, we knew, the theatre would simply be empty. And yet we did nothing. We had not seen Dumat in weeks; apparently we had no need of a translator anymore, and as for tutoring, well, that too seemed to have ended. Days would pass without us speaking to either Hunter or Coffin, who seemed to be spending more and more of their time away from their lodgings. Often, a folded note, slipped beneath our door, would give the address and time of that evening's performance. Nothing more. More often still, there would be no note.

And so we sat by the hearth, we talked, we read—as best we could—the English novels we had begun reading with Sophia. I had developed a strange affection for them. They had been by our bed the morning I woke still believing I would be with her in an hour's time; they had lain on the table next to me as I had hurried my brother through breakfast, worrying we would be late. Outside on the avenue, a hard wind etched the cloaks and shawls of passersby against their owners' backs, revealing the shape—like fingers in a wet glove—beneath the carapace of cloth. Gentlemen hurried by with their hands to their hats. Shoved along by an unseen hand, ladies in bonnets would suddenly hurry their steps, then slow.

We knew we had to do something, and yet, trapped by indecision, tired of talking endlessly about a situation that seemed to have no remedy—where could we go? whom could we turn to?—we did nothing. For four days it rained, trapping us inside. The cobbles were slick with mud, the country roads impassable. We could have taken the opportunity to speak to Hunter and Coffin, to demand what was owed us. We did not. We stayed in our rooms. Had the black boughs scraping against the outside wall been exchanged for palm fronds, we might have been back in Saigon. As soon as the rain eased we took to the fields and woodlots, once again circling the immovable core of our predicament like small muddy planets unable to escape the gravity of their situation. I can still recall the irregular orbit we walked—along broken, cracking streets, past stone walls and statuary black with rain—guided less by whimsy than by a simple lack of will, turning left or right on the basis of nothing more than the vague play of light on a warehouse wall or the suggestion of a smell—a smell like wheat and ash and wetted wool—brought in on the breeze.

We were drowning, of course. Years from home, in a foreign land, at the mercy of two men apparently intent on defrauding us of all that was rightfully ours, we were in more danger than we realized. Unable to turn to the authorities—how could we explain our case?—unlikely to receive a sympathetic audience if we had, we sensed the situation was growing desperate, yet seemed strangely unable to struggle. It was easier to do nothing. The rent on our rooms was still being paid, we told ourselves; the envelopes slipped beneath our door every two or three days still contained enough money for us to feed ourselves. To move at all might tip the balance. Nearly thirty years later a man I never met would write the words that would capture for me, as accurately as any daguerreotype, the helplessness of our lives that spring: "For in tremendous extremities human souls are like drowning men; well enough they know they are in peril; well enough they know the causes of that peril;—nevertheless, the sea is the sea, and these drowning men do drown."

On the afternoon of April fourth, my brother and I had found ourselves in a district of Paris unfamiliar to us; a well-kept neighborhood of respectable homes and carriage houses protected by huge, muscled trees that spread their budding branches over the street. Soon enough, however, the trees began to fall back, their branches parting over our heads. The streets grew slovenly and disordered. Warehouses and vague, unnamed buildings—offices of some sort, we assumed—rose on both sides. We continued on. A thin drizzle wet our faces, then stopped. We watched a small, three-legged dog hunch-trot along the side of a wooden building, then raise its stump to the wall. It began to rain in earnest. Before us stood an imposing edifice with a huge glass dome. On either side of the entrance stood a pair of small, snarling lions, once bronze, now green with time. Gargoyles with monkey faces grinned down from the pediment, slow ropes of rain dripping from their jaws. A small sign above the portal read MUSÉE DE L'HOMME ET LA NATURE.

Was it some vague, undefined curiosity or just the thickening rain that made us seek shelter there? Both, perhaps. Except for the dog, at that moment disappearing around a pile of broken bricks, the street was empty. Passing between the lions, we grasped the heavy, two-handed knobs. Nothing. We tried again, this time bracing ourselves against the left portal and pulling on the right. Slowly, the huge, intricately carved door swung open.

We found ourselves in a vast, cathedral-like hall, cavernous and still. Strangely enough, there seemed to be no one about. No lamps had been lit. No one answered our calls. We looked up. Clouds were rushing past the glass ceiling. Massive steel girders rose and arched above our heads, as if bearing the vault of heaven on their backs. We moved further in, our footsteps echoing against the marble. On either side, circular, wrought-iron stairs connected narrow wooden balconies that rose, one atop the other, nearly to the ceiling. Extending the length of the hall, each balcony contained two tiny alcoves with just enough room for a desk and a chair; the balcony walls themselves appeared to be lined with glass-fronted display cases and cabinets. From the third level up, reflecting the ceiling overhead, these appeared as long, broken strips of cloud, or, stranger still, as rows of windows onto some other, tilted sky.

At the center of the room, towering nearly to the ceiling, was a pyramid unlike anything either of us had ever seen or dreamed: a pyramid of life itself, or death, rather; tier upon tier of antelopes and zebras, foxes and wolves, yellow-tusked boars and long-tailed monkeys. Miraculously preserved, they stared out of glass eyes so liquid, so dark and lifelike, one half expected them to turn and blink at any moment. Inspired by nature's profusion, the creators, whoever they were, had seemingly gathered specimens from all four corners of the earth. One side of the pyramid contained no fewer than thirteen reclining zebras, another a small herd of chestnut-spotted antelope with long, whorled horns. Here was an entire pride of snarling lions; here a pack of hunched and bristling wolves. Four seated leopards marked the corners, their tails turned around their frozen haunches.

We walked slowly around the base, speechless, reverent as acolytes before the altar. On and on the pyramid rose—looking up, we could make out layer upon layer of hawks and herons, badgers and hedgehogs, squirrels and cats—a dusty edifice ascending through ever-smaller increments of feather and bone to sediments of mice and voles and shrews and, finally, heaped piles of finches and warblers, bats and thrushes, small hills of sparrows. Above it all—a touch of whimsy—swallows and butterflies, apparently suspended from the ceiling by hair-thin wires, seemed to swoop and flutter against the actual sky even as, behind them, living birds separated themselves off from their stationary brethren and, tossed by the wind, disappeared from view.

The sun appeared, blazing painfully from a cabinet window on the third balcony, bathing the south side of the gallery in pale, wintry light. The wooden walls instantly reddened; the furred mountain before us seemed to stir slightly. So still was it that when my brother spoke, breaking the silence, I actually started. "We shouldn't be here," he said, uncertainly.

"Why not?" I said. "The door was open . . ."

"I know that." He looked around. "That's not what I meant."

"I know what you meant," I said.

"I know you do."

But we didn't leave. No longer concerned about being discovered, or having to explain to the authorities how we came to be inside an establishment that, despite its unlocked doors, was obviously closed to the public, we began to walk around the perimeter of the room. I became aware of a strange, yellow smell, distinctly chemical yet not unpleasant. We wandered from case to case, past displays of walrus horns and monkey skulls and small, jewellike beetles on pins until we found ourselves, quite unexpectedly, by a door in the wall. The hall had grown dark again; high above our heads, rain was beating anxiously against the glass. All talk of leaving forgotten, we tried the door and, finding it unlocked, passed beneath a small, dark rectangle that suggested there had once been a sign in the wood above the portal.

The room we found ourselves in, though still of considerable size, seemed narrow and cramped in comparison to the soaring grandeur of the main hall. Ill lit by high, dusty windows, obviously unkempt, it stretched into the vague distance, crowded with a silent, hulking company of cabinets and display cases. Seeing them standing together in groups of two and three about the floor, I had the uncanny impression of having interrupted something, as though the shapes before me had only just frozen into their inanimate form. Indeed, for a moment I imagined I could still hear the dull, murmuring echo of their voices—the departing hubbub of the crowd—then all was silent.

Slowly, we walked over to the cabinet nearest to us. After a moment, we walked to the next. We couldn't speak. It was as though our tongues had grown fat and strange in our mouths, as though our throats had decided to choke themselves off. In the first cabinet, set against a dark velvet background, were the jewellike bones of seven tiny hands. Lovingly disarticulated, delicate as shells, some showed six digits, some seven; one, spreading in a miniature fan that could fit easily inside a man's palm, a full eight. In the second cabinet a dried flower arrangement, dove-gray and dun, flax and wheat, framed an allegorical wilderness scene. At its center, atop a craggy hill of gallstones the color of rust, was a skull. At the base, reclining like a tiny bather in the sun, was a miniature human skeleton. In the bones of its right hand it grasped the papery wing of a moth.

If this had only been all, we might still have left the Musée de L'homme et la Nature disturbed but unscathed. But it was not.

It began in the third cabinet with a two-headed kitten (the left looking off to the side, the right licking its paw with a tiny pink tongue); next to it, suspended by wires, was a stuffed viper whose body, like the trunk of a tree, had divided two-thirds of the way down its length. The fourth cabinet showed what appeared to be the skeleton of a dog with the fully formed haunches of another extending from its side. "Oh my God," I heard my brother whisper, "what *is* this place?" I shook my head, unable to speak. It was then I realized he was not looking at the dog at all.

In three cabinets facing each other at oblique angles were detailed anatomical drawings—portraits, really— of twins much like ourselves and yet at the same time horribly different: men and women who had melted into one another in ways one would not have thought possible. Here, as though they had run together at great speed, two young women had been fused face to face, neck to thigh. I understood immediately: They had never been able to turn away from one another. Chin to chin for life, they had died looking into each other's eyes. Here were two boys, reclining on their backs, whose hips had simply, unbelievably, disappeared into one another, forming one, uninterrupted midsection. Though two pairs of withered, rudimentary legs extended from their sides, they would never walk, nor would it be possible for them to see each other except by raising themselves on their elbows. Here another pair, also boys, no more than six years old, had been smashed together side to side with such power that their ribs seemed grown together, their stomachs one; though a single male organ could be seen between the central pair of legs, it seemed to belong to some third brother whose upper body had been lost in theirs.

It was the faces that held us, that kept us there for as long as they did. Faces so real, somehow, so human, it would be years before I would see their like—in the paintings of the masters, in the daguerreotypes that now and again would capture, as if by accident, the agony of our race: faces from some other, parallel world of experience, faces seemingly about to cry or absurdly smiling, ironic or ashamed, frozen in attitudes of stoicism and courage beyond my comprehension.

It was as we turned to leave that we saw him: a full-grown man— olive-skinned, almost handsome—staring out of a picture on the right-hand side of a double-door cabinet. With both hands, he was holding something that protruded directly out of his chest. Prepared though we were by this point to credit whatever our eyes showed us, it yet took a moment for us to realize that this something was another, smaller human being, or, rather, the waist and legs and feet of a human being— a half-grown child, apparently—whose upper body had seemingly been absorbed into his older brother's.

It was not the horror of this that seared itself on my memory, nor the utter cruelty of the predicament. It was not the full-sized skeleton on the cabinet's left side, which clearly showed that the little being had ended, as a recognizable human at any rate, at the waist; that the illusion had disintegrated into a chaos of bone—a bit of twisted spine thrusting, headless, through the brother's ribs, a nub of an arm—only a short distance below the skin. Nor was it even the fact that this ghastly growth, this parasite (for this is what he was) had been dressed in well-fitting trousers and stockings and laced shoes. Even this I could have borne.

What I could not endure was the look on the older brother's face: it was a look of unmistakable pride, unbowed and haughty. One strong arm reached across the little one's thighs; the other supported him from beneath. Thus we were born, he seemed to be saying (though the other could never hear a word he said, nor think, nor breathe), and thus we will go on.

· · ·

We turned and fled, past the cabinets in that ghostly anteroom, past a small wooden sign leaning sideways against the wall—GALERIE DES ANOMALIES, MONSTRES ET PRODIGES—our footsteps knocking hard and close against the stone, then fading into the vastness of the main gallery. We ran under the sound of the rain scattering itself against the glass dome and out into the thing itself, not even bothering to button our coats as our hair quickly plastered to our foreheads and our shirt fronts clung to our chests. The dog was gone. The warehouses disappeared. The streets grew tidier. The trees on either side rose and linked their branches over our heads, as though to protect us from the rain.

It took us an hour, maybe more. Did my brother know where we were going? Did I? Though neither of us said a word that entire time— not one word—I believe we both understood from the moment we turned and began to run that we really only had one place to go, which is why there were no arguments or moments of indecision as turn followed turn and the world grew familiar around us once more. Walking down her street at last was like seeing the windows of home—the same rise, the remembered trees . . . There was the stone fence we had cleared of snow with our hands. There we had walked arm in arm, huddled together against the cold. There was the carriage step I had lifted her onto in the midst of some joke or other (I could still remember the warmth of her breathing, the sweet weight of her body) from which she had made a pretty little speech and curtsied to her audience. My God, she had loved me. I knew that now. I could feel the rain running down my face. There was the house! After what seemed like a lifetime of wandering, foot-sore and soul-weary, sad to the core, the traveler had returned.

There was no one home. No curtains in the windows. At last the door was opened by a well-dressed elderly gentleman in spectacles, wearing a hat and coat as if on his way out. It was clear immediately: She was gone! "I'm afraid Mademoiselle Marchant left Paris three days ago . . . A message? I'm afraid not." Did he know when she might return? That would be impossible to say. Nor was he at liberty to say where she had gone. He had been retained for the express purpose of arranging for the removal of Mademoiselle Marchant's things, no more.

He was not unkind. Seeing me blinking stupidly at the drops catching in my lashes, he stepped aside in the passage. We were soaked through. Would we like to step in out of the rain for a moment? He made rubbing motions, then hurried off, returning with a pair of towels. In one hand he carried a bottle; in the other, crossed stem to stem between his fingers, two small glasses. But I couldn't drink. There was a strange pain in my chest. I looked around. There were the doors to the parlor that Claudine would swing open every morning to the light. How the sun would break in like a toppled column! There was the parlor, just as we had left it—the sofa and the armoire, the mahogany-and-horsehair chairs, the pianoforte on which she had played for us . . . I could hear her voice! It was impossible, impossible that she should be gone. The patterns of the rain, swimming over the furniture, made the room seem submerged.

And then, as though the weeks and months since I had seen her had suddenly come together and overwhelmed me, I began to cry. I didn't make a scene. I just stood there like an idiot, my jaw clenched and the tears streaming out of my eyes and dribbling off my chin. When I asked, absurdly, whether we might have a moment alone in the drawing room, the man looked at me a moment, his head tipped slightly to the side, his lips pursed, then nodded and stepped out, closing the doors behind him.

She was there. I could smell her, hear her. I could feel her touch on my arm. I had never felt this kind of pain. It was as though my chest were caving in, crumbling inward like walls of sand under a rising tide. And then—I'm not ashamed to admit it—I walked around that parlor (a small madness) and kissed the things that had known her, one by one: the arms of the sofa and the pillows on which her head had rested, the book on the spindle-legged table which she had been reading, the silver candlestick holder she had bought in Spain. My brother said not a word, following me from point to point in that dark, watery room, kneeling quietly beside me while I knelt before the sofa like a suitor proposing to a ghost and then (out of some misplaced rapture, some terrible lack of her), pressed the red, embroidered cushion she had always held on her lap like a lover to my face.

I don't know how long he had been in the doorway before we noticed him. We thanked him and turned to leave. "You are very welcome," he said, his voice somehow gentler than before. He looked at me as we stood by the door. I had regained something of my composure. "I am sorry Mademoiselle Marchant was not here," he said quietly. "I am sure she will be sorry she missed you."

A kindness. We walked back into the rain, back to our lodgings. A week later, when Coffin and Hunter made the decision for us, we left Paris for London without an argument. We were never to see that city again.

For thirty years I asked anyone I met who had traveled to France if they had heard her name. But the moment had come and gone, and the years had buried us both.

IX.

We returned to London, once again enduring the long hours in the company of our unscrupulous guardians as we had on our arrival in Europe. Ah, but things had changed, this time around. Our companions, no longer flush with our early success, spoke hardly a word. The prevailing mood was one of sullen desperation; poverty fluttered along behind us like a rag caught in the carriage door.

Reflecting our straitened means, the wayside inns had grown small and grim in the six months since we had passed. Broken-roofed and silent at dusk, these places often had such a desolate air about them that it was only by the smell of the pigsties that we knew they had not been abandoned altogether. Clay-colored water stood in the rectangles of turned earth on either side of the walk. Two or three mossed and cracking steps and a short length of tilting rail (invariably peeling off in sharp flakes of rust) led to the knockerless door.

It would be answered, night after night, by the same shapeless old codger in a hairy cap. There he would be, complete to the hanging flaps of skin, the wattled neck, the mouth, wrinkled and soft as a fallen apple, chewing on itself, working, working . . . Raising the lantern to reveal our faces, he would stare at us for a long moment through watery eyes as though trying to decide whether the reaper, perhaps, had begun doing his work by committee, then, turning about by degrees, lead the way to a dusty railing hung with a pewter pot or dinner rag and up a creaking set of stairs.

Low, damp ceilings, tallow-stained walls decorated with small paintings invariably depicting some cheering scene from the Scriptures, a hearth that gave off volumes of smoke but no heat or light to speak of . . . these were the rooms to which we retired, night after night, after a meal of cold mutton and bread in a cellarlike room by the kitchen. And there they would be to welcome us: Abraham with the knife poised over the panicked Isaac; Lot's wife forever turning, freezing into stone. With little else to look at, we would study them by the light of the candle: Isaac's mouth, round and black like a hole in the canvas; Abraham's bristling beard and horrible, canary-yellow robe; the rent in the sky through which, presumably, God's voice was about to speak, staying the father's hand. Lot hurried on with his companions, looking disconcertingly like a peddler in disguise; behind him, sowed by angels, the plain blossomed with fire.

We had not been the first to make a study of the artwork these rooms contained; above each painting—a record of desperation as touching in its way as the prisoner's cross-hatched picket fences tallying the years— an arc of candle smoke marked the wall like a dirty rainbow. But soon it grew too cold for art. The fire hissed and spat. Chilled to the marrow, we would retire to our straw mattress. Snuffing out the endlessly guttering candle with wetted fingers (there seemed to be no snuffers between Paris and London) we would plunge into bed and be burrowed down beneath the moth-eaten quilt, breathing it warm, while the ribbon of candle smoke still twisted in the air.

How quickly fate, like a wrestler, can throw us to the ground. A room with a wooden floor, a quilt, a hearth . . . how soon these would take on value in our eyes. How soon those walls, that hearth, would begin to glow in our memory. Shivering in the darkness beneath our quilt, making small jokes to keep up our courage, we had no way of knowing that the day would come, and soon enough, when the jokes would end; when we would, without too much hesitation, have willingly offered a finger for another night like this one—laid our hands on the block and turned our heads, and another for one more—had there only been someone to take our offer.

For a time—a brief time, true—it appeared we might be able to revive our fortunes. For a few precious weeks in May the performance halls—though a fifth the size we had commanded a year earlier—were once again full. Once again our names and likenesses appeared in the pages of *John Bull* and the *Universal Pamphleteer*—a far cry, admittedly, from the days when we had appeared at the Egyptian Hall before Queen Adelaide and the Duke of Wellington but, given our situation, encouraging nonetheless.

Emboldened by our success, we began to talk again between ourselves of how best to confront our guardians. For over six months now, Eng had carefully recorded the totals he believed were owed us; returning to England, he had set about reconstructing, as accurately as possible, the performances we had given the first months after our arrival. He estimated the size of the crowds and the probable ticket sales; he noted, whenever the opportunity presented itself, the cost of the halls in which we had appeared, then deducted the probable expenses for our meals and lodging. I helped him as much as I could—recalling dates and places, writing letters of inquiry—but the lion's share of the task fell to him. Night after night he labored. Fearful of losing the evidence, or having it stolen, he took to carrying the notebook in which he made his calculations with him wherever we went. For months, I realized, his outrage over the injustice that had been done to us had been quietly boiling inside of him.

I knew my brother. This was the same man who had saved us after our father's death, who, on emerging from the king's harem, had pulled up his pants and doggedly insisted on selling duck eggs to the citizens of Bangkok; the man who had plotted and planned our survival, engineered our triumph, until the day God, in the shape of a typhoon, had laid his plans to waste. What Hunter and Coffin had done was wrong. He would hang on to their heels like a terrier, jaws clenched and eyes closed, until justice was done or he was beaten to death, one or the other.

I had rarely seen him this happy. "Prepare yourself, brother," he announced one warm evening as we sat in our rented room off Rosemary-lane. He shut the notebook he had been scribbling in. From below came the shoving, jostling clamor of the streets: hooves and shouts and startled whinnies, the cry of a peddler hawking her wares, the clang of steel against steel . . .

His eyes were shining. "I've checked the figures, then checked them again."

"Fish, ha'penny fried fish!" came the cry from below.

"And?"

He cleared his throat, trying hard to sound like a solicitor. "Assuming, as I think we can, that any expenses we've overlooked are more than balanced by the performances we've forgotten—"

"Fish, ha'penny fish." Again the cry rose from below and was buried beneath the knuckled clatter of hooves on stone. A particular London smell—part stable and wetted stone—moved in on the warm air.

"—and subtracting an extra ten pounds so there is no excuse for complaint or argument, Messrs. Slumber and Muffin"—for that is how we, in our childishness, had come to refer to Hunter and Coffin—"owe us not one ha'penny less than 4,653 pounds!"

I stared as though informed that I had inherited the throne of England. The sum he mentioned was enormous, enough to live on—and live well—for years. It could get us home. It could care for our mother to the end of her days. It could buy us that house in Bangkok we had dreamed of. Or two. Properly invested, it could support any venture, cushion any fall.

"My God," I whispered. The noise of the street at that moment seemed lessened, as if Rosemary-lane with its smells and cries, its costermongers and bird sellers, had suddenly, quite literally, dropped away from us.

My brother nodded. "I know," he said.

"Are you sure?"

He nodded. "Quite sure." I could feel something, a high, wild laughter, building inside me. My brother's features, however, had shifted from controlled giddiness to sober determination. On the street far below us, a loud argument had begun. "We'll not get a penny from the bastards unless we're careful," he said quietly. He shook his head. "We don't know the rules here. It's like fighting someone in the dark."

"But we have this," I said, tapping the notebook. "We know the truth."

"The truth?" My brother smiled. "I'll tell you the truth. The truth is that they've made at least *eighteen thousand* pounds on us while for six months we stuck out our tongues and turned somersaults like a pair of organ grinder's monkeys."

Somebody was pounding on a door. "Open the door, y' bitch, or oil beat ye 'ead in," came a man's voice from below. Voices rose around him.

My brother glanced toward the window, then back. "I can feel them moving . . . planning something . . . but I don't know what."

From below, as though the air had grown animate, came the sound of barking, then a quick, lunging snarl.

It was not a big event as events go. That year there would be riots in Bristol and Nottingham; in America, bushy-browed Nat Turner would kill fifty-five in the name of truth and be hanged from a yellow oak; Charles Darwin would step aboard the *Beagle*. And yet, to us—though history would rumble along like a carriage wheel, recording the words of princes and parliaments, mindless of the pebbles pressed into its steel or flung into the ditch—an empty room on Aldgate High-street was of greater import than any invasion of Syria.

The date was May 23, 1831. We had just returned from Temple Bar, where (ignoring the stares of the clerks who scurried this way and that like large, frantic mice) we had spoken briefly to a tall, impatient cadaver named George Francis Rump, a solicitor. It had not gone well. Continually glancing off to the side or over our shoulders, glances accompanied, eerily, by a nod, a raised eyebrow, a small, tight smile, he had seemed mildly interested in our case until we explained our financial straits, at which point the enthusiasm seemed to drain out of him like air from a punctured bladder. Tilting his head, he began exploring his right ear with a finger. My brother, undeterred, continued to explain our predicament:

"And so you see, even though there is this matter of the paper we supposedly signed, we feel that . . ."

Turning his hands palm-up, Rump now began inspecting his nails, a worried look on his face. He reminded me of some pale, ground-dwelling creature studying its paws. I half expected him to lick them.

". . . we feel that since neither of us saw this paper—" my brother was saying.

"Mmmm."

"—much less signed it—"

"I see."

"—it must be a forgery."

Noticing that my brother had stopped, he sat up abruptly, then glanced around the room, as though unsure of quite how to proceed. "Yes, well . . ." he said, moving some papers a short distance to the left, "but you say you and your brother performed before the public these past months?"

"Of course."

"And that these gentlemen acted as your agents in this?"

"Yes, of course. This is what we have been saying all along."

He nodded, clearly irritated now. "I see. Well, this is all most interesting"—here his thin lips stretched slightly in an attempt at a smile—"but as you can see"—patting a large pile of books by his side—"I have a great many cases before me already and not nearly enough hours in the day to attend to them properly." He stood. "I shall be in touch, gentlemen," he announced, not explaining how he intended to do this without knowing our address. "And now, if you will excuse me, I must bid you good day."

A warm brown dust was blowing in the streets. Hoping to save the money on the cab, we returned to Rosemary-lane on foot, breathing through our hands. George Francis Rump had been the third man we had tried to convince to take our case. It had been days since we had heard a word from Hunter or Coffin. And suddenly—as precipitously, as automatically as we had turned toward Sophia's house after emerging from the Musée de L'homme et la Nature—we turned toward Hunter and Coffin's spacious lodgings on Aldgate High-street. It was time.

They were gone. For the second time in as many months we found ourselves standing outside an open door letting in on a darkened, half-empty room. Messrs. Hunter and Coffin had given their notice two weeks earlier, we were told. Their ship had sailed for Singapore on the twentieth.

My first reaction, albeit a fleeting one, was a pang of loneliness. I knew it was absurd. We had dreamed of being free of them, talked of it endlessly. And yet, though the apparent effect of being left and leaving is the same, in the heart they are January and June. We had known Hunter for years, after all, and though we had come to despise him, and Coffin as well, even hating can make a history. At certain times in our lives, given the right combination of vanity and weakness, it can be as difficult to abandon as love.

My brother, on the other hand, was beside himself. I had never seen him so furious. He roared with frustration, splintered his walking stick over the railing, then swung his fists at the empty air, wrenching me about. I tried, uncharacteristically, to console him. A crowd had begun to gather. A small boy ran off, presumably in search of a constable. "It's all right," I said stupidly, unable to think of anything else to say.

He turned on me with such fury that we nearly fell. "Do you know what this means?" he screamed, his right hand closed around my shirt front, shaking me. "Do you have any idea what this means?" He let loose a string of profanities such as I had never heard him use before. If either Hunter or Coffin had appeared at that moment, I truly believe he would have crushed the life out of them with his bare hands.

"We'll be all right, brother," I said, letting the fury work itself out. "Calm yourself."

He laughed. "Calm yourself? Calm yourself?" Letting go of my shirt, he snatched my stick, a fine carved piece I had bought the week after we stepped off the *Sachem,* and smashed it across the rail. "I'm calm. I'm as calm as a babe. I'm as calm as a calf in summer clover. I'm—so—calm"—the stick snapped, sending the handle flying off across the street—"I could rip—this—railing out with my hands and calmly bend it with my teeth."

Turning back to me, he jerked me as close as our bond would allow. "Do you know what this means?" he said again. "No? I'll tell you what it means. It means we have nothing. Nothing. Do you understand that?" The fury was ebbing now, the tears rising closer to the surface. He shook me again, a last departing gust of rage. "They'll eat us alive, brother. Can't you see that? They'll eat us alive."

But I couldn't see it. I was younger than he was, young in a way he would never be. Though I knew what he said was true, though I understood—or thought I did—the direness of our predicament, I didn't feel it. My own moment of weakness, cleansed by his fury, had passed. Not only did I feel no panic now, but down in my heart some small part of me thrilled to the drama of our situation, the adventure of it. We were strong, resourceful. Somehow we would make our way. Perversely enough, I felt a kind of elation rising in me, a feeling of rude health. I glimpsed our freedom. It was deep, beautiful, a wedge of summer sky between buildings at dusk. We were shut of the bastards.

My brother, no weaker than I, just older and wiser, knew the price we would pay for that liberation.

X.

In another lifetime, well fed and warm, we would put another log on the fire, shove our feet under the nippled bellies of the hounds, and tell the tale of how it was. It would make a fine story too, full of color, harrowing yet ultimately redemptive . . . Ten thousand logs would burn to ashes before we told it all.

There were some things we left out, of course; every labor has its leavings. And these, like all omissions, forced adjustments, substitutions. Things grew complicated. When the children (who had committed our tales to memory, and who would cry out the slightest change in the retelling), called our attention to the fact that the dress had been green, not blue, or that the lodging house had been on Sandy's-row, not Boar's-head-yard, my brother and I would thank them for their help and, tapping our foreheads with our fingers, explain that the memory, like the middle, grows soft with age. But we had not forgotten. We had merely lost control of our lies, allowed reality, like a carpenter's ghost, to open a crack and momentarily skew the joints of our tale.

We improved. We learned from our mistakes. Our stories, beveled and smoothed in the retelling, grew so tight no uninvited truth could slip through. Our children rarely interrupted us now; our wives, who had heard it all before, nodded over their knitting.

Perhaps it was necessary. But it was not the life we had lived. To tell *that*—really tell it—I would have to get on my knees and sweep up the bits and pieces that wouldn't make a story, the fragments we'd left aside. To tell it right I would have to force them into the shaped and polished thing we had made, crack its joints, pull the tongue from out its groove.

Where would I begin? I would begin with fear. Fear like a smell. Like sweat, rank and unfamiliar. Like the short, sharp thrust of a five-inch knife in the dark. The kind of midnight fear, so rich with self-loathing, that can keep you from hearing the sounds coming from the other side of the room: the strenuous wheezing, the hand-muffled cries, the grunting plank . . . I would put that in. I would put in the cloud-shaped stains on the woolens above the stove, the caking shoes, the canvas trousers heaped by the wall. I would put in the jump and flinch of a man's skin as he washes himself with a pocket handkerchief, the dip and trickle in the bucket, the way he opens the cloth with shaking fingers—carefully, reverentially—as though it were parchment and might tear. I would put in the lifted arm, the trembling flesh hanging off the bone.

I would put in the September morning I woke on a board in a quiet room with a dirt floor and didn't know where I was. Ten feet away, a swirling chimney of light rose up to a fist-sized hole in the roof. In the gloom just outside it, like a figure in a Flemish oil, sat an old man, naked from the waist up, holding his face in his hands like a bowl.

Everyone else still slept—long bundles of rags lying against the walls. I watched him. I could see the fingers pressing into the speckled, alabaster skin, the dusty strands of hair, the ball-and-joint of the shoulders . . . He was wearing a pair of ladies' side-laced boots with the toes cut off so he could get them on. He sat with his knees pressed together and his feet pointing toward each other, like a child.

I cried on my brother's shoulder that morning, quietly, without waking him. Eventually, I fell asleep. When I woke again, the old man was gone. There was a caving pain in my stomach. I looked at Eng. His skull—the shape of it—had begun emerging through his skin. His lips, stretched tight by invisible fingers, had cracked and split; the sockets of his eyes, enlarged, were pooled in shadow. He looked as if he were play-ing a child's game—sucking in his cheeks, making himself look ghastly to frighten me.

I remember wondering—almost dispassionately, as though it were someone else—which one of us would wake to find the other dead. And then, careful not to disturb him, I pulled aside my clothes so I could see, yet again, the strangeness of my own ribs and hipbones rising to the sur-face, appearing like half-familiar shapes from an eroding cliff.

Boil it down and it comes to this: Death is a conjugation. The *I* dies. The narrative of your life, newly orphaned, is picked up by a third per-son. *I lay my head on the table by the iron gas-pipe, and slept / He died Tuesday afternoon in a lodging house off Black-horse yard.* But when, when—that is the essence at the bottom of the pot.

If only we had known then that someday we would have the privilege of being the narrators of our days. How quickly our despair would have vanished, our courage bloomed! The days would have passed like pages and we would have folded them back (absorbed in the narrative yet already half outside it) secure in the knowledge that their number, after all, was finite; that soon enough the book would end and we would snap it shut, and sigh, and wondering at the strangeness of life, take ourselves off to bed.

XI.

But that June afternoon in 1841 we knew nothing of where our lives
would lead. We walked back to Rosemary-lane through streets crowded
with ginger beer and lemonade stalls, the warm summer air smelling of
old clothes and tar one moment, watercress and marigolds the next. The
wind had died back to a breeze, the dust settled. The world was at peace.
We passed by young men carrying trays heaped high with sponge cakes,
and barefoot girls selling snails at two pennies a quart. Thin strips of
meat and onions, heated by pans of charcoal, frizzled from the ledges of
open windows. At the corner of Glasshouse-street, as always, stood the
molelike little man with the pointy face, selling chickweed and ground-
sel from the bristling basket on his back. We were surprised to see that
nothing had changed. We were still so young we believed the world
would somehow mirror our fates, that the leaves would droop along the
Meklong at the moment of our death, and children, playing in the dust
in Tangier, raise their heads from their games, believing a small cloud
had passed before the sun.

That evening we spread our possessions out on our coats and sold
them on the curb in front of our lodging house. I kept a small jade Buddha and an English novel with two letters pressed in its pages. My
brother kept his watch (we would only need one), the notebook in
which he had figured what was owed us, and our father's knife. When

the coats were empty, we put them on and left. It was almost dark. A small argument had broken out among the crowd of errand boys and broken-toothed costermongers that had gathered around us. "Show us yer stitch," someone yelled as we pushed through the crowd of faces.

We started walking. We had no idea where we were going. We simply sought the close and narrow the way an animal will seek a burrow or a pipe. Stepping over the puddles left by the watering cart, we turned away from the pickling smells of the Jews' shops and the eerily fluttering cages of the birdsellers, alive with goldfinches and redpoles, blackcaps and thrushes, and headed into the dark. Our method was simple: Where two ways presented themselves, we chose the poorer—the guttering candle over the lamp's coin of light, broken cobbles over whole ones, dirt over both.

Walking north toward the river, we left behind the Irishmen smoking their short pipes on rough wooden stools before their doors, the walnut sellers with their nut-stained fingers, the barrows purple with cabbages. For a time, turning this way or that, we could still hear voices calling "Eight a shilling, mackerel!" and "Large penny cauliflower!" and "Eels, live eels!" but it was as though we were dropping down into a well, and soon enough even these ceased, and the noise of the streets fell behind us. This was a world of smaller sounds: the creak of a lamp, the quick scrabbling of claws in the dark, a small cough in a wet fist. We could smell the river: a cool breath of mud, the rot of low tide.

We walked on. As though light and noise were one, the alleys here had grown both dark and silent. Some were so narrow we could have spanned them simply by stretching out our arms. Very few people seemed to be about. Here and there a vague mass turned into the shape of a man sleeping against a wall, his hands trapped between his legs.

We found it at the end of a narrow court hung with clotheslines and crowded with costermongers' carts—a nameless lodging house consisting of nothing more than a kitchen (containing a stove and a big, pitted table) and a dirt-floored room with forty bunks, or planks. We purchased a tin ticket for two pennies at the wicket in the office and entered through the kitchen door. A line heavy with wet gray clothes bellied down over the pipe. A rag had been stuffed into a broken pane. A half-dozen men, most of them naked from the waist up, looked up from where they sat at the table and stared. There was a moment of silence.

"Sweet suffering Mary," said one.

"And the baby Jayzus, too," added another, a grizzled older man with a thick, hairy back. I looked at him. A broken, pugilist's face, small, tight ears, heavy brows, stepped and broken. No one said anything. I could now see that his big arms, which at first glance had appeared strangely diseased, were in fact covered with small, triangle-shaped scars.

Sizing us up a bit longer, he abruptly turned his attention back to the table in front of him, where a pair of dead rabbits with flies about their mouths lay next to a Dutch cheese, a silk shawl and an iron file. "Tommy, ye little ganef," he said, picking up one of the rabbits and indicating a small, runny-eyed boy squatting in the corner. "Ye'll be stayin' outa Hairbrine-court and Prince's-street till I tell ye otherwise. We kin let the princes take care a theirselves for a while," he added, under his breath. The boy nodded. As though suddenly remembering us, the man turned back around to where we still stood by the door. "Ye can't sleep here, gents," he said matter-of-factly.

"We paid our money like everybody else," I said. "We'll sleep where we want."

For an instant, something like amusement registered in his ugly features. "Suit yerself," he said, turning his back on us once more, "but 'less you have a key to that hinge a yours, one a you will be sleepin' on the plank whilst the other's hangin' off the edge like a side a beef." One or two of the others chuckled.

Unable to think of anything to say, we walked to the door to the sleeping room. Knobless, it had been rigged with two pieces of rope strung through the hole and attached to a pair of short, fat sticks. Stepping in sideways, we pulled it shut behind us, then stood still for a moment or two, letting our eyes adjust to the darkness. Far off, on the opposite side of that long room, a single candle, set about waist-high, waved at our entrance.

"Freaks," we heard a voice say behind us.

"Next thing you know'll be trippin' over bleedin' midgets," said another.

"Chinese or some such. Wot's next?"

"I seen 'em down on Peter's-court," said a young voice.

"Shet yer gob, who gives a shit where you seen 'em, ye little crapper."

"Imagine 'avin to go about all yer life chained to yer fuckin' brother," said another, raspy and weak. "I'd stick a knife in me throat, I would."

"He'd do it for ye," somebody grunted.

Narrow planks along the wall, stacked four-high like giant shelves, were coming out of the dark. Vague semicircles became the rims of two buckets by the wall. The floor was appearing now, a pair of toppled boots rising like a thick-leaved plant out of the dirt. The stench of human sweat—aged and ripe—filled that room like a physical presense.

In the kitchen behind us, someone hawked luxuriously and spat. "They'll lose that shine in a day or two," we heard a voice say.

"You should know, Jimmy," said the man who had spoken to us. His words silenced the room like a blade drawn from a scabbard. "You're the crowned king of losing. Why, next to you we're all just dukes and counts."

"I was just—" the other began.

"Ah, but don't be troublin' yourself, Jimmy," the voice went on. "We're grateful. Really we are. Any of us here ever begins to feel the weight of our riches, like we needs to lose somethin' but don't quite know how to go about it—ye followin' me here, Jimmy?—we'll know just who to ask." We heard something crash on the tabletop. "Now you goin' to bring that strip over here, Tommy," we heard him say calmly, "or do I have to kill 'em all myself?"

This was when the counting began. It never stopped. A few weeks earlier, as though suspecting something, my brother had begun putting a few shillings aside from the small allowance Hunter and Coffin gave us for food and travel. In this way he had managed to secrete away a pound and two shillings. Added to the three pounds eleven shillings we had in our pockets, this left us with exactly four pounds thirteen the hour we discovered we had been cast off.

It had been on our return to Rosemary-lane that evening that we discovered our rooms had not been paid for for nearly a week. When the landlord threatened to call the constable, refusing to accept anything less than a full and prompt payment of our debt, we were forced to reduce our worth by just over a pound, a sum we made up—and a bit besides—by selling off what we had on the street. And so it went. The dusty blankets—or flannels, as they were called—that we bought on the street (we didn't find out until days later that they were infested) cost us nearly a shilling. Though we slept on the floor, the twopenny lodging houses charged us double.

I used to wonder why, in those first few days before our poverty began to show itself on our clothes, we didn't seek the help of former acquaintances. The only answer I had was that, first, we had never known these personages well, but only entertained them, as it were, and second, that we knew, or sensed, that charity is always most gladly bestowed on those who need it least. A year ago, when we had neither asked for nor wanted aid, we had been made offers by gentlemen in silk hats and satin waistcoats who had read *The Times* of London and smelled our success. They would be less generous now.

But there was another, deeper reason for why we didn't seek help from others. Simply put, we were ashamed. We were ashamed of our failure. We were ashamed of our appearance and our smell. Most typically, perhaps, we were ashamed of our bad luck. I had always believed the story of Job was somehow untrue, that most men would assume their guilt, accept their boils and their pain, curse themselves before they cursed their God. Now our behavior proved me right. Though we never said as much, to each other or anyone else, we felt vaguely guilty, as though we'd done something indecent, committed some crime, and were now being forced to pay for our deeds. And how very quickly we looked the part! By the first morning we looked as though we'd been dragged through the streets by our heels. By the second we had lice. By the fourth we offended not just well-born strangers who came too close to us on the street, but ourselves as well.

Yet how could it have been otherwise? We slept each night, as best we could, on two straw mattresses we took from the planks and laid out side by side on the floor of the gangway between the rows of bunks. Having no leather or rug to cover ourselves that first night, we used our coats. Our fellows—even the cleanest of them—crawled with vermin. There were neither towels nor basins nor wooden bowls for washing—just a large bucket by the wall. We cleaned ourselves, as best we could, using the tails of our shirts.

We wasted three precious days looking for work among the dredgers and the ballast heavers on the river, wandering from Leman-street near the London docks to Sparrow-corner. There was none to be had. Some took our request as a practical joke, as though we were eccentric princes grown bored with life in the palace; these answered with exaggerated formality, begging a thousand pardons, doffing their caps. Some stared in disbelief, struck dumb by the sight of us standing in their door. Some swore us off their property as though we were the devil himself, come to demand his due. A few—older, sadder men, generally—replied politely enough, but they, too, had nothing. By the end of the week we were back to selling ourselves on Rosemary-lane; a halfpenny a look, a penny a touch. To make sure no one got a look for free, we would wait till a modest crowd had gathered (keeping them entertained all the while with tricks and jokes) then pass around a cup and then, and only then, pull up our shirts. The touchers, on the other hand, paid one by one.

For a time, we did well at this. Soon enough we learned to judge which streets were workable; which, that is, were neither too fine (risking a run-in with the constable) nor too poor (containing too few with money to spend on a moment's diversion). By moving about from street to street, we were able to keep a fairly steady stream of customers. At the end of three weeks' time we had nearly seven pounds and had moved to a threepenny house with a wooden floor and cut bedsheets for towels. Such is the perversity of human nature (or the power of habit) that for a moment we almost missed the warren we had left behind.

Though it was true that the other residents had hardly ever spoken to us except to grunt or ask for something, the rough-looking man with the cut brows had always exchanged a word or two with us when we sat by the stove or ate at the table. He had seemed amused by us, and, as the undisputed leader of that little community of beggars and bone grubbers, his willingness to acknowledge our existence had made our lot marginally easier.

He was crouching by an empty slop bucket as we left, calmly lancing an ugly, festering cut on his thumb with a knife. "Onwards and upwards, eh, boys?" he said, nodding to the folded blankets under our arms. "Well, good luck to you then."

"God be with you, Jack," said my brother, touched by his generosity.

He chuckled. "You take 'im," he said, squeezing a few drops of evil-looking liquid from the opened cut. "I'd be 'appy jest to stay out of 'is sight."

Which was more than we managed to do. Two days later my brother, on waking, reached inside his shirt to where we kept our tattered clip purse (for we always slept with it next to our skin) and found it gone. For a few frantic, desperate moments we thought it might have slipped down into his trousers, or out into our blanket. Clawing through our bedding, we turned and shook it, then shook it again, looked inside our shoes (as though the purse, grown animate overnight, might have hidden itself away), even paged, absurdly, through the novels by my side of the bed. Feeling increasingly sick to our stomachs, we searched the floor for ten feet around, crawling about on our hands and knees like beggars scrabbling after pennies. Nothing. It *couldn't* have been stolen, we told ourselves. Not only would the thief have had to know where we kept it, but my brother had always been a light sleeper, and the purse had been securely wedged against his skin under two layers of clothes which had been securely buttoned in the morning. And yet the unassailable fact remained—it was gone. The purse had simply—impossibly—disappeared.

We made less than a shilling that day peddling our condition in a city that seemed to have lost its taste for freaks, though small packs of runny-eyed urchins still came to taunt when they heard our carnival barker's cry of "Si-amese Twins! Penny a look to see the incredible Si-amese Twins, connected since birth!," squeezing their eyes half-shut and walking about stiff-legged with their arms around each other's waists until Eng, with a sudden furious lunge that sent us both to the ground, managed to grab one that had come too close by the hair.

It was late in the afternoon on Rosemary-lane near Fisher's-alley. For weeks—while I raged and fumed—my brother had quietly endured the chanted rhymes and crude jokes, the quick darting raids of those who bet on whether they could pull our coats or trip us, the occasional peltings with speck fruit (the dwarfish apples or mud-soft plums tossed on the streets by the fruitsellers) that left us no choice but to take to our heels. Now, nearly weeping with rage and frustration, he slapped and cuffed him about the head mercilessly as the little beggar tried to wrench himself loose and passersby stopped to laugh and stare—perhaps thinking it was a show of some kind, a pair of circus freaks beating a pauper.

Growing tired, finally (twice we'd fallen to the cobbles in a tangle of arms and legs), my brother took him by the shirt and the scruff of his pants and sent him on his way. He fell a short distance away, more stunned than hurt, and was just gathering his wits when a well-dressed man, seemingly walking right into him, gave him a good hard kick to the middle. We called out at this injustice and started after the man, but he walked on as though nothing had happened. When we turned around the boy was running down an alley, holding his stomach. The crowd had dispersed.

That evening we bought three onions and a halfpenny's worth of soft pears off an Irish refuse seller who waved away the wasps crawling over his browning, syrupy produce and loaded up the brimless hat we had found the day before. Later, still hungry, we bought a baked potato from a street vendor, who pulled it steaming hot out of the can with his fingers and laughed while we juggled and danced the thing between us: "Aye, be glad there be two a you, lads," he said, rolling his *r*'s. "Y'll burn yer fingers half as much."

That was the first night we slept on the street, curled under a cart in a dead-end alley just off the river. We woke before dawn. It was so quiet we could hear the rattle of the milkmaids' cans in the next street. Gathering up our blankets, we crept away before the owner of the cart could discover us there, and having nowhere else to go, made our way back through the silence to Rosemary-lane. Nothing moved. At the cab stand a horse dozed on his feet, his head hanging down as though grazing on invisible fields while his driver slept peacefully behind him. We didn't talk. There was nothing to say. In the distance the fires of the first coffee stall sparked in the darkness. I could see the coffee man tending his steaming cans—blowing on the charcoal, setting the white mugs between the railings on the stone wall.

To another man the scene might have seemed familiar, even welcoming. To us it was just a reminder of how utterly exiled we now were: already distanced from the world around us by our culture and language, distanced further by the insurmountable fact of our condition, we had been exiled a third time by the loss of our money. Most daily discourse, we now realized, revolved around some transaction; money was the fuel, the oil in the lamp. Without it there was no particular reason to speak to anyone, and even less reason for them to speak to you. You passed through the world like a ghost.

The coster girl selling watercress, bonnetless and sleepy, was already in place. Behind her we could see the rabbit man lift the crate of warm jostling bodies off the barrow with a jerk, then begin setting up his table. They were both somewhere else now, in a world far removed from ours. In all my life, I don't believe I've ever felt as lonely as I did at that moment.

XII.

I had heard it said that imprisoned men would weep and fight to keep from being moved from one cell to another perfectly identical to it, that they would kill to be allowed to eat their bread first and then their broth, and not the other way around. Now I believed it. Stupid with hunger, unable to think of anything else to do, we clung to habit, walking the same pattern of streets, returning to the same cart every night, creeping away each morning before dawn . . . Over the last ten days, by a kind of logic as irresistible as the settling of silt, we had been reduced to picking over the discarded vegetables left on the stones. Every night we would bring our collection of marshy stems and stunted roots to a pump we had found not far from where we slept and wash the dirt off of them by feel.

He came up to us as we stood on the street near a man selling a boxful of wet-nosed puppies, still crying our wares.

"Can't say as the change had done ye good," he said, planting himself in front of us, the folds of his trousers shiny with grease and his brown, threadbare shirt rolled up his arms. Next to him lay a wooden cage full of twittering sparrows. Something in his hand caught my eye. I realized it was his thumb. Swollen to the size of a hen's egg, it had turned a smudged yellowish-black—the color of a winter sunset.

"You're not looking so well yourself," I said.

He chuckled. "See this here?" He patted the cage by his side. "Three dozen sparrers. Got the order yesterday for a shootin' match this afternoon. Two pounds for the lot I says and not a penny less."

"Toasters! Come and look at 'em. Toasters!" screeched a rusty-haired boy a short distance away, holding up a yellow-brown fish impaled on a fork.

He contemplated us for a moment, his hands deep in his pockets. He seemed solid as a wall. "When's the last time you boys put yer teeth to a good Yarmouth bloater?" he said.

He bought us two fried fish and a bun apiece, then walked us over to a coffee stall where a man in a tattered cap and trousers brown with tar refused pay for three cups of coffee. "Don't even be thinkin' of it, Jack," he said gruffly, as he busied himself getting the cups off the wall and wiping them out with a rag. "I'll be owin' ye more 'n a few cups a coffee." He peered into one of the cups, scratched at something with a thick wedge of a nail, then carefully poured the black liquid from the can without spilling a drop. "There ye are, gentlemen," he said, grandly, and then, turning to our friend: "Not a day goes by, Jack, but the little ones says to me: 'Say hello to Mr. Ratty for us, Father,' and not a day goes by but the wife and I're glad they're there to say it."

We walked off a short way along the wall to a pile of bricks and ate our food—slowly, savoringly, almost giddy with gratitude—drawing out the bits of meat around the gills and sucking on the bones, then pulling them out to see whether the job was complete. Our friend, whose full name, we now learned, was Jack Black, seemed disinclined to talk about himself, and so it was only by persistent prodding that we learned that years earlier he had been known throughout London as "the Queen's Ratcatcher"; that he had had a wife and family and a fine house in Battersea; that for fourteen years he had had a thriving business complete with a cart with rats painted on the panels and printed handbills that read, "J. Black, Rat and Mole Destroyer to Her Majesty."

"Water rats, Norway rats . . . I don't know as there's anybody livin' could tell ye more about a rat than I could," he admitted finally, not without a touch of pride. "The Norway rats is bigger—light brown atop with a dirty white belly, almost gray. The water rat's got a larger head and thicker hair so the ears scarcely show; tail's got more hair. I killed thousands and thousands of 'em. I killed 'em with ferrets, I killed 'em with traps . . . If I was in a tight space I just grabbed 'em with my hands. A rat's bite is a particular thing: It's got a triangle shape to it, y' see—like a leech, only deeper. Twice I nearly died—once when I got bit on the lip, the other when I forgot to tie my shirt and a big Norway rat ran up my sleeve and bit me on the muscle of me arm.

"I never known anything like it. I just went numb—I bled awful bad. By the next day the arm had swole and gone so heavy I could hardly lift it. Like a brick it was. I was bone cold with fever one minit, rollin' with sweat the next. The bite grew an ulcer big as a boiled fish eye, and every time I lanced it and squeezed the humor out it grew back." He paused and took a long slurp of his coffee. "I remember the doctor opening me eyes with his thumbs to see if I was still alive. Young chap he was. Told me to have the arm off, but I wouldn't do it, and it got better."

"What about the coffee man?" Eng asked.

"Tom? Ay, that was a bad case. Last winter his lady wakes in the middle of the night. The little ones is cryin'. When she goes into the room and strikes a light, she sees rats running into the holes in the lath and plaster. The children's nightgowns is kivered with blood, as if their throats 'ave been cut—the rats'd gnawed on their hands and feet, you see."

"What did you do?"

"Poisoned 'em. Nux vomica an' oatmeal. Worked like a charm until they got smart to it—clever beasts they are. The rest I got myself, though not without a bit o' trouble."

We walked back to the coffee stall, where Tom took our cups, wiped them clean with the rag, and set them back on the wall.

Jack Black picked up his cage. We started walking. "Sparrers is the rats of birds," he said companionably, tapping the bars with a finger. "See how they pile up in the corners? Just like rats in a pit. Why, I once got fifty or sixty in the royal kitchen—rats, that is—and me with a cage no bigger 'n this. Thought I'd have to carry 'em out in my coat, but they stacked up neat as cups, one on top of the other." He nodded to himself, remembering. "I didn't do too badly then."

A Jew clothesman had spread out his wares on a folding table: coats and bonnets and reheeled boots, a soiled doll in a blue dress, a child's blanket, its small-rose pattern faded nearly white.

"So what happened?" I asked. We had stopped at the corner of Stoney-lane and Meeting-house-yard. Not far away a pretty girl was standing behind a wet table piled with perch and roach and gudgeon.

"How do ye mean?" he said. "I carried 'em out and put 'em in the cart."

"Not that. I mean . . ."

"Ye mean to Jack Black, Rat and Mole Destroyer to Her Majesty?" He smiled. " 'Hammer become the nail,' 's the song says." He looked off past a man in a dented top hat selling oysters. "One minit yer walkin' fine, the next yer on yer arse, lads. Like ice in January." He ran a hand through his thick badger hair. "Nothin' to be done about it. Run—ye fall. Try to walk slow an' careful—ye never get anywhere an' ye fall just the same." He smiled. "I s'pose ye can crawl on yer belly like a snail, but what's the use a that, eh?

"No, I let 'er rip and went down." He paused, turning to look at us. "Not so very different from the two a you, I suspect. No more 'n a year since I saw the bills for yer show at E-gyptian Hall. Ye seemed to be quite the thing for a spell there."

"It feels like somebody else's life now," said my brother. It was the first thing he had said all afternoon.

"Did well, did ye?"

"We met the king of France."

"That so?" We had started walking again. "G'mornin' t'ye, Sally," he said to a woman behind a table-sized tray of walnuts. And then, to us: "So where's yer king of France now, eh?"

We said nothing.

"Ye want a word of advice? Give it up."

"We *have* given it up," said my brother, irritated.

He laughed. "Yer hangin' on like a baby to its mother's tit. And the might've-been tit is dry, boys, take my word for it. Ye can suck till ye draw yer arse t' yer neck. It won't do ye any good."

Suddenly he turned to face the ragtag group of coster boys and pickpockets who had been following us at a distance of twenty feet or so—yelling and laughing, gathering steam—since we had left the coffee stall. There were eight or ten of them—more than usual—some hovering along the walls, some appearing now and again in the crowd, backpedaling against the current. Now and then a twelve-year-old wit would yell "Freaks!" or "Lookit the freaks!" or "Whyn't ye get a saw, ye bloody freaks!" and the rest, thin as jackals, would grin and show their teeth.

We had grown used to this. Rarely did an hour pass without at least a few of the little ruffians in attendance; they attached themselves to us like burrs. Still, though a thrown rock had cut my brother's scalp a week ago, we had found that most of their work was limited to insults and an occasional rotten plum. Eventually, if we were lucky, a constable would come into view or the other costers would threaten to beat them for interfering with their business (though often as not they would turn on us for having brought them), and we would have a few minutes of peace.

The crowd had thinned for a moment, the current slowed. Our friend stood with his hands, as usual, deep in his trouser pockets, his feet planted as firmly as though his shoes had sent roots into the cobbles. Seeing him turn and come toward them, the group had shifted back, step for step, until he stopped.

"Billy," he called out now to a tight-faced, older-looking boy whose skin seemed to have been forcibly drawn to the back of his head. "Who am I?" His voice was warm, familiar.

"What d'ye mean?" replied the youth, uneasily.

"Who am I, Billy? I want you to tell me who I am."

"I don't . . ."

"Tell me who I am, Billy."

"Yer Jack Black, king of the ratcatchers."

"That's right, Billy," said our friend, looking at him pleasantly. "An' yer a lad with ten toes, an' two whole ears, and a pair a seein' eyes." The group fell back. Prodded by some unseen signal, a full-grown rat had struggled out of our friend's baggy shirt and scrambled to his shoulder. A second took the other shoulder. A third climbed up his collar to the top of his head and sat up like a small dog.

"I want you to spread the word, Billy," he went on, as though he hadn't noticed. "Ye listenin'? I hear a *one* a ye troublin' me friends here, *one* a ye as much as forgettin' t' say 'g'd mornin' to you' when ye sees 'em about, and by Christ I'll sick the blood rats on ye in yer sleep." He smiled.

Five or six of the boys nodded. They seemed mesmerized, not just by the rats but by that calm, caressing voice, gently cutting into them.

"They'll cover ye like a blanket, me boy. They'll shear ye smooth. Ye hear?"

They nodded again, rabbits in the viper's eye. For a moment, I almost felt sorry for them.

"Now off with the lot a ye."

The boys vanished. He waited till they were gone, then gently picked the rats off his head and right shoulder and slipped them back in his shirt. The third he handed to my brother. "Gentle as cats, they is," he said by way of explanation. "Sleeps next to me at night."

"We had ducks when we lived in Siam," said my brother to no one in particular, petting the beast between its transparent little ears.

And just for a moment the distance we had come seemed as unbridge-able to me as time itself.

We did whatever we had to do to survive. Unable to climb trees, we were prevented from joining the birdcatchers who swarmed out to the country lanes after the redbreasts and linnets and thrushes that began to fly about at dawn; everything else we tried. Pushing a broken barrow we found near the London dock, we joined the scavengers who poured each morning over the refuse heaps. Stuffed birds and broken shaving boxes, shoehorns and pocket ink-bottles, decanters and files and trivets and chimney cranes—all these we cleaned as best we could and sold for whatever we could get.

For a while we joined the community of waste-paper gatherers who collected everything from tailors' bills and hymn books to cheap editions of Molière; tearing the covers off the books, wrapping the rest with twine, we would sell them by the pound to a waste-paper buyer on Cartwright-street. At times it seemed to us that somewhere in London there was a buyer and seller for almost everything, from secondhand harnesses to African cowries. Unfortunately for us, we had nothing of value to sell. For a time we joined the small army of bone grubbers and rag gatherers who dug through the heaps of ashes and dirt thrown out of the houses with spades and hooked sticks, looking for anything sellable.

And we survived. Every morning we would divide our rags into lots, separating off the white rags from the colored ones, and both from the canvas and sacking we sometimes found as well. The white rags were the scarcer, and brought two or three pennies a pound; the colored ones, which we sold along with the bones at the rag shop, sold for just two pennies for five. Eventually, when we saw that the rag trade would never bring us more than five or six pennies a day, if that, we joined the grubbers of cigar ends, then the dredgers and the sewer hunters. For two memorable days, thinking our size and strength might be to our advantage, we even went out with the mudlarks, working the river's edge, until we found ourselves beaten to the prize, time and again, by children who seemed to run over the muck, jumping from broken barrels to boards even as we floundered knee-deep and stuck fast, like a coal-laden lighter trapped by the tide.

Now and again, when we had the four pennies for our beds, we slept with a roof over our heads; more often we saved the money and slept where we could. For two giddy weeks in July or August we walked about with a mongrel bitch given to us, along with a bottle of evil-smelling stuff to rub in her fur, by one of the tribe of broken-nailed urchins who had previously delighted in tormenting us. What this substance consisted of we never discovered, but whatever it was, it made our charge, who was already in heat, enormously popular. Every dawn (for this was when business of this nature was customarily transacted), we would walk our white-spotted bitch, well perfumed, up and down the alleys. And every morning, dogs of all shapes and sizes and dispositions would drift out of alleys and yards like enchanted poets following the first scent of spring and (after only the briefest of introductions) ask for—and generally receive—the love they sought. We would let them start to have their way, then walk them—two-legged and foolish—around the corner, where, having completed their business, they would happily consent to the rope around their necks. My brother, not surprisingly, disapproved of this line of work; I saw the humor in it, I recall, and rather enjoyed it. But our attitudes had little to do with it; the success it brought us was undeniable: We sold them one and all to an individual known only as Carrots, who sold them to the stokers and seamen on the *Hamburgh* and the *Antwerp* and the big French steamers scraping against the docks, who in turn, we were told, sold them abroad.

An unworthy line of work? No doubt. And yet we would be about it still, I believe, had we not run out of that magic potion. For a time we tried to acquire some more—even offering a substantial sum—but the urchin in question, having secured himself a sound night's sleep by his generosity, would have none of it.

The fifteen pounds we made that week—a princely sum—we put in a purse I had sewed into the inside of my shirt. It was late September now. On cold mornings the coal smoke made everything look as though it had been rubbed with a soiled eraser. The costers by their coffee or potato stalls stood a little closer to their coals now. Inspired, like ants, by the approach of winter, the armies of want now combed the city for every gap-toothed comb and crushed bonnet, every cracked spittoon. Our one fortnight of prosperity had been followed by two of increasing desperation. Despite our best efforts the money we had saved dwindled away—penny by penny, shilling by shilling, pound by pound.

Yet again it was Jack Black who showed us the way. A ready market existed, he told us, for all the "pure," or dog dung, we could collect. The tanyards in Bermondsey, he said, used it for purifying the leather for book covers and kid gloves and such, rubbing it into the flesh and grain of the skin to remove the moisture; they would pay ten pennies a stable-bucketful, sometimes more, depending on the quality.

And so, for a month or more, we were pure finders, scouring the streets at first light, carefully mixing a bit of mortar from old walls into the mixture to give it the desired quality, finally wending down to Lamont and Roberts's or Murrell's or Cheeseman's before the offices closed at dusk to sell our take.

Strange to think how familiar this world was to us once: the tanyards where we sold our pure, the back-door office at Murrell's with the candle on the shelf (a thumb stub, no more, drowning in its wax), the little hedgehog of a man who would always poke about in the bucket with a piece of wood he kept standing against the wall, as though expecting to find a brick. Every day, after we had bought our bit of bread and penny-worth of herring, we would walk out to a space between the back fences and add as much as a shilling to our savings.

It was on a windy early morning in mid-October, when the yellow flames of the coffee stalls lay sideways like miniature banners and the costers stood hunched with their backs to the dust, that I found myself thinking, less than a third of the way through our daily route, about how much further we had to go. Midway down Blue Anchor-yard I had to rush into a back alley and, praying no one would happen out at that moment, relieve myself against the wall.

Less than half an hour later it came again. We rushed into another alley. Holding on to the side of an old wagon, my legs trembling, I let the water pour out of me while my brother, squatting beside me, held me up. Just then, with the harsh scrape of metal against metal, a small window in the building over our heads was thrown open. A woman cried out. We looked up just in time to see her cross herself and disappear.

Unable to make it to the tanning yards, we hid our half-bucket of pure behind a fence near our lodging house, covering it with whatever refuse there was to be had. Somehow we made it past the woman in the office, through the kitchen and into the nearly empty bunk room. Every half hour or so my brother, who could do nothing but lie beside me in the darkness, would drag me to the buckets, then back to our blankets, laid out on the dirt. Eventually the light outside the small, dusty window began to fade. Then it was dark.

They wanted us gone. Though at any given time fully half the residents might suffer from some manner of complaint, true illness had always been cause enough for eviction. And though it was cruel, it wasn't without reason: Disease brought into the close quarters of a boarding house would spread like fire through tinder.

I had no strength left to fight or argue; curled up on the floor or staggering to the bucket, I seemed to draw inside myself. The voices around me grew faint, then disappeared for stretches of time altogether. It was my brother who saved us, arguing from the floor where he lay next to me, helpless—bargaining for our lives. We would pay double if they let us stay. We would pay a penny to anyone who brought us food, another to anyone who offered to help us to the buckets, a half a shilling to anyone who fetched a doctor.

In many ways it must have been worst for him. He could do nothing. Though healthy and strong, he could neither work nor go for help. Lying beside me, hour after hour, he could not so much as relieve himself without first having to wake me. Having roused me sufficiently, he would have to stand me up, then drag me, half-unconscious, across the room, then lower me, floppy as a rag, down to the bucket next to his, and then, finally, answer nature's call, all the while trying to keep me from collapsing forward or sideways (inevitably spilling the bucket's contents) before he was finished. A pretty picture we must have made, the two of us—bound together, for richer, for poorer, in sickness and in health, till death take you both, amen. But so it had always been, and so it would be. Illness, like love, made our prison visible, revealed the bond for the iron ring it was—the symbol and substance of our arranged marriage. The same strip of flesh that had cost me my one chance at happiness would jealously drag us down, together.

As the fever took hold I babbled and tossed till the residents threatened to throw us out on the street. For a while I was back in Muang Tai as the palms thrashed and scraped in the wind; we were in our boat again. Ha Lung called out to us from the shore. I was so glad to see he wasn't dead. He was holding something out to us, something I couldn't see. It was wound between his arms, like bands of light. I realized it was a length of gray intestine.

He disappeared around the curve. A black-haired painter was standing before his easel. He waved us along irritably as we slowly drifted through his painting. And suddenly she was there, brushing my wet hair back from my face. "My love," she whispered. I tried to speak but no sound came out. I wanted to tell her everything, to explain. Her face, her voice, were as familiar as my own. "Please don't think badly of me," she said. "I looked everywhere for you."

Something was wrong. There was a tickle, an odd burr inside her voice. The touch of her fingertips along my temple disappeared. A heavy hand now lay across my forehead. "I looked everywhere for you," I heard her say again, her voice falling back into some place I couldn't follow, changing, by some uncontrollable alchemy, into something heartbreakingly unfamiliar to me. "Can your brother hear me?" it said. And then: "I represent the interests of Mr. Phineas T. Barnum, sir, and our first task, I believe, is to get you to a physician."

PART FOUR

I.

And so, properly cleaned and restored, we were brought (vomiting all the way, for the passage was rough) to the happiest land in the world—the land of Sabbaths, as Charity Barnum once called it. Delivered from Egypt, we stepped out onto the wooden docks of Canaan. Around us, men of all ages and races were scrambling over mountains of boxes and barrels, pulling on ropes, tying down canvas. Standing in a quiet eddy, we took it all in: the smell of vinegar and wood, sand and stone; the man wrenching at a horse trapped between piles of lumber, the three bedraggled gulls standing on the roof of a shack advertising COLLIN'S INVIGORATING ELIXIR. We looked up. Far above us, thrusting like bayonets against the white December sky, was a tilting forest of masts, leafless and black as though ravaged by fire. We had never seen so many ships. In the distance, the webwork of rigging gave the air a woven, spidery quality, as though the world we had found ourselves in, seen rightly, were nothing more than foolscap.

And, indeed, at times it would seem as though this world we had found ourselves in was just that: a blank page on which anything might be written, any, even the wildest narrative ventured—and if believed, made true. Or true, at any rate, by the definition of truth that seemed to hold sway here: If they believe it, it's true; if they buy it, it's real. For this, we were made to understand, was the promised land of puff, the happiest place in the world for quacks and schemers and frauds. And floating above this Elysium of liars whose depths no plummet could ever sound, forever trolling for suckers, was none other than Phineas T. Barnum.

Years later, long after we had left his employ, we would read about him (and little Charlie Stratton and Anna and some of the others we had known) in the newspapers. Barnum, we heard, had just acquired a pair of long-necked camelopards (as giraffes were called then), or a red-lidded albino child that had never seen the sun. He had built a house in Connecticut encrusted with Turkish towers and minarets. He had bought a thousand acres aligning the railroad tracks to New York and hired a man to plow the fields with an elephant. And so on.

And it seemed to me then—I can't speak for my brother—that even Phineas T. had served a purpose; that without him we might never have found the will to be anything more than freaks. Such is the privilege of survival: to be allowed to fashion the means that fit our ends, to cobble together a narrative that reveals (as by the divine light of illumination) the predestined arc of our days. This is no small gift. With it we can neutralize all but the greatest losses, reduce even the greatest bastards to nothing more than bit actors in the drama of our lives, put on this earth for the sole purpose of forwarding our cause. Blessed are those who can believe their own stories.

Barnum's representative returned from England with a learned pig, a dwarf woman, a white Negro, a two-headed calf, and us. We outdid them all. We were bigger on Broadway than we had ever been in Piccadilly, more popular in Boston and Philadelphia than we had ever been in Paris. "The nigger's the worst suck I ever had," Barnum complained to his friend Moses Kimball, in a letter found and given to us by a friend, "and the calf shits so I can do nothing with him, but the twins will *draw*, I tell you." He went on: "They're an unlikable pair, I'll admit, much inclined to take on airs and question expenses and talk about what *we* are doing, but I'll have them down to their old level soon enough. They're worth the aggravation. Give me a fortnight, and I'll have the community ravenous for them. And when the public maw is ope, my dear Kimball, then, like a good genius, I'll throw in, not a 'bone,' but a regular tid-bit, a bon-bon, and they'll swallow it in a single gulp."

The maw opened, the good genius threw us in. Three years later, to pursue the alimentary metaphor to its natural conclusion, we emerged, properly masticated and digested at last—as celebrities. We had clothes, we had money—and the airs to go with them. It was time to go. We could have stayed, of course—allowed ourselves to be cycled through once more, passed like a pearl through America's second stomach, puffed and sold and consumed again; indeed, if one thing seemed certain, it was that the Almighty Audience—a fatted ox with the head of a lion and the soul of a barnyard chicken—would always be up for another serving. We chose to leave, instead. Some appetites can make you uneasy.

But if the public's hunger seemed insatiable at times, it was as nothing compared to Barnum's; after all, if the masses paid to see 161-year-old Joyce Heth, "Washington's Slave," or "the Feejee Mermaid," a dried-up monstrosity consisting of the tail of a fish, the body and breasts of a female orangutan, and the head of a baboon (a thing with all the appeal of a giant piece of hair-covered jerky), it was because their appetite had been artificially stimulated. Barnum's was real. His was a shameless, a prodigal gluttony. Gorged and stuffed to surfeit, glutted to the gills, he hungered for more.

"I must have the fat boy," we heard him bellowing once from the back of the museum on Ann Street in a voice that must have shaken the guests and rattled the windows of Astor House across the way. "I must have him, you hear?"

And he got him, just as he would get all the other sad, triple-chinned seven-year-olds that followed over the years—"the Carolina Prodigy" and "the Baby Goliath," "the Great Wisconsin Boy" and "the Infant Hoosier Giant"—each one, in turn, ceremonially escorted up the steps of the American Museum (and out of whatever childhood might have remained to him) by his proud, diminutive mother. No, whatever Barnum's failings, excessive self-restraint was not among them. He got them all—"albino beauties" and "dog-boys," African sloths and Nile crocodiles, "man-monkeys" and musclemen. He got "shaking Quakers" and German midgets, twelve-fingered flute players and horned Ethiopian comedians. He got Madame Josephine Cloffulia, whose dark, virile beard extended a full five inches, and who was never seen in public without the brooch containing the portrait of her bearded husband. He got a four-and-a-half-foot-high, twenty-six-year-old armless man named Mr. Nellis, who could fire a pistol and play the violin and cut out paper valentines with his feet. And, of course, he got us.

I disliked him from the moment I saw him—a sentiment shared, for once, by my brother. I disliked the bushy hair, the well-fed face, the pork-sausage fingers. I disliked the air of self-importance—the almost suffocating atmosphere of self-regard that filled the room. Most of all, I disliked the calculating I sensed taking place behind that pasty brow, those quick little eyes, those bunched and meaty cheeks—the ceaseless, machinelike calibrating and recalibrating of opinion and tone, the parrying and probing for weakness, the constant figuring and refiguring of the probable odds of success.

More than any other man I ever met, Barnum had an instinctive, almost doglike nose for power. Those greater than himself he flattered instinctively and shamelessly; those he deemed below him he bullied or ignored. He could turn on a dime—wheedle and whine one moment, bare his teeth the next. Worse yet, he could be charming, with an irrepressible, childlike enthusiasm and a hearty, booming laugh that made him difficult to hate. A connoisseur of the varieties of human desire, he could set the table to suit the guest, and have him signing on the dotted line before the second course. Meeting him, one had the distinct impression, above all, that this man would do anything to win; that it mattered supremely to him; that everything in him was trained, like a cannon, to his purpose.

"Of all the sons of bitches in the world," Gideon once said to me, "the worst are the ones that can make you laugh right after they've stuck a fork in your chest." I disagreed. I said the worst were not the likable ones but the ones who knew what you wanted. The ones who could align themselves with your needs. These were like a river—benign enough, even useful, so long as you happened to be going their way. But try to turn and they'd roll right over you. This was Barnum.

He saved us, I suppose, or, more accurately, his representative in London did. By the time he found us on the floor of the boarding house off Parson's-court, we were down to our last ten shillings. I was more gone than here. Barnum's man arranged for everything. We were transported to decent rooms, bathed and fed. A regular physician attended us. In less than a month we were on our feet. Passage on a steamer had already been purchased, we were told. We signed a preliminary contract, designating Phineas T. Barnum as our exclusive representative; details to be worked out on our arrival in New York. We were in no position to argue. We sailed a week later with a single carpetbag between us. Our possessions, besides the few necessities that had been bought for us, consisted of two English novels and a miniature jade Buddha. My brother had sold his watch and our father's knife that last week in the boarding house. The Buddha would have been next. The novels had survived because they were worthless.

It was not until late in the spring of the following year that we met again the man who had found us—a Mr. Timothy O'Shay, a tall, dignified gentleman in whiskers who nonetheless gave the impression of having, at some earlier point in his life, seen a ghost and been marked by the experience for life. His hands, in particular, seemed to have registered the shock; quick and nervous, they would periodically sprint away like runaway children, rising halfway to his head or quickly picking a hair off his tongue before he could manage to bring them under control; these actions he would attempt to cover over, like an embarrassed parent, by casting attention elsewhere, by laughing loudly or suddenly growing irritated over some matter that until then had gone unremarked.

We were sitting in the cool dimness of Barnum's drawing room in the back of the museum, waiting, as usual, for him to decide that we'd waited long enough. From the front of the building, sounding deep in shade one moment, filled with sun the next, came the din of Broadway: hooves and carriage wheels, shouts and oaths, bits of songs and laughter. Now and then a particular voice, no louder than the rest, would rise and we would hear the words, perfectly clearly, as though the city had momentarily disappeared or the speaker sat beside us, invisible, in the leather chair by the grate. "Masie? Too tight a wicket for me," said one with a laugh. "Turn him, you fool!" bellowed another. "The vexations I've had with that darky, I can't begin to tell you," a young woman's voice complained to some unseen companion.

It was partly to cover these voices that came in from the street (it felt vaguely indecent to sit there listening to them) that we asked him how he had come to find us.

"Purely by chance, really," said O'Shay, taking a deliberately casual sip of port. He scowled, an expression that seemed to come naturally to him. "Of course I had heard of you. Everyone had. Mr. Barnum had even instructed me, on leaving for the Continent, to try to find you. But nothing had worked. Thieves and scoundrels, when they heard I would pay for knowledge of your whereabouts, claimed to have seen you here and there, but nothing ever came of it."

As he spoke O'Shay's right index finger, seeing its opportunity, had begun drawing quick little circles along the inside rim of his glass. Noticing it, he quickly placed the glass on the table beside him. "Of course, one never knows with these people," he continued, quickly sitting back in his chair and waving his arm in an expansive gesture meant to suggest the generally unaccountable rabble just outside the walls. "It was because of one such mongrel that I—"

"O'Shay?" It was the imperial summons.

Our companion leaped to his feet as if kissed by a tack, one hand automatically jumping to his hair, the other to his waistcoat. "Yes, Mr. Barnum," he called, looking about for his coat and cane. "Coming, Mr. Barnum."

"Timothy, Timothy, Timothy O'Shay/Gathering flowers in the month of May . . ." It was Barnum, amusing himself.

"It was the sheerest chance, really," O'Shay concluded, whispering.

"Eating them raw like a horse eats hay . . ." rhymed Barnum. "Tell us why you do it, O Timothy O'Shay."

There was a pause. "O'Shay?" he roared.

"Coming, Mr. Barnum." Snatching up his cane, O'Shay gave us a quick little bow and hurried into the office, closing the door on Barnum's bit of doggerel and our two-year sojourn in the Old World.

II.

It was around this time that we made the acquaintance of Charlie Stratton and Jesus Christ. The first we would leave behind, eventually. The second "took," as they say, quietly padding along behind us on his bare, martyr's feet, insinuating himself into our lives . . . For seventeen years he sat on our porch in North Carolina, picking his toes and damning our pleasure, speaking through my brother's mouth.

Barnum, of course, thought Stratton and God were one, and if one exchanges the currency of heaven for the baser coin of Broadway, one can see how he might. To Barnum, after all, Stratton *was* the savior—his own pint-sized personal savior—and recognizing a good thing when he saw one, he prayed fervently for the little man's continued well-being, consecrated his heart and his purse to him, knelt daily at his thumb-sized feet. The image is as appealing as it is appropriate: Barnum on his knees, supplicating himself; the General, standing bolt upright, staring imperiously into his disciple's navel. How *like* the little homunculus to accept such a tainted reverence. And how like the other—forever praying with one eye open and one hand on his purse—to offer it.

What an exhibit they would have made—Phineas and the General. "See them Talk Out of the Corners of Their Mouths, ladies and gentlemen! See them Gull Their Closest Friends!" As the evangelical strain grew louder throughout the land, and everywhere song turned to hymn, they adapted their tune without missing a beat. "Small in stature but big in Christ," was how Stratton described himself now, always adding "and there's not a day that passes that I don't fall on my knees and thank God it's not the other way around." Sometimes, particularly if the members of the press were present, he would do just that, and falling to his knees (hands clasped and tiny ankles touching), thank the Almighty for having made him as he was.

Who could resist such submissiveness? So profound a resignation? Who could fail to note the lesson in humility it taught those of us (like Mr. Nellis, perhaps, or Lettie "the Leopard Child") who might have thought they had a bone or two to pick with fate? Not the press, apparently. Nor the public, who never tired of his piety *or* his antics. "Such a vision of courage and Christian acceptance was Tom Thumb as he knelt before the Almighty last night at the American Museum, that few could look upon him without weeping," wrote the reporter for the *New York Observer,* an observation with which I could readily concur.

Carefully, of course. Barnum's American Museum, as we all knew, was not a democracy; despite its name, the give and take of the streets stopped at its doors. Obeisance was expected. On a bad day, an inadvertent smile or a stifled snort could put one on the corner, bag in hand and heart in throat. Of course, as in a regular monarchy, dukes were afforded liberties peasants could ill afford: The biggest attractions could risk the occasional ironic smile. To others it could be fatal.

It was a lesson I was taught soon after our arrival. I had made the mistake one evening of allowing my feelings to show on my face while listening to one of the General's self-aggrandizing little speeches. I had quickly found myself on the receiving end of a furious little sermon. "We must accept our fate with humility and gratitude," he quacked, poking an indignant finger up at my belt and accusing me, as a stranger to Christian lands, of not understanding the danger I ran in resisting the Almighty's will. So surprised was I by the vehemence of this onslaught that I actually found myself retreating a step, then two, dragging my brother along with me, all the while resisting the urge to put him over my knee.

"I am well aware," he went on, by this point addressing the crowd more than myself, "that there are some who have lately wondered at the American fancy for exotics, and even objected to the public's disgraceful preference for foreigners over native-born curiosities. I have never numbered myself among these critics and yet, when I see such un-Christian behavior in foreigners who know nothing of our noble land yet seem ever ready to accept her bounties, I confess I can see how they might take the position they do." And here he turned to me and declared, "I have been blessed, sir, blessed, and am properly grateful for it. In the eyes of God, sir, I am a giant." And for one absurd, irreverent instant, I imagined the Deity peering through Sophia Marchant's microscope at the downy growth beneath our hero's nose, miraculously transformed into a robust crop of hairy wheat springing from the soil. He gave me a curt little bow and turned on his heel. The crowd burst into applause.

I saw right through him, of course. I saw how the veneer of piety made it easier for the ladies to pass him around like a rare, hairless cat, to pet and fuss over him, to exclaim over his feet and his eyes and his adorable little hat. I saw how expertly he milked it, snuggling into their skirts, allowing himself to be kissed and stroked and fondled. He had made himself into an infant, you see—a Christian infant at that—and like his famous predecessor (preternaturally wise, surrounded by donkeys, staring up from the straw), he did well for a time.

I held my tongue. We all did. The only one who ever stood up to the pair and lived to tell the tale was Anna. She was fearless in a way we couldn't imagine, routinely speaking her mind or laughing out loud at their absurdities with a freshness, a spontaneity, that never ceased to amaze us. Strangely enough, when faced with this unaccountable insubordination, the two seemed to accept it much the way one might accept a force of nature—grudgingly, even angrily, but in the end, with something like resignation. Anna was simply Anna, and there was nothing that could be done about it. The rest of us—awed, respectful—never dreamed of adopting her ways. Hers, we understood, was a special dispensation.

Which is not to say that it was easy for her, or that the two conceded defeat with anything like grace. Barnum, especially, hated her continually and creatively, threatening to send her back to Nova Scotia or starting rumors of some other giantess, newly discovered in France or Fiji, who would cut her down to size. Whereas the General (who would sit in the palm of her hand during their act with his legs crossed, smoking an inch-long pipe) instinctively realized he had met his match, Barnum raged on. Unmanned by a woman a full two feet taller than himself—a woman, moreover, who had sent him sprawling at their very first meeting when, wishing to see if she was standing on a platform, he had lifted her skirts without warning—he never missed an opportunity to cast aspersions on her popularity, or to remind her of precisely how much she owed him.

To which our Anna would invariably respond with a sweet, disbelieving laugh, and go her way. "And how is Mr. Bunkum?" she would ask on coming to his office, or, if things were particularly strained between them, "Tell me, is the sham-man in today?" In the evenings we would gather in the sitting room to play pinochle and she would entertain us with stories about Barnum's latest bit of humbuggery: an idiot brother and sister plucked from an asylum in Ohio and turned into "the Amazing Aztec Children"; a "Circassian Beauty" who had been overheard screeching at one of the geeks in a way that suggested the Hudson poured past the minarets of Wall Street directly into the Bosporus; an "Incredible Three-Horned Bull" whose stock in trade had unaccountably tilted like the Tower of Pisa in the middle of a performance, thereby earning its owner a quick trip to the stockyard . . .

It was a dangerous game, and it made our little circle—Madame Cloffulia and Isaak, Mr. Nellis and Susan—visibly nervous. Barnum, however tyrannical, was still their savior; it was his will (or whimsy) that kept them suspended above the poorhouse. And though this mercy—if mercy it was—was compromised by the fact that he never let them forget it, it did not entirely erase their sense of debt. They laughed uneasily, lowered their voices, glanced around continually to see if they were being overheard. Of them all, I realize now, only Anna grasped the true nature of the covenant between Barnum and his flock; only she understood that the connection was less a lifeline (thrown from him to us) than, well, a Siamese bond; that just as he held us above the pit, he, in turn, continued to exist only by virtue of our continued belief in him.

Forty years later I can still see Isaak Sprague, with his hair slicked and combed, slowly dealing the cards with arms no thicker at the wrists than my finger. I can see Madame Cloffulia smiling to herself over a good hand, her husband's portrait peering from her chest like a miniature chaperon. I can see Susan, like a genial mountain of flesh, sitting four feet back from the table on an iron stool; Anna, next to her, handing her her cards. I can see Mr. Nellis, leaning back in his chair, reaching across the wood with his smooth, splay-toed feet. With marvelous dexterity he raises his glass to his lips. Now he gathers the cards in a neat little pile, brings them to his chest, fans them out like a peacock's tail.

They were our friends. We saw them nearly every day, shared a stage with them, traveled in their company. For three years we argued and commiserated with them, negotiated their moods (and they ours), shared their griefs and grievances. We even grew to love them, I suppose.

We might never have managed our escape without Charity Barnum. Sincere to a fault, plain as a pudding, she had about her a humorlessness that stopped just short of being terrifying. Utterly incapable of grasping even the simplest joke (observing others' mirth she would smile vaguely, like a deaf-mute, or a traveler in a foreign land), she seemed overwhelmed at times by a husband who lived for the laugh (preferably at someone else's expense), a husband who looked upon her the way an unrepentant sinner looks upon the flesh brush and the scourge.

Most of us, in our ignorance, felt sorry for her. We might have done better to pity Barnum. For Charity was in every sense her husband's match. Pale and prone to fainting, she put her frail evangelical faith up against his omnivorous appetite for bare-legged French girls dancing in tubs of bursting grapes, and fought him to a draw.

Barnum loved the theatre. Charity disapproved. Barnum smoked like the locomotive on the L&R Railroad. Charity disapproved. Barnum took a solicitous interest in the latitude of his female performers' hems and necklines. Charity, not surprisingly, disapproved. Like Hunter before him, Barnum scrabbled for every cent, blissfully unconcerned that his wealth would in any way impede his entrance to heaven. For Charity, no labor could be so sweet, no employment so exalted, as holding up Christ to a dying world.

And so it went. Returning from abroad, Barnum ridiculed her, publicly, as a sickly, carping hypochondriac who had very nearly ruined their European tour. She endured—and prayed for him. When asked by the press, she opined that she had found Paris the most vulgar place she had ever visited, filled with half-naked trollops eager to show their legs and expose their nakedness on the stage. "They should be horse-whipped and kept on bread and water until willing to gain a decent livelihood," she had added, stopping just short of offering to do the job herself. Barnum gnashed his teeth. When his beloved Charity, "always piteously moaning about something or other," fainted on the staircase leading down to Niagara Falls, he continued on alone, smoked a cigar over the roaring cataract, then tossed the butt into the abyss.

If Barnum had been less of a hypocrite, or his wife more of one, I might have sympathized with him. As it was, I preferred to keep them both at bay. When Charity sought us out, month after month, determined to drag us under the protective wing of God, I resisted as politely as I could. When she informed us, in her tremulous, fainting way, that all were equal in His eyes, I marveled at her blindness. And his.

This, I see now, was when the forking of our lives began. I might have anticipated it, forestalled it somehow. I didn't. I saw no need. It was only later I realized that even though my brother and I had been listening to the same words, we had been interpreting the sermon differently.

Sitting before us, ankles pressed together like a schoolgirl, Charity Barnum told us all—Madame Cloffulia and Mr. Nellis, the Albino Twins and the Aztec Children—that our female beard or lack of arms, eggshell skin or feeble mind, were invisible to Him. That these things were as the deceiving fog, which momentarily obscures the house in which we dwell, and that, just as the wise man disregards the mist and recognizes it for the slippery, insubstantial thing it is, so God in His Wisdom would disregard what was passing and concern himself solely with what is real. The shining house of the heart. The soul. Just as the morning sun inevitably burns away the morning mist, she would add, her eyes glistening, so he would one day send his only Son to burn away all the vanity and falsity of the world—expose, as with a burning flame, the rock of the Church within us all.

"When?" asked Anna, once.

"When what?" asked Charity Barnum, momentarily confused.

"When will he come to burn the mist away?"

"Soon, child. Look about you." She waved her arm generally in the direction of Broadway. "The last days are clearly upon us."

"Mmm."

I looked at the others. Madame Cloffulia, eyes shut tight as if in pain, had bent her head and was praying earnestly. Susan was looking off at a spot on the floor where bits of sun and leaf-shaped shadows waved on the wood, thinking her own thoughts. Mr. Nellis stood up, and reaching for his cap with his toes, flipped it expertly on his head.

And it seemed to me then that almost everything Charity Barnum had told us was precisely backwards. To every one of us sitting there, whether we admitted it or not, the mist was as stone—neither slippery nor insubstantial—and would never burn away. Though we might wish it otherwise, our earthly shape *was* our house, our soul, and his inability to see that truth, to acknowledge it, to prostrate himself at our feet for it, made it forever impossible for me to see him. He could keep his Son at home, as far as I was concerned. Save him some pain. He would be too late in any case.

We left. We left Barnum in one blow—took our money and went—

at least in part because I had realized, thanks to his wife, that only on this earth, and not in heaven, could I hope to find some approximation of the equality she promised. I would leave the world of freaks and attempt to live like a man, equal to others in my own eyes, if not in theirs. But my brother—my baby brother, as I always thought of him—had been touched. The seed had been planted. In the eyes of Almighty God, we were all the same. It was only men that misread his creation, seeing differences where none existed. To stay in Barnum's employ, therefore, continually exploiting these differences, would be to live a lie, to fly in the face of God's truth. And so, though inspired by different motives, we went our way.

III.

Our leavetaking is something I look back on with a great deal of satisfaction. No one could accuse us of not having learned our lesson.

When the time came, everything had been planned; every move anticipated. Barnum, we knew, rarely lost what he considered his; once he had his paws around a thing it would either remain inside the American Museum or be rendered so unattractive that no one else would want it. Though smaller than Tom Thumb, we were still one of his biggest attractions, part of the central stable on which the museum depended; he would fight like a bear to keep us, and whatever else one might say about bears, they were not gentlemen. By the mid-1840s, Barnum's reputation for ruthlessness was such that even the truly famous dealt with him carefully.

But Barnum had never met anyone like my brother, who still carried about with him, like a goad, the notebook in which he had painstakingly recorded all that Hunter and Coffin had owed us. When the moment came he unloaded all the anger and resentment he had stored, all the humiliation he had endured at their hands, on Barnum. Every slag heap we had picked through, every piece of pure we had sold, every moment he had endured on the floor of that boarding house watching our money disappear as I faded away beside him—every one of these he turned into a weapon. The first target had escaped him, had slipped away into the forest of the world. The second sat, close-eyed and fat, just across the room, preparing, if necessary, to bargain us back to the poorhouse.

He never knew what hit him. For the first time in his life, I believe, Phineas T. Barnum found himself overwhelmed—quickly, decisively—by a force whose will was greater than his own. Scrambling desperately, he tried to take cover behind our contract. My brother had committed it to memory, and recited it back to him, chapter and verse. Barnum quoted expenses he had incurred, implied we owed him money. My brother knew our financial situation to the penny. We owed nothing. Mr. Barnum, in fact, by even the most conservative estimation, owed *us* just under three thousand dollars. Two thousand nine hundred and seventy-six dollars, to be exact. We would expect payment in full within two days.

Barnum allowed himself to grow angry, then hurt. He called us ingrates, and reminded us of how he had saved us. My brother noted the sum we had made him over the past three years. He threw himself at our mercy. Times were particularly hard at the moment. The American Museum, appearances notwithstanding, was struggling. Surely we could stay on another six months, a year at most, if only for the sake of the friends we would be leaving behind. My brother replied that, regretfully, we could not. When all else failed him, Barnum, as expected, bared his teeth. He threatened to ruin us forever. We would never be able to show ourselves before the public again, he said, pounding the desk. He would grind us up like corn in the masher. He would not be intimidated. He would not be threatened by stripling boys still wet behind the ears who thought they could come into his office and throw their weight around any time they chose. Who did we think we were talking to? He had half a mind to throw us out on our Siamese ears.

I could feel the blood rushing to my head, my heart beating indignantly against its cage. Barnum seemed to loom up behind his desk, red-faced and huge, his meaty hands spread on the wood before him as though to keep him from lunging at us. I resisted the instinctive desire—which I had always felt toward anything that frightened me—to throw myself at his throat.

My brother waited for him to finish, then looked him in the eye. We were retiring from public life, he said, quietly. We would be staying at the Spencer for two days, waiting to hear from him. And we took our leave.

An hour after we confronted him in his office, the papers were served, announcing our suit. Less than twenty-four hours later our lawyers had extracted the three thousand dollars we were owed as neatly as a tooth, along with a signed statement setting us free of any and all contractual obligations to Phineas T. Barnum, the American Museum, or any representatives or subsidiaries thereof, effective immediately.

We knew exactly where we were going. Six months earlier, on a tour through the South, we had stopped in the little town of Wilkesboro in the state of North Carolina and decided that someday we would return there to live. We would build a house. We would be farmers. The corn wouldn't care if two men walked behind the plow instead of one; it would grow as it would for any man.

This thought, above all others, seemed like an opening window to us that last winter as we sat on our divan watching the snow blowing this way and that against the red brick facade of Matthew Brady's gallery. We would outwork them all. Farmers from across the state would travel to see our fields. In time, our neighbors would learn to judge us as they judged each other—by the labor of our hands. And if they didn't, we said, with fine, twenty-three-year-old bravado, well, then, there was no help for it, and our fate would have been the same wherever we chose to meet it.

IV.

I know in my mind there was a time when I had not yet seen the meadows that would become our fields, when the road, like a meandering stream, was nothing more than a brief pause in the thigh-high carpet of wildflowers and weeds that stretched, unbroken, all the way to Stoneman's woods. I realize there was a time when there *was* no house, when the patch of deep, tangled grass between the chestnuts was empty of everything but the wind rubbing up against the stems and those invisible, scurrying things that people a place before we have come to it. I know this is true, but I can't believe it. I can no more imagine a time when I didn't know the view from our porch—the generous sweep of open land, the pond, gray with rain—than I can a time when I didn't know my own son's voice.

Looking back, it seems to me that certain places, like certain people, can rearrange our lives so utterly that even though we may still recall, as in a dream, the time before we knew them, we no longer quite recognize the person we were. The new life, piling year on year, overgrows the old. So it was with me.

On a wet April day, two boys stepped down from a wagon and walked up through a soaking field. Clouds rolled against the tops of the trees; a fine mist wet their faces. Reaching the top of the rise, they turned around to admire the view. And felt a sudden recognition. From that moment on, everything speeded up: The wheel picked them up like a lost weed, pressed them into a crack in the rim, tamped down the dirt with each revolution. And the years passed. The rain fell, the crops grew. A slave died. A war came—like a storm over the land. His son and mine disappeared into that storm. And then the storm was over.

A lifetime later it seems to me as though the world that grew around us just happened, as though the months and years of labor had never been, as though we had waved our arm and said, "Let there be a house," and in the shade between the chestnuts a house had appeared, a fine, two-story affair with a veranda on three sides, extra-wide staircases, and a chimney big enough to sit a bench in. Around it, the fields were suddenly mowed, turned under, rustling with corn. Stumps disappeared, leaving only a slight depression in the dirt, a slight quickening of the plow. Rocks, pulled from the ground on rollers and inclined planes, washed clean by the rain, turned overnight into walls spotted with blackberries in the open sun or patched with moss in the shade. They seemed to have been there always, marking our holdings, separating field from field.

Addy and I were married for thirty-one years. I never loved her, really, though when she went she left behind a well so dark, so full of her voice, that for a long time I wanted nothing more than to fall into it and be drowned. In my life I had loved someone else, and though I had no desire to sacrifice one woman on the altar of another, it could not be helped. Loss begat loss. I argued with myself, of course, but all I succeeded in doing—and that badly—was pushing the one out of my heart; the other did not take her place.

Not that she would have wanted to, necessarily. Very early on she had realized there had been someone before her and, not wishing to live in a house another had called her own, so to speak, had chosen to live her life outside it. It meant nothing to her. When, during the first year of our marriage, I asked her to be careful with the two English novels on the bookcase because they had once been important to me, she simply smiled and left them undusted for twenty years. Which of course made me care for them all the more—and all the more conspicuously.

And so it was with everything: The less willing she was to acknowledge my past—to ask me about it, to admit its importance—the more I clung to it. The more ridiculous she made me feel, commenting—not without justice, I suppose—on the absurd figure I cut, or pointing out, ever so reasonably, my many shortcomings, the more devoutly I polished the memory that might otherwise have faded, and made sure to keep it in a place where she would see it. All I wanted was for her to acknowledge that someone might have loved me once; that I was worthy of that love. All she wanted, in turn, was to be told that the past was the past; that she was my wife and the mother of my children and that the other no longer ruled my thoughts. Each of us wanted the other to go first, saw the other's admission as prerequisite to their own. After you. No, after *you*.

My God, how absurd it seems to me now! How useless. Eventually, as time went on, we forgot the original motivation behind our behavior—to gain the other's respect, or love—and continued on as we were from force of habit. It was as though all we could remember was the last unkind word, the last weary smile, the last small act of generosity denied us. And yet there were good things in each of us. How easy it would have been to let them live. To break the spell. How little it would have taken to risk a kindness. After you. No, after *you*. I would go first now, if I could.

An old man's regrets. Even I find them annoying—all the more so, perhaps, for being unavoidable, given my personality. "Enough, Bunker, enough," Gideon would say on those nights we sat on his porch drinking his good whiskey: "Give it a rest, for the love of Christ." Tipping his chair off the wall, he would point at me with the hand holding the bottle, one long finger unwrapped from around the neck: "Cast off your regrets, my son. Dwell not in the land of couldeth and shouldeth and mighteth. And if your tongue speaketh in the subjunctive tense, root it from thy mouth, for better it is to bray like the ass—or hith like the athp, for that matter—than to traffic in things that were not." And so forth. And I would for a time—cast off my regrets, I mean—hardly even noticing my offended brother sitting stiffly beside me, sober as a church.

But now Gideon's gone too, damn him, and every year it feels more and more as though some great event were taking place outside in the churchyard and we were the only ones not invited. I miss them. I miss them all—Josephine and Catherine, gone with the scarlet fever in less than a week . . . And it's hard, as the house grows quieter and everyone leaves, to keep back the regrets, to keep from looking back and trying to make sense of what happened while they were all still here. What the story told.

The rain fell, the children grew, the war came. One by one, the people and things I loved in this world were pulled from my grasp. All but one, that is. And even that one I didn't save, but received instead as a gift, a morsel snatched from the jaws of God.

V.

My son was born on December 19, 1845, six days after the United States Congress, in its wisdom, annexed the territory of Texas. We named him Christopher. He was four months old when General Taylor reached the Rio Grande, a little over a year at the Battle of Buena Vista. By the time he was two the United States had gained a great deal of sand (although what we would do with it, precisely, was hardly clear), and my life had been transformed forever.

Let me say this: All of my children were dear to me. Every one. I had no shortage of love to give them. But Christopher—well, Christopher was the first. He was the one who broke the mold that had begun to harden around my heart, the one who (even as an infant) brought a rough kind of grace into my life, who made the world a negotiable place for me. Looking back now, I realize that Mount Airy was only a home as long as he was with us.

I remember the night he was born—a night not unlike this one. We had sent for the doctor, who had moved into a house two miles down the road, as soon as Addy's pains began in earnest. Eng and I, unable to stay inside, had walked out to the road with a lantern, our steps crunching against the frozen dirt. The sky was all around us: huge, close, furious with stars. A thin paring of a moon hung to the east, sharp enough to draw blood. We had hardly reached the fence when we heard the horse's hooves and in the same instant saw the wagon emerge from the shadow of Stoneman's woods. It came up the road like a child's exercise in perspective, shrinking the world behind it.

Horse and wagon pulled up at our gate. A dignified-looking man, perhaps ten years older than ourselves, bareheaded but wrapped in a heavy coat, sat on the buckboard, smoking a cigar. "Easy, Sarah," he said, and the horse was still. He took the cigar out of his mouth. "I prefer June deliveries," he said.

My brother and I said nothing. He carefully tapped some ashes on the floor of the wagon. "You are the father, sir?" he said to me.

I nodded.

"I thought so. And this is your first?"

I nodded again.

"Mmm." He took a meditative puff. "Cold for December," he observed.

We agreed it was. Very cold.

He nodded. We were silent for a moment. "Well, gentlemen," he said, "what do you say we go in and join the ladies?"

I had never thought of myself as one of those unfortunate souls condemned to stand, all observant, on the shore of the moment, but never take the leap. I bucked and snorted, plunged and sank. My brother, withdrawn inside himself, increasingly layered in reserve, was the one I would have chosen for that fate. He was the one whose temperament left him only half-present at any event, the one who ran the considerable risk of only knowing life at one remove.

And yet, in the months before, when I had tried to think about what it might mean to have a child, it had felt as though I were imagining it for someone else. The more I pinched myself, the less I felt it. I had been happy when Addy told me, of course. I had snatched her in my arms, even danced a few steps around the parlor (my brother sweeping along with us, grinning as though I had just won a foot race), but in my heart I had felt as though this thing had little to do with me. I was like a guest at a banquet given in honor of some distant acquaintance. Though pleased for him, I saw no need to get exercised over it. It was good news. Everything was fine. But dinner was waiting.

It was no different now. Left alone downstairs (Sallie and the doctor having disappeared into the upstairs bedroom), Eng and I busied ourselves as best we could, walking out to the shed for more wood, stoking the fires, petting the dogs . . . When Addy's cries began to grow harsh and raw, exploding from her like steam under pressure, my brother tried to reassure me, assuming, naturally enough, that I was suffering as he was. I thanked him, touched by his concern, reassured him in turn. If it hadn't been for the fact that he obviously needed my help and support, I could have used the time for any number of tasks. To fix the door to the pantry, for example. Or replace the floorboard in the hall. "Should we get more wood?" I would ask, to keep him distracted, and "Why do you think Sam took so long getting back?" Every now and again, the realization of what was happening would flash across my mind like a pheasant bursting from cover—and be gone.

By three o'clock in the morning I couldn't move. My brother tried to talk to me. I couldn't answer. A profound despair—a gray November dusk—had settled over me. I had never felt so alone, so utterly orphaned. I knew now it could never be. Something would go wrong. The seed would turn. And suddenly I realized (as I never had before, in a flash of truth like steel on flesh) that the moment would come, inevitably, when I would cease to be. And for a moment—just one moment—this seemed like the saddest thing in the world to me.

And then we heard voices and the bedroom door was open and Gideon Weems was handing me a blanket wrapped around a face as small and blotched as a windfall fruit. "A son," I heard him say, and, hardly breathing, I stroked his cheek with the back of my finger and he looked at me out of eyes as swollen and red as my own and wouldn't look away. And in that moment the father was reborn in the image of his son. "You can look at him if you like," I heard Gideon saying from somewhere far away, "it's warm enough at the moment," but by now I was crying ugly and sharp as a child, my body shaking with the kind of sobs that can look so much like laughter, and someone came to take him from my arms—trying to help, I suppose—but I wouldn't let them. I held him for a long time. Nor did I take him from his blanket. I had no need to see him, you see, to know that he was perfect.

And he grew, my boy. An independent and curious soul, precocious and straight, he seemed to emerge from the womb intent on making up his own mind about things, on quietly, and without any undue fuss, going his way. If the proffered finger suited his plans as he toddled, bow-legged, across the wooden floor, he took it; if not, nothing could induce him. It was a quality he never lost. When I whipped him (as I did often, those first few years until he was eight or so), we both understood that the exercise had nothing to do with changing his mind. He'd look at me sometimes, after I had carried out my fatherly duty and he was pulling up his britches, and it was as though he were saying, "I know you have to do this, because it's written somewhere, but you and I both know it won't make a bit of difference." Indeed, at times, despite the tears he'd smear irritably across his cheek with the heel of his palm (tears that never failed to trouble me, despite my brother's admonitions to be firm), I almost felt he was sorry for me. He loved me. And he knew I'd lose, eventually.

By the time he was eleven I had learned to pick my battles. When I found out, for example, that he had been spending time in the company of the blacks (by now he had struck up his friendship with Moses), I checked my natural reaction and wisely said nothing. The boy was a strong swimmer, I reasoned, and he wasn't alone. Lewis, whom I could make out only as a faded pair of pants moving in and out of the shore-line greenery, always seemed to know where he was. Lewis would watch out for him.

No, as was more and more often the case where Christopher was concerned, I saw no particular reason to stand in his way. A small part of me even saw his side of the thing: with his cousin Samuel off to Leesburg for a month to visit his grandparents, that left only Patrick to play with, and Patrick, though decent to the core (and as obedient a son as any father could hope for), was quite irredeemably dull. Not unlike his father, at times.

No one could say the same for Moses.

"Mornin', Mistah Chang, Mistah Eng," he would say, coming up to the porch where my brother and I sat trapped like clerks behind the old dining-room table (for this was already 1856 and my brother, thirsty for salvation, had determined to commit Charity Barnum's red-leather edition of the King James Bible to memory). "I brought y'all this string of cats." And swinging them out from behind his back, he would hold up a length of rope packed with yellow-bellied bullheads, tracing a string of drops in the dust around his feet.

At times his familiarity (a matter of tone more than anything else) overstepped its proper bounds. "This isn't the kitchen," I remember my brother saying curtly one Sunday morning when Moses appeared, interrupting him in the middle of his devotions.

The smile almost disappeared. I watched him tip his head slightly to the side and back—a gesture of resistance, even insolence, common to all men. "Yessuh, Mr. Eng," he said. He shrugged: "I thought y'all might want to see 'em, is all." And then, under his breath: "I knows where th' kitchen is." The instant the words were out of his mouth he knew he was in trouble. I could see it in his face, and, unaccountably, I felt sorry for him.

My brother's head was up in an instant. For weeks now (goaded on by what he saw as my unforgivable laxness regarding Christopher) he had been going on, none too subtly, about the importance of maintaining proper relations with the blacks. Now he saw his chance. "What did you say?" he said, leaning us forward.

I couldn't help myself. "He said he's going to take them to the kitchen, brother," I said, and then, to Moses: "Are you sure your mama doesn't have any need of them?"

"No suh, Mr. Chang," he said, recovering quickly. "She got plenty."

"Well, bring them around," I said, and then, just to turn the knife in my brother's side a little: "They'll make a fine breakfast."

The bullheads, of course, were hardly the point. Nor would I have been inclined to excuse the boy's tone had it not been for the greater good of getting my brother's goat. A few weeks earlier, when Christopher had been found out and hauled out of bed by his mother in the middle of the night, my little brother had taken her side.

I hadn't forgotten it. I had been asleep, dreaming that my brother and I were back on the stage. As we answered questions from the audience I kept looking at a kindly-looking older man in a white shirt, sitting in the fourth row with his hands on his knees. Something about the way he held himself, leaning slightly forward as though trying to pay attention, alert yet deferential—was familiar. I realized it was our father. He nodded at me—gave me a small, reassuring smile. I was about to call on him (though he hadn't raised his hand) when I was distracted by sounds from somewhere outside the hall: a woman yelling something I couldn't make out, and a strangely familiar crying. I felt a terrible uncertainty. I looked back at our father. He nodded at me, as though giving me permission, though for what, exactly, I didn't know.

I jolted up, dragging my half-sleeping brother to a sitting position. It seemed to be coming from the boys' bedroom. Wrapping a blanket around ourselves we ran upstairs, following the lamplight, where we found Addy (her sister next to her) holding Christopher by the ear, shaking his still-damp britches in his face. It was just after midnight. Shadows leaped and shrank against the wall. I could hear the baby crying. Down the hall I could see the children's heads, like mushrooms on a tree, protruding from their doorways.

She had come to look in on them, she explained, and found him gone. Nearly frantic with worry, she had been at the point of waking up the household when she had heard the back door open and seen him creep up the stairs. Unable to think what it might mean, she had determined to wait till morning to confront him, but had found herself too agitated to sleep. There was no time like the present, after all. She would raise no liars, she said now, lifting him up till he yelped. No, sir. There would be no liars in the Bunker house.

That was when my brother entered into it. He had counseled against it, he said. He had argued against it, not once, but a dozen times. It was unnatural. A corrupting influence. But I wouldn't listen.

Addy turned to me, still holding Christopher by the ear. For a moment she seemed to be trying to understand what she had just heard. "You knew about this?" she asked, in a strangely calm tone of voice, disbelieving.

"I did," I said. "I've known about it all along."

She shook her head as though it were a sieve and she was trying to sift some essence from this bit of information. "You . . . you're saying you *knew* this boy was spending his nights lazing about with niggers, and you didn't say anything to me?" she said.

"It was all I could do to keep from saying something myself," said my brother.

"I think you should resist a bit longer, brother," I said. I turned to Addy. "The boy's been spending a few evenings by the river. Swimming. Fishing. I saw no reason to make a fuss. I didn't want to worry you."

"You didn't want to worry me?" She adjusted her grip, cranking him up like a foul-hooked fish. "It didn't occur to you . . ."

"It occurred to me," I said, feeling myself growing angry. "I just didn't do anything about it."

She smiled. "Oh, I see. You didn't think that maybe—"

"Why don't you put the boy down," I said.

She stared at me a moment, then laughed, incredulous. "What?"

"Let go of his ear."

"I'll do no such thing."

I could see her lip beginning to tremble. Her chin looked like a peach pit now. I didn't care. I took a step forward, jerking my brother along.

"Oh, yes you will," I said.

"I'm his mother . . ." she began.

"I'm not going to say it again," I said quietly.

"Fine," she said, almost whispering, fighting hard to keep her features from rearranging themselves against her will. "Fine. If you're bound and determined to make a liar out of him, go ahead." And letting go of Christopher's ear (who sank down to the ground, crying less from pain than from what was happening around him), she turned around and walked away, her sister behind her.

For a few seconds the only sounds in the world were their steps on the wood and the creak of the lamp, swinging on its handle. "Go to bed," I called into the growing dark, trying hard to sound like I always did. Uncle Chang. Father. I reached down and lifted Christopher up by the arm. "Come on," I said, "stand up now." He wrapped his arms around me, crying as I hadn't seen him cry in a long time, and buried his head in my chest. He'd grown so tall. I petted his head, feeling him shake against my ribs. "I'm sorry," he sobbed, "I'm sorry."

"It's all right," I said. "It was my fault as well."

My brother sighed. "This is what comes——"

"Don't say anything, brother," I said. "Don't say anything at all." And he didn't.

I felt sorry afterwards—something I'm good at. This was my wife, I told myself. The mother of my children. Someone who loved them as much as I did. I had never threatened her before; never raised a hand against her. That was changed now. Though we would both do our best to pretend otherwise in the weeks and months to come, something had been broken between us.

But it couldn't have been helped. For an instant, as Christopher had turned in her grip, trying not to cry, his eyes had caught the lantern's light. I knew it was nothing—just the wetness in his eyes; a matter of perspective, nothing more. But in that moment, so help me God, they had looked blind to me, and before I knew what was happening I was wading in to save him—this one child of mine who probably needed saving least—from the one person in the world he least needed saving from.

And yet here's the thing. Though I knew all these things to be true, I also knew that given the same situation, I would do it again.

VI.

Unlike things, the primers say, cannot be summed: The smell of sour milk. The taste of whiskey. The screaming of children playing in the wind.

How do you sum a life? You don't. You don't even try. You leave it as it is: irreducible, ungraspable. A torrent of things, of days—unlike, often unlovely—cutting a channel through your heart. The faces of your children, still red from the womb. The ripeness of the nursery on still winter mornings. The hoarfrost in the parlor windows, shot through with small oval thumbprints. The garden, that one brief season, burgeoning madly as though under a spell, bowing down with fruit. You don't add these things. How could you?

And yet you try. You must. One possum, hissing sheepishly, hunched forever on the crossbeam of a porch. Wind. The shadows of small clouds hurrying across the fields. An open door at the back of a house—like a well-lit painting at the end of a long corridor. In it, two boys, already far off, are caught mid-leap, disappearing over the edge of the bank.

Loss, loss. How to hold against this steady seepage, this never-ending subtraction? Go ahead: Herd them together, make a pile of them—the perfect days, the hours of life, the moments of utter happiness, brought on by nothing more than the smell of tobacco and the warmth of your coat on a cool night. A small joke, perhaps. Remember your son standing mid-calf in the stream that day, half-buried in orange butterflies. Add your daughter, watching him. Now recall the crawdad you noticed passing by his legs. You could see it there, below that air-clear current spreading and respreading itself between the banks, hurrying over and around the brown, furred rocks . . . And for just a moment, everything held. Everything was right. And then, in a puff of silt, it was gone.

Gone. The saddest word in the language. In any language.

You fool! What are these things you hoard, compared to their leaving? To your father, trying to smile while dying against a bamboo wall. To your lover—lost. To a baby toddling across a wooden floor while her nurse, a child herself, stares out the window and, lulled by the fire in the hearth behind her, dreams of boys . . .

VII.

Did I know he was teaching him to read those long summer afternoons he was gone? I did not. Am I sorry for it now? No, I am not. I am sorry for many things—that is not one of them.

Christopher did what he would do. He always had. And having decided, for some reason forever unknown to me, that he would teach a slave to read—a decision still astounding to me for its implicit anger, its utter disregard for the laws of the day—he proceeded to do just that. Perhaps he thought I knew. Or that I had given him tacit permission, somehow, by defending his nights by the river. I doubt it. I doubt he would have cared.

I still find myself wondering, at times, how long it took them. How many weeks and months of days, the two of them holed up in some deadfall with a view of the woods below, always alert for movement—*any* movement, for black or white were nearly equal threat to them now—Christopher pointing, saying, "Naw, it can't be that, 'cause there's an *e* at the end of it," first scraping the words in the dirt with a stick, then unfolding newspaper pages smuggled out in his boots, smoothing them against his knee. I can see them snorting with laughter ("That ain't '*Kan's-ass*,' you donkey. You just forget the other *a*. I don't know why"), picking out the words together as the first few drops smack the dust, the blackberry leaves, pock the page itself . . .

I missed it all. All those years he worked in our house (for I brought him and his mother in from the fields the week after his father died), I had no idea he could read the books on our table. Even now I find it a bit disconcerting, just as someone speaking a foreign language for privacy might find it disconcerting to discover that the people he had assumed were ignorant of his meaning had in fact understood every word. Moses never let on, never gave himself away. And Christopher never told me. Until the day, nearly five years later, when I received a letter stamped with the circular seal of the Union Army and signed by one "Private Moses Bunker," I had no idea.

I had excuses, distractions. That was the year—the last, before the world accelerated like a runaway cart—when the rains didn't come. The ponds shrank, the lettuces bolted, the corn burned. The mud banks of the river widened, growing out of the sluggish flow, then cracked into brown continents. Already you could feel the changes stirring in the land, hear the first high wind. We had no idea of what was coming, of course, no way of knowing that for the rest of our lives a listing of the years that followed—1857, '58, '59, '60—would bring to mind a child counting out the distance between the lightning and the thunder; and yet it seems to me now we must have known it, must have sensed it in our bones.

Day by day my brother grew more taciturn, more irritating. Morning after morning—or so it seemed—we'd sit sweating behind that damned table while he (a man born on a bamboo mat!) imbibed the Holy Spirit, battening like a tick at my expense. I found it difficult to talk to him now. Though nothing dramatic had happened (it was mostly a matter of silences: head shakings and pursed lips, glances averted in disgust or dis-approval . . .) I could feel him growing away from me. Confused and resentful (the thought that *he* should be backing away from *me*, after all I had borne for him!), I quite naturally took every opportunity to punc-ture his sanctimoniousness, using whatever weapon came to hand.

That was the year the bright leaf tobacco barely saved us from ruin, the year Lewis died. I was sorry about Lewis. I still am. We had our troubles (just weeks before his death he had quarreled with us about getting his son a knife, as though we were a mail-order catalog he could order from whenever he pleased), and yet I see now that, just like certain other members of his race, he had about him a quality that set him apart from his kind. I can't say that I liked him, but I was sorry when he died. So much so, in fact, that the week after we brought him back from Belle-fonte in the back of the wagon (he was buried in the Negro graveyard off Sorghum Road) I interrupted my brother's studying one warm October afternoon to inform him that I had decided to bring Berry and Moses into the house with us.

I knew it would not be easy.

For a few minutes, as we sat there on the porch, I tried to figure out a way of making my case in the least objectionable manner possible. I couldn't do it. More importantly, I discovered I didn't want to. The more I thought about it, in fact, the more I resented having to justify myself to my own brother. I looked at him. There he sat, with his hairy ears and his reproving look, looking like some wandering apostle sniff-ing the air for sin, while I twisted myself into knots trying to figure out a way of asking his approval for something I had every right to do on my own. It was absurd. To hell with him.

"I've been thinking about bringing Berry and Moses into the house," I said, plunging in. "It seems to me Aunt Grace could use the help."

"Oh?" he said, without raising his eyes or his finger from the book. "Have you noticed her falling off from her duties?"

"It's obvious she's getting on," I said. "The house is too much for her."

"Is it?" He turned the page.

"I think it is," I said. "Besides, we have to think about the future. Bet-ter now, it seems to me, than when she's too frail to properly train her replacements." My brother said nothing, letting me run on. I could hear my own voice—false and ingratiating.

"I've made up my mind," I said, feeling myself growing hot in the face.

He smiled, pulled the tassel to mark his place, closed the book. Some-thing about the movement—its deliberateness, I suppose, as though he

were a schoolteacher dealing with a stubborn child—infuriated me. "I
believe I still have some say in these matters," he said, looking off across
the fields.

"Some."

"Be so kind as to hear me out, then."

I waved my hand. He paused, while I marveled at the absurd formality that had recently crept into his speech.

"It's inappropriate. She's needed in the fields. Trust me, brother,
she'll be best off among her own kind, not separated off from them in a
world she doesn't understand. Not to mention that—"

"Are you finished?" I said.

"Would it matter?" he said, stung.

"Probably not."

He stopped. "I can't say I'm surprised. I never expected you to take
anyone else's opinions into account."

"Really? Why did you offer them, then?"

"Because I foolishly thought I could talk some sense into you. I
should have known the time for that was long past."

"Oh, but how Christian of you to try anyway, brother."

He was trembling now. "You're an arrogant and selfish man."

"And you're a prig and a fool."

"Don't bait me, brother. I won't stand for it."

I laughed. "Bait *you*? You're a fish on a plate."

He stood up abruptly, jerking me to my feet.

"Enough reading for today?" I said, smiling.

For a moment I thought he was going to hit me. A long moment
passed. From inside the house came the quick clanging of pots. A cow
lowed in the distance. "I don't care what you say," he said at last, quietly.
"They're not coming into my house."

So they came into mine, instead. Over the next four years, for exactly
two weeks out of each month, Berry would help Aunt Grace about
the house—washing, mending, spinning flax into linen, preparing the
midday meal out back by the old brick oven—while Moses would do

whatever needed doing; for the other two they would stay on with the others under the general supervision of our overseer, Tim McDaniel (though I often thought they could have managed just as well or better alone) keeping up the house for our return. I never regretted it. Unlike Lewis, who could be difficult, both mother and son generally knew their place, and never took advantage of the good fortune that had come their way.

But though the obvious success of the arrangement should have brought some peace to our affairs, it did not. The original argument covered over but didn't heal. How could it—when every two weeks one or the other of us would be forcibly reminded of the limits of his domain? Though we had always deferred to each other to some extent when in each other's homes, the gesture had always been voluntary. It was so no longer. Submission had become a requirement, a mandate neither of us hesitated to impose on the other.

And as the months passed, we expanded it joyfully, allowing it to encompass nearly every part of the day. When in Eng's house now, I would be forced to retire early because he preferred it, to walk when he wanted to, to sit for hours on end while he made his way for the umpteenth time through Charity Barnum's Bible, refusing to admit he was tired even though it had been an hour since he had turned a page and I had been watching him fighting sleep the entire time—his body sagging, then jerking awake—just to spite me. I responded in kind, fighting to stay awake into the early hours when we came to Mount Airy, moving about to wake him if he started to nod off before me. I canceled our Bible mornings, swore as colorfully as I knew how, attempted, at every turn, to anticipate his wants, so as to know how best to frustrate him. Now, if there was anything to be done at Mount Airy, it was done my way; if there was any disagreement—over anything, really—my decision was final.

None of this was ever addressed directly. We remained superficially polite. *If you wouldn't mind. If it's not too much trouble. Certainly, brother, have it your way.* We smiled. Whatever we endured, we endured in silence, unwilling to give the other the satisfaction of seeing our irritation. Now again, for the first time since childhood, our bond became an issue between us—the most convenient thorn with which to torment the other. Bit by bit, a lifetime of small but necessary accommodations was abandoned. The signal before sitting up in bed. The willingness to get up immediately when nature called the other. The thousand small adjustments of weight and balance that made bending, or turning, or reaching for something, less difficult for each of us.

Now, if my brother reached for something to his right, I held my weight back just enough to force him to move me around. If I turned to speak to someone as we walked down the street, he would jerk me back slightly, making me stop and back up, instead of coming up ahead. And so on. Gone, seemingly overnight, was the coordination that had always struck outsiders as very nearly supernatural, the unthinking alignment that had allowed us to swim and run and fight, that had saved our lives that day on the *Sachem* when, running at full speed from one of the mess boys who delighted in chasing us about the deck, we had suddenly seen the open hold yawning at our feet and, too late to stop or swerve or signal, had instinctively lifted off at precisely the same moment—I off my left leg, Eng off his right—and cleared the pit by so little, with only the front of our bare feet hitting the wood, that had it not been for our momentum, which threw us tumbling across the deck, we would never have made it. Now we twitched and lurched about like men continually hitching their pants or getting at some hidden itch or suffering from some strange nervous disorder. *It's fine. It's nothing. I'm sorry, brother, did you mean to turn?*

And we got used to it. Month by month, as we went along, we grew accustomed to the new dispensation, adjusted ourselves to its demands. Habit took hold, as it will. The furrow grew deeper. Whereas at the beginning a good quarrel might still conceivably have wrenched us out of our path, now it just confirmed our course. We would argue, accuse each other of mendacity and all manner of crimes, and in the morning resume precisely where we had left off. The year came and went. Another began. Nothing anyone said could sway us.

Not that they didn't try. Addy and Sallie, singly and together, wept and begged us to be reasonable. The Reverend Seward, having gotten wind from some conjugal quarter of our situation, preached a repetitive sermon on tolerance and brotherly love, taking as his inspiration the First Epistle of John 2:9–11: "He that saith he is in the light, and hateth his brother, is in darkness even until now. He that loveth his brother abideth in the light, and there is none occasion of stumbling in him. But he that hateth his brother is in darkness, and walketh in darkness, and knoweth not whither he goeth, because that darkness hath blinded his eyes." And so on. I let it pass. We hardly spoke now except to convey the most essential information, and when speaking to a third person, would communicate through them. *Tell your uncle Chang she'll need a second dose of Cook's pills. Ask your father if he's hungry.*

That particular Sunday morning in 1859, if I recall correctly, we had not spoken directly for days. Which may explain why, at first, I didn't realize he was speaking to me.

We had just settled ourselves behind the table for our Bible-reading session (it being my turn to wear the ball and chain) when, opening one of Sophia's English novels, which I was rereading at the time, I thought I heard my brother say, "I really wish you wouldn't." It took me a moment to realize he wasn't talking to one of the boys.

"I'm sorry, brother," I said, confused. "Did you say something?"

"I said I wish you wouldn't," he repeated.

"I beg your pardon, brother, but 'wouldn't' what?"

"Read that book."

I couldn't believe what I was hearing, but I still managed to remain calm. "Why on earth not?"

"You know why," he said, going back to his book. "Don't make me say it."

I could feel myself trembling. "Why not, if it gives you pleasure."

"It doesn't. It gives me no pleasure whatsoever."

"Why don't you just say it," I said.

"I'd rather not."

"Go ahead. Say it."

"I don't have to say anything. You know exactly what I'm talking about."

"You coward," I said.

"Because it was hers," he said, almost hissing it. "There's something unseemly about it. Something weak. Like stroking a piece of her clothing or . . . or fondling a lock of her hair."

"It's none of your goddamn business," I said.

"Oh, but it *is* my business. This is my house."

I opened the book. "Go to hell, brother. I'll read what I want."

He jumped up, wrenching me to my feet. I had forgotten how strong he was. "There will be no more reading today," he whispered, his jaw clenched and his face almost disfigured with rage. "And don't you dare, ever, tell me to go to hell when it's because of you that I . . ."

"Because of me that you what?"

"Nothing."

"That you what? That you'll—" Hearing footsteps in the hall behind us, I paused, shaking like a blade of grass in the wind.

"Daddy?" Nannie appeared behind the screen mesh. "What are you doing?" she said, seeing us standing there behind the table.

"What is it, Nannie?" I said.

"Have you seen Aunt Grace?"

"She's probably out back by the oven," I said.

"Aren't you reading today?"

"No," I said. And then, after a pause: "Your uncle Eng and I have a few things to talk about. We're going for a walk."

We didn't get far. "So that's what's keeping you up at night, brother?" I whispered when we were halfway across the yard. I could see Lester pouring a bucket of slops for the pigs. The sound of excited grunting rose in the still, hot air. "That you'll go to hell because of me? Is that it?" I leaned closer. "Are you worried that God won't bother to cut us free? Hmmm? That he'll just toss us out like a half-rotten apple?"

We had passed out of the shade of the locusts. We were walking faster and faster, jerking and wrenching each other about. Aunt Grace was out back by the brick oven. I remember seeing Frank rolling a wheelbarrow full of wood toward the shed. He called something out to us, but neither of us heard him.

"The lake of fire, brother," I whispered, wanting to hurt him, to run him down to the ground like a winded animal. "Is that what's worrying you? That your name won't be written in the book of life because of me?" We were plunging across the tobacco field now, oblivious to the plants being trampled underfoot. "Well it's too late, brother. Do you hear me? It's too late." I leaned closer. " 'He that saith he is in the light, and hateth his brother, he is in darkness even now.' " We were almost running. "Are you listening, brother? 'He that hateth his brother, he is—in—darkness. He that—' "

The first blow broke my nose. A great gout of blood gushed across my shirt and I fell into the furrows with him on top of me, my hands around his throat. I could hear him strangling even as I felt a dull hammering on the side of my face and wondered what it could be. We rolled and wrenched, punched and gouged. He was my brother—as boys in Siam, we had wrapped our arms around each other and rolled down the hills, laughing and screaming—and yet at that moment I swear to God I would have left him dead in that tobacco field, cut him loose like a piece of cloth, and walked back to the house alone. But I did not have a knife. He did. At some point, I remember, he rammed a handful of dirt into my face, grinding it up into my nose and eyes with the heel of his palm. Choking and thrashing, I managed to raise a knee between his legs. I heard him grunt and felt him curl toward his middle, the strength draining out of him, just as a searing pain flashed through my side—once, twice—and I heard him scream and wondered, for one mad instant, if someone else had hurt him, but by then my hand had closed on something hard and I was swinging it wildly, not knowing what was happening, dimly aware of voices yelling something somewhere, and then a huge weight was on my chest and my arms were pinned to the ground and I was crying and spitting dirt and that, as they say, was that.

VIII.

It took six men to carry us back to the house and up the stairs, where they laid us on the bed from which we would not get up again that year. We bled through everything they put under us. My brother couldn't move his neck. I had two broken ribs. I would learn, in time, that I had very nearly smashed in his skull with a rock, and that for four days he had drifted in and out of consciousness and I with him; that for a time it had looked as though I might lose my right eye; that my nose had grown so horribly infected that Addy and Sallie had had to cover it up before letting the children come into the room. Eng's knife, we found, had cut almost a full third of the way through the fleshy bottom of our bridge. Only the fact that he had been unable to get the blade in his right hand, but had been forced to slash, awkwardly, with his left, had saved us.

It was Gideon, of course, who sewed us up like a torn sheet, who came galloping up as he had fourteen years ago when Christopher had been born, and delivered us from ourselves. Not that he was happy about it. I still have a vague, dreamlike memory of hearing his voice as we drifted in and out of the world those first few weeks, speaking to someone sobbing out in the hallway. I could hear the rain dribbling off the eaves. "Not a thing," I heard him say. "Men will do what they will, my dear, and until they find a cure for idiocy, or the kingdom of heaven comes down to us at last, I'm afraid there's not a blessed thing I can do about it."

To us, he was more forthright. "Ah, you're awake," he said one afternoon, noticing us stir. He threw a soaking yellowed bandage into a bucket by the window. "That's good. I've been wanting to say something to you." Coming around the bed, he sat, none too gently, by my side. There was no one else in the room. "Are we listening?" he said, and I could tell he was furious by the economy of his movements, the way he slapped tight a crease in the sheets with a single backhanded sweep. I couldn't see my brother at all. I couldn't move. My entire face felt as if it was on fire. I closed and opened my eyes. "Good," he said. "I want to make sure you can both hear me."

He went on: "For two weeks now, I've been ministering to a house of crying women and terrified children. I take no pleasure in this. It annoys me, particularly as they are silly, emotional creatures who can't understand why their fathers and husbands would want to kill each other, and who insist on carrying on even after I've explained it to them. So this is my point." He leaned closer to us now, not smiling. "First, if you ever try something like this again, I will kill you myself. Second, since, in the current situation, I have sixteen patients, I have decided to charge you accordingly. If you fail to remit in a timely manner—I am reasonable enough to wait until you are able to move about—then so help me God I will haul you into debtor's court and squeeze you like a lemon in a vice. Stupidity, gentlemen, must be paid for. Take my word for it: When you see my bill, you will wish you had either finished the job you began or refrained altogether." He stood up to leave. "Oh, and one more thing. The longer you convalesce, the larger my bill. I have no one else to talk to in this godforsaken county, and I'm too old to start drinking alone." And he turned and walked out of the room, closing the door quietly behind him.

I don't remember much of those four months of my life. I remember waking up once at dusk (no lamp had been lit) and seeing Addy sleeping in a chair beside the bed. I remember opening my eyes another time (it could have been the next day, or the next month), and finding the whole family standing around the bed like pickets around a garden plot and Nannie asking me how I felt. I remember the sudden gust of shame that traveled through me at that moment, and how, unable to speak, I simply nodded. I remember Frank and Charles struggling to get the bedpans under us, their black arms hard and warm around our waist, saying, "All right, Mistah Chang, Mistah Eng, you can set down easy now." And I remember a certain breezy fall afternoon when I woke to find Christopher sitting in a chair, knees to his chest, looking out the window. Now and again the curtains would billow gently, spreading sunlight over the wooden floor, then drawing it back, and I looked at his face a long time, wondering what he was thinking. Eventually he turned and we just looked at each other—not smiling, not anything—and I knew that he had already forgiven me, and worried about this, knowing that it was not good for eleven-year-old boys to forgive their fathers so easily, to know them so well. "I'm sorry," I said.

He nodded—so much a man already, expectations cut to size. "It's all right," he said.

My brother, his head still heavily bandaged, stirred, tasting something in his sleep, and was still. "How is everybody?" I asked, unable to think of anything else to say.

He nodded again. "They're all right."

The curtain billowed; a tide of sunlight rose to the top of his frayed overalls, then fell back like a wave. He turned to look out the window, his left hand picking at the loosening seam on his pant leg, thinking.

"What's new in the world?" I said.

He smiled then, not the way most young men would have, but quietly, almost shyly, as though he were about to tell me he'd fallen in love.

"Looks like we're gonna have us a war," he said.

That January, bundled against the wind like old men, my brother and I climbed the steps to Gideon's porch with our first monthly payment of three dollars and fifty cents. Nineteen months later—the Yankees' gold on the one hand and our own Congress on the other having succeeded in making the exercise absurd—we delivered our last. By that time, a single bar of soap cost seventy cents, nearly four times what it had, and we were drinking a vile liquid made from chicory and acorns, and calling it coffee.

It was an evening in late August, as I recall, four months after Shiloh. We had not yet heard of a muddy little creek called the Antietam. Certain cornfields, rustling quietly in the sun, had not yet been tapped into history. Sunken country roads, bent cowlicks of grass falling over their banks, had not yet been chosen over others. Others had: Gaine's Mill, Frayser's Farm. Malvern Hill.

Rolling the three faded bills into a long taper, Gideon held them to the lamp's flame, then brought them to his pipe. "Consider your debt paid, gentlemen," he said. Dropping them on the boards of the porch, he slowly, thoughtfully ground them out with the toe of his boot. "We'll all have debts enough, before this is through."

Around us, the clamp tightened slowly—relentless as frost. Stoneman's sons were suddenly gone—all except Billy, who was still too young—leaving him to manage as best he could. We could see him moving about the place sometimes, wrenching on a mule, or pulling two-handed on a rope attached to a pulley in the oak. From a distance he looked like a man stabbing himself in the stomach. In town, the stores began to empty, the streets grew quieter. Benjamin McCullough's son Tommy had been killed at Shiloh, Thaddeus Stark's boy, Tad, at Seven Pines.

Richmond was being evacuated. We heard of streams of refugees crowding the roads; of ransacked stores and burning farms; of baggage wagons—heaped with trunks and boxes—creaking and rattling through the night so endlessly they seemed, one man said, to form a giant, wheeling circle (here the little girl on the buckboard again, crowded into her father's coat, there the kid with the bristle-brush hair, legs dangling over the wagon's end, shaving down that stick) revolving around some unknown hub.

Eng and I lived, those first few years of the war, in a republic of our own. We didn't speak. We didn't fight. We received the news of the dead in silence, and went about our work. There was nothing to be done about it. I had known that since October of '59. We had been lying beside each other for over two months at that time when I awoke one afternoon to find us alone. The room was empty and still. High up on the window, a yellow jacket tapped and crawled about the pane, too foolish to know the glass was open just below. I remember being surprised that the trees had turned so suddenly.

I knew he was awake without having to look at him. "Think he'll find it?" I said, knowing he had noticed it too. It was the first thing I had said to him since that day in the tobacco field.

There was no answer. The yellow jacket tapped against the glass, buzzing furiously. Someone said something downstairs. I thought perhaps he hadn't heard me. "You think he'll find it?" I said again.

"I want you to know something," he said, speaking steadily, and even without looking at him I could tell that he was crying. "Even though God has apparently decided that we should live out our lives together, you're not my brother anymore. I just want you to know that."

IX.

For a time, as I remember it, everything held. The war, though all around us, was still elsewhere. Pope, we heard, was looting farms in Virginia, threatening to hang anyone suspected of aiding the Confederacy. There was no dye to be had in town. No rope. One day—it could have been in '61, or even '62—we came upon Aunt Grace using a hawthorn for a needle, and knew that the war was coming closer. We were like children looking at a volcano through a wheat straw: we could see the part—the trembling blade, the rising spark—but the whole escaped us. Or we escaped it.

When we heard, in early '62, that the Congress had extended all enlistments for the duration, we walked over to Stoneman's and offered him whatever help we could spare, then went on with our planting. There was nothing else to do. It was so with everything else. The Conscription Act had nothing to do with us. Though fully recovered (and willing as any other man to fight for independence) we were who we were—no regimental commander, we knew, would give us a second look, and Christopher, our oldest, was not yet fourteen. Besides, there was work to be done: sheds to fix, cotton to scrape, tobacco to top and sucker and worm . . .

Then Moses ran away, and our world—slowly, almost imperceptibly—began to tilt. He left in August 1862, removing himself from our lives as neatly as if, like his namesake, he had simply parted the fields and forests and let them close behind him. We were so inept, so trusting—and yes, so preoccupied with not paying attention to what was happening around us—that by the time we realized he was gone it was nearly noon of the next day, and there was little to be done. He left nothing of himself behind: a stripped bed, a neatly swept floor. I remember joining a half-hearted search party that blundered about for a time, sweating and cursing, crashing through the briars behind McCullough's blue tick hounds, but nothing came of it. The trail, such as it was, simply disappeared into the river, and though we waded across, carrying the dogs in our arms, then tracked a full mile up and downstream (working our way around the backwater sloughs through thickets of thorns as tough as wire), we never found it again. When it started to rain, we allowed ourselves to be talked out of going on, and turned for home.

There was nothing to do, no one to punish. The father had gone, and now the son. We had heard of others who, wishing to make a statement, had had the families of runaways whipped or sold, but though we could see the point, neither Eng nor I had the heart for it. We had watched Berry's face collapse by degrees when we told her, breaking apart—lip and cheek and quivering chin—like a mud castle built too near the current. It was obvious that she had known nothing. Neither, I felt sure, had Christopher.

We knew where the boy had gone, of course. Everyone did. Only two weeks earlier the *Richmond Enquirer* had informed us that "the Great Ape from Illinois had decided to swap the goddess of liberty for the pate and wool of a nigger," and authorized the enlistment of persons of African descent. Fourteen slaves had run off that week in our county alone, three of them belonging to Joseph Price. Only one had been caught. Nor had our area been the only one affected. A great cry of outrage had gone up throughout the Confederacy the week the news was received, accompanied, as always, by the martial clash of metaphors: the Illinois Ape was now the diseased sputum of despotism, a fungus from the corrupt womb of fanaticism, a hireling traitor picked from the vomit of a fallen civilization.

Only Gideon seemed unsurprised that hot, still afternoon he read us the news. We had, by this time, begun spending an hour or two in the afternoons on his porch again, though it was not as it had been, and my brother rarely spoke. Tipping his chair against the wall as always, pipe clenched between his teeth—for tobacco was the one thing we had plenty of—he would read the news aloud (so that for years afterward I couldn't hear mention of Antietam, or the fighting at Sharpsburg, or, indeed, the Negro Conscription Act, without hearing his voice, as though the war, those first two years, had been some horrible serial appearing in consecutive numbers of the *Richmond Enquirer,* narrated by Gideon Weems).

"What I don't pretend to understand," he said, "is why everyone seems so shocked." He wiped his forehead and the back of his neck with a handkerchief. "What did we expect? That having entered into this war, he would refrain from hitting us with every weapon at his disposal? That he would hold back from using the Negro, or anything else for that matter, if he felt there might be some advantage in it?" He shook his head. "Why would he do this, gentlemen? To keep from upsetting us, perhaps? To protect our good opinion of him?"

Transferring the newspaper to his left hand, he poured the two of us another drink. My brother, as always, was staring off across the fields. In the distance, three women (a light-colored kerchief and two red ones) were slowly making their way side by side down the furrows, checking the plants. I watched them move in and out of the lengthening stripes of sun, passing through the long, narrow-trunked shadows of the trees like ghosts.

"A good harvest," said Gideon musingly.

I nodded. "Now if we could only figure out who to sell it to."

"Why don't you try the Yankees? Seems to be working for Price well enough."

We sat in silence for a few moments. "How's Stoneman?" I said.

Gideon looked down into his glass. "Hard to say. Bearing up, I suppose. I went by yesterday to check on him."

"John was his favorite, you know."

Gideon nodded. "I know. I'm just glad May didn't live to see it."

"How's Billy?"

Ellen stepped out on the porch to see if there was anything we'd be needing, and to ask if we'd be staying for supper.

"You look very nice, Ellen," I said.

"Thank you, Mistah Chang," she said. "You sure you and Mistah Eng won't be stayin' on for supper now?" She smiled. "Mama's always sayin' you can't get enough of her ham hocks, an' mine's twice as good."

"She's just like Grace," I said, when she had gone inside.

"I don't know what we would have done without her all these years," said Gideon. We sat quietly for a long while, not saying anything. In the field, the shadows of the trees had grown longer. The hot bands of sun were now just thin, reddish strips, cutting across the green; the light, midge-speckled and low, had been herded east across the furrows to the edge of the woods. The three women were gone. A hot breeze stirred the branches hanging above our heads, then died.

Gideon was looking into the distance, seeing nothing. "Strange," he said. "Evenings like this you could almost believe it hadn't started yet." He took another sip of his drink, then, noticing the newspaper on his lap, laid it by the side of his chair.

"It'll be over sooner than you think," said my brother.

Gideon hardly missed a beat. "Oh?" he said, as naturally as if these were not the first words of actual opinion we had heard my brother speak in weeks. "Why do you think so?"

"Because it won't work," said my brother, as though he'd been part of our conversation all along, and for a moment I felt a pang, remembering how good it had been once, the three of us arguing over something or other late into the night, then walking home, our shadows rippling across the wall of corn or pouring over the stubble.

"Conscripting the blacks won't work," he went on. "The Yankees won't fight over slavery."

"Why not?"

"Because they won't. Union, maybe. Slavery? Never."

"You don't think it will work."

"No, I don't. One out of fifty is an abolitionist. The rest don't care about the blacks."

"And even that one out of fifty may not want to lay down his life for him," I said, careful not to look at my brother. It had been so long since I had agreed with him about anything, I was fearful of seeming to curry his favor.

"The war is as good as over," said my brother. "Six months at most, we'll go our separate ways."

"You really believe that."

"I do. Absolutely."

"What about you?" I asked Gideon. "What do *you* think?"

"What do *I* think?" He looked at us a moment, then out across the peaceful abundance of our fields. "I'll tell you what I think." He tapped the paper by his side. "I think the diseased fungus from the womb of despotism has just won the war, gentlemen, but that it will take us a while to realize it."

Eng snorted. In the distance, I could hear a dinner triangle begin to chime, calling the slaves in from the fields. I could smell the cooking coming from inside the house. "That's what worries me most," Gideon went on, "that it will take us a long time to see it. No," he said, that small, sad smile I loved so much momentarily passing across his face, "it can't be over. We haven't suffered nearly enough."

X.

I think I knew he was gone the moment I heard the door slam and saw
Addy running toward us across the yard, running not the way a woman
runs—even a frightened woman—but like a woman escaping a demon,
clawing and flailing at the air as though pulling herself along by invisible strands, or fighting her way through them. She tore straight into the
early cotton as if it weren't there, plowing across the furrows, whirling
at the plants grabbing at her skirts. When she went down, hard, I knew
for certain, but by this time the moment had burst its shell and we were
running as we'd never run before—quietly, ferociously—cutting a
swath across that vast green expanse, and then we were there and she
was sobbing in my arms, gasping, "Oh God, oh God, what're we going
to do?" and Eng was yelling, "What? What is it?" and I was reading the
note behind her back. The paper folded in the wind; Eng took the other
side. "Tell Father not to worry," he'd written toward the end. "I'll look
out for myself."

"Stand up," I said to Addy, raising her up. "Stand up now." I could
hear my own voice—familiar yet strangely detached—as though it
were coming from inside a well.

"What are we going to do?" she said.

"We're going to get him," I said.

"Tell me what you want me to do," said my brother.

.　　.　　.

We were gone within the hour, our bedrolls in the wagon behind us, the one daguerreotype of Christopher, taken when he was not yet ten, safely tucked between the blankets. The date was April 20, 1863. A warm, wet wind blew from the south. Christopher had taken the mare. "I'll pay back for Sal with my wages," he'd said. By nightfall we'd gone no more than twenty miles. No one had seen him. Boy on a roan mare? Fifteen? No, don't believe so. Dark hair, little bit like us in the eyes? No, can't say 's I have. Two hours out of town we were freaks again, back in the land of the long pause, the uncomprehending look ("Say, ain't you the two I saw . . . ?"), the body turning with the head as we passed as if welded solid at the neck.

That first night we made a fire in a small patch of woods off the road, ate our meal, then bedded down in the wagon, the shotgun by our heads. We lay quiet for a time, listening to the stream where we had dipped our water. "He's smart enough not to try close to home," Eng said suddenly.

"I know," I said.

"They may not take him."

"They'll take him."

"He doesn't look eighteen."

"He doesn't have to." I could hear the water, chuckling to itself in the dark. To the left, an irregular strip of sky in the leaves overhead showed the direction of the road. "You know him," I said. "He'll talk his way in. He's good at that. He'll try one place and then . . ." And suddenly it was as though the thing I'd been holding in all day had to get out somehow and I could feel a strange, helpless rage rising up inside of me and hear myself saying, "I won't lose him, brother, I won't," but it wasn't until I realized Eng had put his arm around me and was patting me awkwardly on the back, saying "It's all right, brother. It's all right. You're not going to lose him," that I realized I was crying, something I'd forgotten I knew how to do, and something I wouldn't do again for over a year.

We were up at dawn, traveling north and east as the roads would allow, hunting the war we'd spent the better part of two years trying to avoid. It didn't take long for the first signs to appear—odd things: an upturned wagon, a house with a door hanging crazily off its hinges . . . One morning we spotted three men running far off across a vast, untilled field, then watched as they leaped a hedge, one after the other, like awkward deer. On the fifth day we came across a large group of male slaves, watched over by four men on horseback. There must have been forty or fifty, all young, sprawled about in the shade of the trees. Some sat with their backs against the trunks; others cooled off by a small grassy stream, pouring water over their heads with a dipper. Five wagons, two of them loaded with supplies, stood by the side of the road.

The men watching them had been talking to each other, their horses nosed in, when they saw us coming up the road. As we approached, one turned his horse partway about while the others shifted slightly in the saddle to face us. They looked like a father and three sons to me; the father a hard-looking man in a dusty black vest with a fine white mustache coarse as a buck tail, the sons quiet, unmoving, watchful and suspicious as wolves in a pen.

"What the hell you want to do that for?" said the father when we told them we were looking for the Confederate Army. "You don't *look* crazy."

"We're not," said Eng.

"Must be damned fools, then. Most people with half a brain are tryin' to get the hell *away* from the war." He paused. "You lookin' to enlist?" he said, incredulous.

"I'm looking for my boy," I said.

"You won't find him."

"I didn't ask you that," I said. Out of the corner of my eye I noticed one of the others tilt his head slightly as though hearing something. Another, who had been chewing on a stem, stopped.

There was a moment's silence. "That's true," said the father, leaning forward a bit in the saddle, "you didn't. But I'm goin' tell you anyway because I'm a goddamned humanitarian and because you seem like the kind of man who just might listen to reason. I've lost two myself—one at Manassas, the other I don't even know where. I'm sayin' you might as well shoot yourself right here and save your horse the trouble. I wouldn't send a nigger into that hell."

The young men shifted uncomfortably in their saddles. There was a long pause.

"How old is this boy of yours, anyway?"

"Fifteen," said my brother.

He nodded. "Tell Lacey to get 'em up," he said to no one in particular, and one of the boys stepped his horse around and trotted off. We watched him come up to the edge of the glade and sweep his right arm up—an abrupt gesture both martial and oddly graceful.

"Go on," he said to the others. "I'll be right there."

My brother picked up the reins. "Where are you taking them?" he said, indicating the crowd of blacks now walking toward the road.

"Wherever it is a man's property can't be stolen away from him for the sake of the Confederacy. Texas, if I have to." He looked at me. "You're a fool," he said. "You want to find the war? All right." He pointed up the road. "Day east, maybe less. Turn left up the Shenandoah. Follow the smoke."

And that is what we did. I can see us still, as in a dream, traveling north up a great valley, past thick woods and open fields, neat country graveyards and small white churches no different from our own, past a straight thin column of yellow smoke rising a mile or so off the road, past a small group of men—three digging with handkerchiefs tied around their mouths, one catching his breath, leaning on his shovel— burying half a horse at the far edge of a weedy meadow. I can see us stopping by a hundred-acre field stamped into dust and smelling of human waste. It started to rain, then stopped. We walked past heaps of oyster shells and broken bottles and cans of preserved fruit with their tops scissored out; past a thousand bits of paper and trash moving, in fits and starts, across the field, only to catch, like pulled cotton, in the tangles at the edge of the woods; past abandoned kneading troughs and blackened fire rings that dogs or coons or crows had dug about in, looking for bits of meat fallen in the ashes . . .

I can see us walking, over and again, down the narrow roads running between tents and cookfires, past men and boys too tired to hoot, past a man playing "Come Where My Love Lies Dreaming" on a mouth harp, following us with his eyes, past another (hair as lank and light as straw) sitting on a bucket, tongue clamped, scratching out a letter against the back of a tin plate . . .

They couldn't help us. At the end of every one of those roads was a captain or a colonel with bloodshot eyes named McGowan or Gordon or Perrin or Field who couldn't divulge the movements of the Confederate Army, who had absolutely no way in hell of knowing where on God's green earth my boy could be and who couldn't find him any more than he could find a particular pebble in a field, or a particular leaf in a forest, or a particular kernel of corn in a cornfield the approximate size of the entire goddamned state of Maryland, but who assumed he was probably home with his mother by now, having discovered that the Confederate Army did not enlist children.

I can see us standing inside the tent of one of them—it might have been Field—who seemed to have more authority than the rest. Behind him, I remember, two bearded young men studied a huge map laid out over a wooden table. Every minute or two the flap would open behind us, letting in a gust of cold, wet air, and a young man would enter, salute, and offer some obscure bit of news, which would be acknowledged, and he would withdraw.

"How long have you been looking?" he said.

"Almost three weeks," said my brother.

"And you just walked into all the other camps the way you did into mine?"

"Yes, sir."

"Amazing." A hard gust of wind shook the canvas. "A drink?"

"No. Thank you."

"What, exactly"—he indicated his own side with the hand holding the bottle—"is the nature of your condition?"

"We're connected, sir," said my brother.

"I see. Can you shoot?"

"Yes."

"Run?"

"Yes."

A young man entered and handed Field a written note. "Tell the captain he did not misunderstand," he said.

"You say you have a wagon, hidden away somewhere?"

"Yes, sir."

"I need wagons." He poured himself a drink. "And men too, connected or not." He paused, considering. "So this is the deal I'll make you. You are free to go. If I see you again, however, I will enlist you, and your wagon, in the Confederate Army. Do I make myself clear?"

"Yes, sir," said my brother. We turned to go.

"Bunker." We turned around.

"I can't help you find him," he said.

"I know that," I said.

"Christ himself couldn't help you find him."

I nodded.

"Go home."

The horse and wagon were gone. When we came to the place where we had hidden them, a patch of dense, scrubby woods rising like an island out of the middle of a vast, muddy field, we found hoof prints and wagon ruts filling with rain, and nothing else. That night we slept in an old, sagging barn with boards missing from its walls and a huge, gaping hole in the roof through which the rain came down all night like a gray column. It still smelled of livestock. In the morning we could see the foundation of the house that had stood just up the hill. We walked outside. Branching streams, like hoarfrost on a window, had cut through the dirt. Bits of yellow hay were moving in the muddy waters or caught against the banks like broken bridges. We passed the teeth of a rusting cultivator, brought down by weeds, and started down the road.

It was late that afternoon, numb with fatigue, that we came to the church at the crossroads. It stood on a rise near the edge of a vast, open plain: untilled fields and young corn, bits of wood and orchards. I remember it well. Though a retreating mass of black clouds still obscured the horizon, the storm had begun to clear. There was, I recall thinking, something undeniably picturesque and dramatic about the scene: the church with its wide, badly weathered boards under that huge, bruised sky; the clouds, trimmed with white like ecclesiastical robes; the grain of light on the broken stones in the churchyard behind the fence . . .

We had spent that day, it seemed, walking out of the world of men. We had no idea where we were. No one moved any longer about the houses and barns we passed. Twice in the last few hours, hearing bursts of rifle fire from the woods, we had hidden in the bushes off the road, then, not knowing what else to do, carefully continued on.

It was partly because Eng thought he had seen the cheesecloth-thin curtain move in the little window to the left that we let ourselves in the gate and walked through the churchyard, glancing here and there at the incriptions (I still remember the name A. Emmanuel Lipp) on the tilting headstones. The sweet, loamy smell of earth, raised by the rain, filled the air. A mockingbird, still as though painted there, sat silently on the branch of a small, dripping elm. We walked up the three boot-scuffed steps and knocked on the door. Around us the road, the fields, the woods, bathed in that stormy light, had turned a deep, undeniable blue.

There was no one there. Eng tried the door. A low rumble of thunder rose from the west, subsided momentarily, then rose again.

"What's that?" I said, but Eng, having frozen for only a second, was already pulling and slamming at the wooden frame as the sound, so different now, rose like a cloud coming up the road that dipped into the woods a quarter-mile to the east, and stepping back, we crashed through the door and slammed it shut an instant before they were upon us, pounding by not like men on horseback but more like the storm I had imagined them to be at first, a charge of thunder made flesh and bone and hoof, transformed in one instant into a river of men clinging to the manes of horses pushing apart the air like a concussion of sound. They seemed one mass, like a torrent loosed from a burst dam, with here and there a leg, a face, a foaming muzzle visible in the rush, pouring by for three minutes, then five, then ten, until it seemed that that side of the world from which they had come must soon be empty of horses and men.

We never heard the rifle crack, but suddenly out of the mass a man separated and flew twisting through the air. Two horses went down in a tangle of hooves and terrified neighing, forming an island in the torrent that quickly parted around them like water around a deadfall. "Oh my God," I heard my brother say. The man lay facedown in the church-yard, his head bent under his chest and his feet propped on the bottom rail of the fence like a diver who had mistaken grass and dirt for water.

It never stopped. By the time the river had passed, leaving behind two more, one crumpled in the dirt, the other lying on his back, half hidden under the body of a horse, we could hear the distant boom of cannon. Thin plumes of white smoke rose above the trees. We rushed to the other window. They were already halfway across the untilled field, a sea of men a full quarter-mile or more across. We rushed back. The edge of the woods at the top of the far rise winked and sparked in the low, sharp light like a rock full of mica.

"Quick," I said, pulling my brother toward the door. "We can still make the woods."

"Which way? We have no idea where the main force is. Where their sharpshooters are. If they take us prisoner it could be years before we're home."

We ran back to the first window. The tide had advanced. We could make out the figures of individual men now against the mass of uni-forms, their faces and hands like spots of light in a dark wood. There were thousands and thousands of them, walking steadily, the ranks dip-ping down into an invisible depression less than a third of the way across the field, then rising again like a flow, like oil, like anything but men, and more were still coming. They would pass within a hundred yards of us, maybe less.

"My God, we've got to get out of here," I remember my brother saying.

"Where? There's nowhere to go."

"If we could get beneath the floor somehow . . ."

"There's no time. We can't get the boards up . . . There's no cellar . . ."

"We have to do something. They're going to tear this place apart, brother."

They were so close now we could see their beards, their caps. They walked bent-kneed and slow as though under a great weight, their eyes on the line of woods ahead. Unable to move, we watched them come on, their boots, their clothes, their breathing making a low hissing sound unlike anything else on earth. In the silence we could hear the men on horseback yelling something, their high-strung charges stepping along the edges of that tide as though afraid of getting their feet wet.

When the guns exploded it was as though a child had tossed a handful of pebbles across the surface of a still pond. A single, sustained wave of sound as overwhelming as a blow and the field was pocked and pitted and torn. Men simply disappeared. I saw dark bits of things fly from the center of a space where a shell had hit, and then the corner of the church was suddenly ripped open to the light and we were flying backwards into the boards of the opposite wall and I was saying to myself, with utter certainty, as in a dream, *I can't die yet. I haven't found him yet. I won't allow it.* A steady screaming—hoarse, inhuman, unbearable—rose above the din of battle.

I'm not sure which of us thought of it, or if we ever even thought of it at all—if thinking was even possible at that moment, and even if it was, if our minds would have allowed us to think such a thing—or if we simply knew what to do the way an animal knows when to burrow and when to bite. Perhaps it was me. I'll accept it if it's so. All I remember is the two of us crawling through a cave of noise, a cave whose ceiling seemed to be lowering down on us like a lid. I had shat myself, though I wouldn't realize it for some time to come. We reached the door—or the place where the door used to be. Something roared behind us like a fire bursting through an open flue. There was the yard. The road. Down the dirt, jerking from side to side like a tortoise, crawled a man with dark hair who had been cut in half at the waist. For a moment, the world started to recede as though I were backing into a long dark tunnel. At the end of it I could see him moving across a diminishing, plate-sized circle of light. *Not yet! Not yet, you bastard!* The plate grew larger. We wriggled across the porch, slid down the steps. The man who had been shot off his horse was still there, at the end of an invisible string thirty yards away, twenty yards away, ten yards away. *They don't kill the dead,* I remember thinking, over and over. *They don't kill the dead.* I never thought to pray. I knew who my enemy was. He had my boy by the arm.

He had managed to turn himself over. A shrieking wind, a swelling chorus of voices, a thousand strong . . . Five yards away and I could see the wound, gulping and clutching below the wreckage of his ribs and the torn fabric of his coat. His lips were moving slightly, as if remembering how to speak, or memorizing a poem. A young man, barely bearded. I could see his tongue pushing against his broken teeth like something blind trying to find its way to the surface. He bubbled up a gush of blood, trying to get something out of his throat. "Please," he mouthed. "Please." I could see the bayonet he'd managed to get into his hand. Another gush and he began to choke, then thrash, and I could see him looking past me, seeing nothing, a man like any other by God but not him, somebody's son, but not mine—and I snatched the steel a second before my brother's hand closed on my own and together we bore down and felt the flesh yield to the bone, felt the shudder catch and stop and still.

Something tore apart the air above our heads; a thick rain of stones and bits of iron fell over us. And I did what I had set out to do: I dipped my fingers into his blood, splashed my brother's face and chest, my throat, my side, then fell into the dirt and lay like the dead—not weeping, not thinking, not anything at all.

·　·　·

I don't know how long we stayed there. When the space beneath our arms had been dark for a long time, we began to crawl toward the road. From the fields and orchards at our back came a strange, wavering sound, sometimes like a child at play, tunelessly humming to itself (or more like a thousand children, ten thousand!) . . . sometimes like the lowing of a cow . . .

I glanced back only once. A half-moon hung motionless in an open sky. As far as I could see, their shadows clearly visible against the pale ground, lay the mounds and heaps of the dead. And yet the scene was not still. The entire valley was moving—slowly, almost imperceptibly—like the minute hand on a watch. We were one of the things making it move.

When we came to the road we kept going. It was only when we had reached the fringe of woods a hundred yards farther on that we dared to stand. I wonder if some sharp-eyed sentry saw us that night, alone among those thousands, suddenly rise to our feet and disappear into the woods as if that particular stretch of dirt just beyond the dip, just past the sycamore, marked a frontier beyond which resurrection became possible, so that those behind us had only to struggle across that invisible line to live, to have their shattered bodies made suddenly whole, to rise and stand and breathe—deep, deep!—like wakened dreamers trying to remember where they'd been, then run a hand through their cooling hair and slowly start for home.

XI.

I think I knew the moment we walked out of Stoneman's woods that July afternoon and started down that long open road—the same one Gideon had thundered down that frozen night to deliver him into this world—that we had lost him. I could tell by the way the house looked, by the shadows of the trees across the yard. We had been gone almost three months. And somewhere inside of me, some small thing very quietly shut.

Addy collapsed when she saw us walking toward the house without him. I couldn't speak. It was as though I'd forgotten how. That afternoon in the parlor Sallie told us that Frank and Charles had been impressed into the Confederate Army as laborers. James had run off a week after we had left. There was no meat left in the smokehouse. I didn't hear her. "We're moving north," he'd written, "I don't know where. I miss you and Mama and Nannie and everybody but most of the men here think a month will decide the war and then I'll be home with you before you know it. The food is bad and most of us crawl with lice which keeps us up all night. I saw General Pickett yesterday. He was dressed very fine and had long black hair like a woman, but those who know him say he's a good fighter and have faith in him. I have to go."

The children gathered around us. I held them all. I wanted to say something. There was nothing I could say.

· · ·

Three days from home, a toothless old man, seeing us coming down the road, had straightened up from hoeing a small, neat garden and walked slowly over to the fence. It had rained that morning. It looked as though it might rain again. "Where might home be?" he'd said, leaning his hoe on the rail beside him. We told him. "We don't have many Chinamen about these parts," he said. Small clouds of mayflies, like tiny white blossoms, had been rising from the hedges all morning. He fanned his hand in front of his face. "What might your . . . I mean, if you don't mind my askin'?" We told him. He nodded seriously, looking past us into the fields. A little fly had stuck to the damp bristle of his cheek. "I heard of a two-headed calf once," he said, "but that was diff'rent." He picked up his hoe. "You boys hear about the fightin' up in Pennsylvania? Fifty thousand dead near some town called Gettysburg." He shook his head. "Hard to get your mind around somethin' like that."

We had been less than a hundred miles away.

I slept, I dreamt. I heard his voice. He came back to me as a three-year-old child, face and legs still soft with fat. He was sitting on a wooden floor in the sun, laughing. He was suddenly grown. I walked past a room and saw him standing in front of a window, and it was him—his back, his legs, his hair, exactly as he was—and in the dream I knew he was gone.

I knew it before the lists of the dead at Gettysburg were printed in the Richmond papers, before they were posted on walls and lampposts. Before I saw Gideon Weems walking up the steps and knew why he had come. Before my eyes had read the names of Francis Bartow and William Beall, Judah Benham and Jefferson Blaisdell, John Bratton and Thomas Buford. Before they had read the words—just words, really—Christopher Bunker, Pvt. Before I had stood there on the porch hearing the sound of my own breathing, my own heart beating on, hearing someone saying, "Quick, get her to the sofa," before I had realized, would never realize, I think, *could* never realize, that I had lost him—the one I couldn't, wouldn't lose—my boy, my heart.

XII.

I remember many things. I remember the night, coming home, we found a greenhouse still smelling of new-cut wood and lay down in a corner to sleep. And slept, waking only twice—once to the sound of rain on the panes overhead, another to the flying moon, just past full, briefly whitening the glass.

We woke just before sunrise, surrounded by the dead trapped in the glass. We stood up. In the pane in front of me, ghostly and inverted, I could see a vast field rising up to a blank horizon, a thin fringe of trees, a rail fence smashed as utterly as if it had been made of matchsticks and some impatient boy had just raked his hand down the line. In the foreground lay two dead horses; one, its neck twisted up against the flank of the other, seemed to be neighing at the sky. Beyond them, very nearly covering that stubbled plain, lay the black heaps of the dead, some singly, others in groups of two and three, diminishing with distance to the crest of a hill where the actual sun, rising now through a low gap between the trees, showed enormous and swollen through the gray November sky like a second, burning earth.

We looked about us. Shattered foundations, splintered wagons, fortifications like the backbones of huge fish laid across the land. A bearded young man had been caught pushing himself across a field with his heels; another slept facedown on a comrade, one leg out like a sleeping child, the skin of the calf exposed against the dirt. On plate after glass plate—for this is what they were—we could see ditches and ravines and furrows, clotted and sown with the dead. Some had apparently died recently; others, their bellies and thighs straining against their uniforms, had begun to grow.

We had left their like behind a week back down the road. And yet there was something here that built in me like a wave. The dead gestured and exclaimed, pleaded and cursed. Some seemed surprised, or simply disbelieving. More than a few still clutched their rifles. Entire companies, bent in ways that men don't bend, appeared to have been flung into the muddy stubble or half-grown wheat from a great height. I remember I picked up a broken pane leaning against the wall: a brown-haired man lay along a picket fence, his neck arched back, his cap still pinned beneath his head. Just above him, a partial crack in the glass ran through a shattered wagon. His arms, frozen at the elbows, pointed straight up from his sides, the fingers straining, as if eager to convince someone of something, or ask a question. Looking at it I couldn't escape the sense that he had seen the sky above his head crack before he died.

They were flawed photographic plates. A sudden change in the humidity on a particular day had made the collodion too tacky, or not enough; a spear of light entering the horse-drawn darkroom had erased half a cornfield; a mosquito or a gnat, settling in the silver nitrate, had marred the picture of the men along the picket fence like a piece of buckshot.

It even made sense, in a way. Glass was scarce; damaged photographic plates, worthless. But my God, what it must have taken—building those transparent roofs and walls with the dead, setting them in place . . . Here and there, the landscape of barns and bridges in the glass was nearly identical to the one beyond it, must have seemed, to those looking through it, a kind of nightmare imposed on the actual land. And that's when Eng noticed it: the images faded as they rose up the walls; to the south, where the sun beat strongest, the panes were already nearly blank—the dead, and the world they had died in, were vanishing like ghosts. I looked at the open mouths, the tumbled hair. Even now I can see them going: brothers and lovers, fathers and sons, kind men and cruel, high in their bier in the hot Virginia sun, their agony for one brief moment laid out to the sky like a reproach to God, then gone.

XIII.

He's asleep, the old fool, his face pressed into my neck like a huge bristly child, wheezing and garumphing and chewing his gums . . . That I should have spent every moment of my life tethered to this man is unbelievable to me. But I have. Time is a narrowing of paths, a pruning away of branches. Nothing like a thing finished and done for ending the debate. Or beginning one, I suppose.

The fire, burning on two logs, is growing down. The ice is silent. I wonder why it is that a fire with two logs will dwindle and die while a fire with three will burn. Is there a third log for everything in this world? A secret threshold that brings it to life, or quietly lets it die?

If it should be now, I'm not unwilling. But I worry about him. He twitches his paws in his sleep, then shifts with the cold. I draw the blanket up around our shoulders.

I can still see them there, waiting in the woods by the open fields, watching the milkweed drifting in the air like a lost squall. Some scribble quick notes against the stocks of their rifles or their brothers' backs or the stones of the old mossed walls that run through those woods like a stitch through a quilt, marking borders long forgotten—"To Miss Masie," "To My Father," "In Case of My Death"—then pin them to their shirts. Most just sit with their backs against the trees, their caps hanging lightly on their bayonets, waiting.

No one speaks. A bee buzzes on a turtlehead blooming in the damp, climbs up the tongue. A hot blade of sun lights the moss on a boulder, cuts the toes off a boot. Here and there men lie sprawled on the previous season's leaves, staring up through the layered branches. Further off, where an old road has shot light through the roof of leaves, a photographer in a black vest and a wide-brimmed hat goes about his business, hurrying back and forth from a small, square wagon.

Suddenly a canteen falls over with a clank; a cut leaf twirls slowly to the ground. Like sleepers waking, they raise their heads. A private's hat flies from a branch. They leap to their feet. The floor of the forest, an overgrown orchard, is stippled with apples, small and hard and green. Within seconds the air is alive with joyful, savage shouting. I can see them, sprinting for the breastworks of pasture walls and broken trees, one hand holding their caps to their heads, the other cradling their bulging shirts, lumpy with ammunition. And for a short space of time, they seem to forget where they are. The wavering heat, the ridge, the order—soon to come—to advance across the open fields (an order Longstreet himself will have to give with a nod, unable to bring himself to speak): All these fade away one last time like distance on a summer afternoon, and they play. As children will play. As though death were a story to scare them to bed, and scarce worth believing.

And I can see him there, my little boy grown tall and lean, his wrists protruding a full three inches from his sleeves. I can feel his thrill at a solid hit, the sting of a little green ball in his side. And I see him take a small bite with his teeth. Then another. His stomach feels tight and hard as a fist. He drops down behind the wall and finishes the four in his pocket, spitting out the bits that won't chew, then reaches for two more lying by his legs. A young man drops down beside him, soaked in sweat, laughing. "I pasted Wiley," he says, grinning, his chest rising and falling, gulping air. "If he was a squirrel he'd be in a pot by now."

Somewhere, once again, Longstreet nods. Pickett scribbles his note to his wife, then gives the order. It's a little after three. The Union guns have fallen silent. The men stop, rise. Ranks form. The mile of open field is still with heat, the air almost white. The world pauses, holds. The order comes. The men step into the light.

.   .   .

All but one, pants around his ankles, shitting himself raw in the corn-field. All but one, retching little bits of apple like a demon, holding to the stalks that barely reach his head—unable to stand, much less walk—as the air explodes with the sound of eleven cannon and seventeen hundred rifles going off at one time and who, soiled and shamed, believing in his fifteen-year-old heart that he'll be shot for a coward and a deserter, wipes himself as best he can, and then, not knowing what else to do, weeping with rage and frustration, crawls through the corn and into the woods and starts walking; walking until Gideon, saddling his mare one hot July morning, looks up the road and freezes, then slowly lays down the reins and begins to run in a way not fitting for a man of his age.

All but one, given back to me like a tidbit, like a bone, after all I'd lived and lost—"Here, take him, if you want him so badly, he's yours . . ." And by God, I did.

A NOTE ABOUT THE AUTHOR

Mark Slouka's story "The Woodcarver's Tale" won a National Magazine Award in Fiction for Harper's *in 1995. His collection of stories,* Lost Lake, *also published by Knopf, was a* New York Times *Notable Book of the Year and won the California Book Award silver medal for New Fiction. He currently teaches at Columbia and lives in New York City with his wife and children.*

A NOTE ON THE TYPE

Pierre Simon Fournier le jeune, who designed the type used in this book, was both an originator and collector of types. His services to the art of printing were his design of letters, his creation of ornaments and initials, and his standardization of type sizes. His types are old style in character and sharply cut. In 1764 and 1766 he published his Manuel typographique, *a treatise on the history of French types and printing, on typefounding in all its details, and on what many consider his most important contribution to typography—the measurement of type by the point system.*

Composed by Creative Graphics,
Allentown, Pennsylvania

Printed and bound by Berryville Graphics,
Berryville, Virginia

Designed by Iris Weinstein